THERE IS A PLAN FOR THE DAY AFTER.
IT'S CALLED THE BLUEPRINT.
AND THESE ARE THE MEN WHO WILL MAKE IT
HAPPEN . . .

Wilson—Expert pilot, sniper and mechanic. Flunked out of combat school for being too aggressive.

Sloan—Electronics and computer genius. Quick with gallows humor. Deadly with a grenade launcher.

Rogers—The group's medic and utility outfielder. He doesn't take prisoners.

McKay—The leader. His maximum experience in land warfare, urban combat and anti-terrorism made him a natural.

THE GUARDIANS
AMERICA'S FUTURE IS IN THEIR HANDS

THE GUARDIANS

RICHARD AUSTIN

A JOVE BOOK

THE GUARDIANS

A Jove Book / published by arrangement with
the author

PRINTING HISTORY
Jove edition / February 1985

ISBN: 0-515-07980-4

Jove books are published by The Berkley Publishing Group,
200 Madison Avenue, New York, N.Y. 10016.
The words "A JOVE BOOK" and the "J" with sunburst
are trademarks belonging to Jove Publications, Inc.

PRINTED IN THE UNITED STATES OF AMERICA

FOR ROB PRUDEN

ACKNOWLEDGMENTS:

Thanks to Robert Pruden and John Brooks for advice and technical information.

PROLOGUE

It's finally happened: the Third World War. Armageddon.

Tension had stretched ever tighter across the years before, as the two superpowers clashed indirectly, choosing sides in every conflict that cropped up in the backwaters of the world. More and more often bloodshed by proxy spilled over to include the actual forces of the U.S. and the Soviet Union. Each such direct confrontation tightened the thumbscrew of tension another turn.

The eighties became the nineties. The tension grew. The world watched. And waited.

It was an innocuous enough incident on the face of it. An East German family busted the border near the oilfields of the Lüneburger Heide in eastern Saxony. Their ancient two-and-a-half-ton truck, armored against bullets and mine blasts by boiler plate welded to the bottom and sides, smashed through the last fence and into the arms of a British patrol. The East Germans followed them right across. The Vopos *fired, wounding a Tommy. When the shooting stopped, five East German border guards lay dead on Western ground.*

A vicious incident, though not unprecedented—but just the excuse the desperate Soviet leadership was seeking to precipi-

1

tate a showdown. Within three hours, the Soviet Army was on the move.

The Warsaw Pact forces swept into Western Europe like a steel wind. Paratroops dropped out of the indigo hours of the early June morning to seize NATO bases and command posts well back of the frontier. Bombers, missiles, and even tanks sowed a deadly wind in front of the onrushing armored columns.

Almost at once they began to reap the whirlwind.

For years the soldiers of NATO had been in effect betrayed by their own commands, who dinned incessantly into their ears that the Soviet Army was an invincible killing machine, that the Russian soldier was a bulletproof giant. The German, British, American, and Belgian troops who faced that awful onslaught were demoralized even before the millions of enemy soldiers began to appear out of the early mists.

But still, they fought. Mostly volunteers, all from wealthy Western nations, they faced an ill-fed army of conscripts. The Soviet soldiers would have fought with superhuman cunning and to the last drop of blood for their own homes and hearths, but now they were being driven forward to die seizing land they didn't want, for no benefit one soldier out of a hundred could envision. The Western troops fought with their backs to the wall and sheer survival at stake, and most of them knowing their homes were a few hours, days at most, from being swamped by a Red tide.

NATO's initial casualties were brutal. Warsaw Pact casualties were worse. As always, the Soviets led off with armor. Though some NATO formations were disrupted by the airborne attacks, Western field commanders, unlike their Eastern counterparts, had been trained to use their own initiative. And use it they did.

Western infantry hugged the rolling green landscape and drove antitank rockets into the steel hides of the encroaching monsters. Swarms of missile-carrying trucks and jeeps stung the flanks of the advancing columns, then darted away to strike again without warning or mercy. Deadliest of all were the attack helicopters: bouncing up from behind folds in the ground, launching tank-killing missiles, dropping below the horizon before anyone knew they were there.

Attack aircraft fell in droves, prey to better built and better *flown NATO planes. The Soviets' vaunted chemical weapons proved a catastrophic disappointment. War gases designed for quick decomposition and dispersal turned out not to have much of a shelf life; millions of rubles and hundreds of lives were spent sowing the NATO lines with what turned out to be harmless aerosols. When the gas had not decayed in its canister, it all too frequently blew back into the faces of the Warsaw Pact infantry following the armored thrust. The conscripts of the Soviet army, frightened and often half-illiterate, forgot much of their training, and those who managed to struggle into their bulky protective suits often learned a brief, lethal lesson about quality control in the workers' paradise.*

Years of propaganda of Soviet invulnerability—emanating from Washington, Bonn, and London as well as from Moscow—died with the cream of the Red Army. Within two hours of dawn, the Soviet invasion had lost momentum and was beginning to come apart. Then the Soviets' problems began in earnest.

In their strategic planning, the Soviet general staff had anticipated that a single body blow would knock NATO out at a stroke. When the Western forces came off the ropes swinging, it was the Soviet logistics that gave—with help from the Soviets' "allies." Before noon of D-day the Polish army had rebelled, cutting the rail lines and seizing a score of airfields. The Czechs and the Hungarians followed suit. In a matter of days the Russians found their supply lines running through hundreds of miles of hostile territory before reaching the stalemated troops on the European front.

Two days after the attack, a year to the day after the People's Republic of China had signed a pact of eternal socialist solidarity with the U.S.S.R., a million Chinese troops rolled across the Amur and Ussuri rivers into Siberia. A million more—predominantly Muslim tribesmen, struck from the Southwest, from the deserts of Xinjiang through the high mountain passes, to be greeted as liberators by their cousins across the frontier.

Rebellions began to explode like satchel charges hidden in the very foundations of the Soviets' empire. Georgia revolted, then the Ukraine, Latvia, Estonia, Lithuania. Fully a quarter of the Soviet Army's manpower had been deployed in the south, along the borders with Turkey and Iran. With most of those men withdrawn for the offensive in the West, millions of fanatic Muslims raised the green banner of Jihad, and poured north to deal a deathblow to the ancient enemy of Islam, and the Muslim republics of the southern U.S.S.R. rose joyfully to join them.

The Soviets reeled from disaster piled upon disaster. Though resupply from America was disrupted by air and submarine attacks in the Atlantic, a NATO counterattack rolled off four days after the Soviet offensive began. At 1350 on D-day plus 6, elements of an American reconnaissance platoon reached the suburbs of Prague. Leipzig and Dresden had already fallen to West German armored forces.

The Russians pressed the panic button.

Just after nightfall, the Soviets struck the length of the European front with the full force of their tactical nuclear capability. The NATO forces reeled—then retaliated in kind.

Red Army troops traditionally bunched. The Soviet soldiers who had learned better, the scarred, battle-weary veterans of Afghanistan, Iran, Uzbekstan, and Kirghiz who might have been able to teach their comrades the vital lesson of staying dispersed, were all on duty in the eastern reaches of their vast homeland. Massed in railyards in East Germany and Poland, clumped in mountain passes in Czechoslovakia, the Soviet troops died in a military catastrophe unequaled since the German defeat at Stalingrad.

The Politburo met in an all-night session. The nightmare the oldest among them had dreaded for half a century was solidifying into inexorable reality: the armor of the "fascist" West rolling like the tide into the Motherland herself. Only, this time the invaders would not make the millions who greeted them dig their own graves and machine-gun them by the tens of thousands. This invader would not suddenly halt his drive on Moscow for a fruitless attack to the south as the bungler Hitler had. This enemy would topple the Russian empire, with the willing help of tens of millions of her subject peoples.

Only one course of action remained. It took time for the hydra-headed Central Committee to face the fact squarely. When it did, it moved with cunning and by not seeming to move at all. The fateful word of their decision was passed on to the super-secret Defense Council, which controlled the U.S.S.R.'s nuclear arsenal. Then, with detached and icy calm, the Soviet leaders settled back, awaiting the moment to strike.

It was past noon in the Union of Soviet Socialist Republics when the Politburo acted. But when the missiles began to thunder upward from their silos, to boil from the launch tubes of submarines secure in the cool embrace of the sea, it was 8:30 A.M. Eastern standard time: rush hour along the Eastern seaboard.

CHAPTER
ONE

"Here they come!" Lt. William McKay, USMC, had just stepped into the doorway of the entrance hall, machine gun held across his chest, when one of the Secret Service men holding the end of the North Portico of the White House shouted the frantic warning. Gunfire ripped humid air already pungent with the stink of a thousand fires burning. McKay flicked his eyes to the dosimeter strapped to his thick left wrist. The glowing red numbers read 0.8 rad. Above background radiation level for downtown Washington, but not dangerous. *But that'll change pretty damn quick, if the wind shifts*, McKay told himself.

The door's glass had been blasted all over the gray-and-white marble floor. McKay half turned, slammed the empty metal framework open with his shoulder, spun through, and raced to the end of the Portico. Glittering shards of glass crunched under the steel-reinforced soles of his boots. A half-dozen agents in dark suits hunkered behind the meter-high marble wall that upheld the four great columns fronting the Portico. One of them started to turn, swinging the muzzle of his Uzi to bear on the newcomer. He checked himself, recognizing the tall, burly ex-Marine in urban-warfare camouflage printed in jagged patterns of gray, black, and brown. The

7

agent nodded briskly, then turned back to the wall.

McKay dropped to his knee beside the agent. He laid the Maremont M-60 lightweight machine gun across the marble barrier, pulled down the bipod, cleared the 105-round ammunition belt from his shoulder, and looked out at a stricken city.

The few brownstones that progress and the proliferation of federal office buildings had left along Sixteenth Street showed it worst. Most of the ones along the east side of the street had dropped parts of their facades onto the pavement. Huge sections of blown-out windows gaped on the sides of the glass boxes of hotels and office complexes. Maybe a quarter of the buildings in McKay's field of vision were on fire, coils of smoke and fluttering leaves of flame sprouting from glassless windows like bizarre vines from modernistic planters. The Farragut West overpass had dropped, becoming a shattered jigsaw of concrete lying across Sixteenth, and the Sheraton-Carlton gazing blankly down on it like a many-eyed skull. Beyond, a single black pillar of smoke rose from the stricken suburbs around the University of Maryland, marking the hypocenter of the first missile strike.

To the west, out of sight beyond the old Executive Office Building and the blazing Blair House, a wall of flame erected by a pair of hydrogen blasts crossed the residential districts of Arlington. And in the southwest quadrant of the District itself, the slums shriveled in the grip of an honest-to-Christ firestorm, ignited by the overlapping thermal-effects zones of the warhead that had detonated over the Virginia Theological Seminary and the groundburst that had obliterated Andrews Air Force Base. Down there the police and firemen had just given up. Most of them couldn't even get water pressure in their hoses, and McKay had heard reports on the radio monitors down in the War Room that fire fighters were taking sniper fire in Anacostia.

At the moment events closer at hand claimed his attention. It was less than a hundred meters to the fence, point-blank for his M-60. He peered along its blued barrel, through the thick shimmer of midday heat haze, through the trees on the north lawn of the White House. The trees had been early-June green when the sun came up that morning. Now they were withered by the dragon's breath of a fusion warhead bursting in the air to the west. Beyond them, the mob that filled Lafayette Park had spilled across Pennsylvania Avenue and was rolling against the black iron fence of the White House like a wave.

White plumes of smoke blossomed in the middle of the mob as the guards in the strong points by the gates frantically tossed gas grenades. "Jesus!" an agent yelled. "It's not even slowing 'em down!"

Coughing and weeping, the maddened horde came on. McKay heard the popping of the gate guards' weapons. The kneeling Secret Service men blazed away with their Uzis, and a black agent at the other end of the colonnade carefully squeezed off round after round from a G-3 SG1 sniper's rifle.

McKay lowered his head to activate the mike taped to his larynx. "Did you get that, Tom? They're in."

"I read you," came back the calm voice of Lt. Thomas Rogers, formerly of the Special Forces. "The Secret Service boys in the West Wing report they're taking heavy sniper fire from the old Executive Office Building too."

McKay gripped the pistol foregrip of the machine gun with his left hand and slipped the forefinger of the right around the trigger, feeling its cool, poised hardness. "Are they finished yet?"

"Chief Justice is administering the oath now."

"Shit. See if you can't hurry 'em up. There must be three thousand fuckin' people hitting the wire. Don't know how long we can hold 'em. Casey?"

"Yo." It was a pure southern California voice, seemingly too young for its owner to have done the things he had.

"Get Mobile One fired up, and make sure the escort vehicles are ready. We're gonna have to de-ass in one hell of a hurry."

"Roger."

For two hours they had been gathering in Lafayette Park, this legion of the lost. Bureaucrats from the shelters dug beneath office buildings, maddened by fear and claustrophobic crowding; dwellers from the few pockets of ghetto remaining in the inner city, fleeing the flames that devoured their tenement homes like a hungry red beast; the wounded, shocked, dazed, and bloody of all kind. At first the crowd milled pointlessly while harried emergency medical teams moved among them, giving what help they could, and the police tried to persuade the uninjured to return to their shelters. Gradually, though, the mob grew angry, hurling threats at the cops or at the battered face of the building across Pennsylvania Avenue. Then with wildfire suddenness they had turned savage. The thin cordon of patrolmen went down like a wall of sand before the tide, and the mob charged the White House, which had become the target of their hatred.

They were clambering over the fence now, beneath a pale yellow sky filled with clouds linked by a dazzling tracery of lightning. McKay took a deep breath, snugged the butt against his shoulder, and briefly squeezed the trigger.

The steel butt plate jackhammered his shoulder. A skinny white kid, long-haired, the right side of his face an oozing red wound, was just coming over the top. He threw up his arms as 7.62 mm rounds ripped through him and clawed him down. Beside him, a heavyset black man still wearing his herringbone jacket and tie lost his hold and fell, impaling himself on an ornamental spike. He hung there, his screams clearly audible above the rippling gunfire and the inhuman roar of the mob as dozens poured past him over the fence.

McKay lowered the muzzle a hairbreadth and triggered another short burst into the onrushing mob. He tried to make himself feel the grim joy that always gripped him in combat, tried to make himself forget that these were his fellow countrymen, fellow survivors of Armageddon. But now they weren't truly human anymore, he told himself. They had become wild animals. And he and this small handful of Secret Service agents were all that stood between their anger, their bloodlust, and the shambles of the Blue Room, where the new President of the United States was being sworn into office.

CHAPTER
TWO

The One-Day War had started in the thin, bleary hours of that fateful morning. Just before, dawn lay in a dirty salmon-colored ribbon across the shopping district to the east of the White House. McKay and the other Guardians stood in a knot next to the helipad beside the Rose Garden. Surrounding them stood dark-suited Secret Service agents, all alert and armed for bear. Well inside the iron ring of agents, a few feet from McKay, stood the commanding form of President William Lowell, head back, jaw thrust forward, gazing out across his capital city and looking as though his craggy profile had already been carved on Mount Rushmore.

A dull warm-wet wind whipped the Chief Executive's tie over his shoulder. Light traffic streamed along E Street beyond the south end of the grounds as if this were any early morning in the world. It was hard to believe that just fifteen minutes ago the National Security Council had advised the President that there was a 93 percent possibility the Soviets would attempt a preemptive strike in the next twelve hours.

This is it, McKay told himself. His entire life for almost the last two years had been directed toward this moment, focused on it. Every one of them had known it was coming soon, ever since the Red Army rolled through Fulda Gap a week before.

But it had never seemed quite real before this instant.

From the southeast came the thupping of helicopter rotors beating air, hard and rhythmic, like the sound of a grinning chef chopping vegetables at a table in a fancy Japanese restaurant. A moment later and three of the craft flashed over the East Wing of the White House. The long, businesslike black shape of the President's personal UH-60 Blackhawk transport helicopter settled down onto the cement apron in back of the East Wing. Engines snarling, its two escort gunships whipped by, then split east and west to take up a protective orbit around the White House as the President mounted the Blackhawk for the trip to Andrews Air Force Base. There a converted 747 was waiting to bear him and his cabinet aloft, above the destruction to come. The 747 had been designated NEACP (pronounced "kneecap"), the National Emergency Airborne Command Post.

The escorts were AH-64 Apaches, lean green choppers with funny-looking dachshund noses. But there was nothing comical about the weight of firepower they carried, the rocket pods and laser-guided Hellfire missiles slung under their stub wings and 30 mm chain guns tucked into barbettes beneath their chins. As anyone would quickly discover, domestic nutcase or foreign hit team, who made a play for the Man himself, on the ground or in the air. Lowell was the first president to have gunships accompany his transport helicopter. It went along with his carefully cultivated image as a hard man, but given the tense situation that prevailed inside the country as well as out, they were probably necessary. *Things are fucking tough all over,* McKay thought.

The big rotors slowed to visibility, doors on the sleek side of the Blackhawk slid open. Bending low, Lowell ran to the chopper, the Guardians and a cluster of Secret Service men with Mini-Uzis keeping pace. He moved well for a man in his seventies. An Air Force colonel in mirror shades waited in the doorway to help the President inside.

The President straightened. He was a big man. At his full height his hazel eyes looked directly into McKay's blue ones. "Thanks, Lieutenant." His deep rich basso voice didn't have to strain to be heard, even above the scream of the two huge GE engines and the swishing of the rotors. "I'll take it from here."

McKay rocked back, for one of the few times in his life unsure of himself. "What do you mean, sir?" He found that *he* had to shout.

The President laid a strong hand on his shoulder. "I mean you and your boys have done your job. I'm flying from here on. I'll be in the hands of God and the U.S Air Force. Nothing you can do for me anymore." Liver-colored bags hung under his eyes. The granitic masses of his face had subtly begun to sag from weariness—and something more, it seemed to Billy McKay. "You look after Jeff if anything should happen to me."

"But we're assigned to *you*, Mr. President!" McKay felt as if the concrete were spinning beneath his feet in time with the rotor turning lazily overhead.

"I told you, there's nothing more you can do for me." Lowell's voice cracked like a teacher's ruler on a student's knuckles. He wasn't used to being contradicted. He turned away and climbed into the Blackhawk.

Without hesitation, McKay clambered in after him. The inside of the helicopter had been remodeled along the lines of a private jet cabin, with airline-style seats and padded sound-proof walls. Aides were helping President Lowell back to a seat toward the rear of the chopper. He ignored McKay.

McKay turned toward the cockpit. The Colonel in the Third-World-dictator shades moved to bar his way. "Just what do you think you're doing?"

"I'm using your telephone, fly-boy," McKay snarled back. "I'm a Guardian. That gives me the right to commandeer all necessary facilities. Now stand the hell aside before I pitch you headfirst onto the concrete."

The Colonel's sunlamp tan lost a few shades. McKay was only a few inches taller but much broader, and one big hand hung suggestively above the butt of his .45 in its custom-built Milt Sparks combat holster. The Colonel knew about the Guardians, who and what they were. This lunatic had every right to do just what he threatened to. He swallowed and stood aside.

McKay shouldered through the bulkhead into a cockpit crowded with instruments. The pilot and copilot turned in their seats and stared. "Get me emergency channel twenty-three double-alpha. Guardian clearance. Make it march."

"Now just a goddamned minute—" the copilot said, starting from his seat. The pilot, a wiry black with captain's bars, touched him on the arm. "Do it," he said softly. The copilot stared angrily at McKay a moment longer, then sank back into his seat.

The President's Blackhawk was fitted with a vast array of the latest communications gear so that the nation's leader need never be out of touch. Sullenly, the copilot worked his comm console. In a matter of seconds McKay heard the rasping voice of Major Crenna, originator of Project Guardian. "What is it?"

"The old man," McKay said. "He says we're not going."

There was a pause. McKay stood hunched over with the earphone pressed hard against his ear to keep the engine noise at bay. Where Crenna was, he had no idea. All he knew was the number of the special channel to be used only in the utmost emergency. And he knew that such an emergency had just arrived.

"Why not?" Crenna asked.

"No explanation. He says we should hang back here and keep an eye on Vice President MacGregor." It was a part of the evacuation plan that the Vice President should remain at the White House in the event the President had to relocate to the flying White House. No point in putting all the country's eggs in one nice basket, waiting for a thermonuclear Soviet brick to land on them.

"Figures. Lowell's making a grand gesture. Trying to get his image back." The aging Lowell had been elected as the man on horseback, a strong, active leader who would pull the country together and get things moving again. But things had moved irrevocably beyond his control, with worsening situations overseas, political discontent and economic hardships at home. Now, Crenna seemed to think, he was symbolically casting aside the shield the Guardians were intended to provide, going it alone—riding off to battle on a flying white steed.

McKay was not normally the type to ask for guidance from above. Just the opposite, in fact. But he couldn't handle this on his own. "What do we do, Major? Insist on going along?"

"Negative. Do what he tells you to: stay behind in the War Room with MacGregor and Chief Justice Shaneyfelt and wait for the smoke to clear. Let him make his grand gesture."

"But we're supposed to safeguard the President!"

"Negative. Your primary mission is to guard the chain of command."

"But—"

"No buts, Lieutenant," Crenna broke in harshly. The Major's breathing was irregular, saw edged. McKay could almost see the intact half of his face twisting in anger at the younger man's near insubordination. "Once the President is on board his plane, there's not a damned thing in the world you can do to help him. If nothing goes wrong, he'll land at an appropriate safe airfield, where a military escort will be available to augment his Secret Service detail. You Guardians won't be needed in that eventuality. You'll stand by here for reassignment."

McKay winced. *Reassignment!* he thought. *After all that training—all that psyching up . . .*

"But if something happens to that plane, you will be carrying out your assignment as per your original briefing: to get President Jeffrey MacGregor safely out of Washington to an alternate command center."

McKay's throat was dry. "Yes, sir," he said. Without waiting for more, he tossed the headset to the copilot and walked back into the chopper's cabin.

Lowell sat in his chair surrounded by aides, a headset over his steel-gray hair, a notepad microcomputer on his lap, monitoring military and intelligence reports on the situation in Europe and the Kremlin. He looked up as McKay came in. "Lieutenant. I want to thank you and your men for helping look after me these last few months. I've been able to sleep better knowing you were on the lookout for trouble." A wan smile. "I didn't sleep well, but better."

"Just doing our job, sir," McKay said hoarsely. Aides and the Colonel hovered impatiently around him. He paid no attention to them.

The massive leonine head nodded. "We're ready to lift, Lieutenant. Good luck to you, and God bless you."

McKay snapped a salute. "The same to you, sir." There was no more to say. He jumped down out of the chopper. The doors slid shut behind him and the big Blackhawk leaped into the air.

He walked away from it without even looking back.

●　　●　　●

There were no niceties of first strike–second strike. The war was like the old dogface slogan, "Smoke 'em if you got 'em." Neither the U.S. nor the U.S.S.R. had solved the terminal guidance problem, in spite of years of propaganda by both sides that boasted of pinpoint accuracy. No one had actually fired a missile over the pole; test firings generally took two or three shots to score a hit over hundred-mile ranges, and the missiles being tested hadn't had to deal with the earth's rotation, gravity fluctuations along the line of flight, and weather, the way circumpolar shots did. Each side's main concern was to smash the other's capacity to smash it, *and the only way to assure that was saturation of primary targets—silos and strategic-bomber bases.*

Nobody could resist getting into the act they later called the One-Day War. The Soviets launched on China at the same time as they launched on the U.S. and Western Europe and, for good measure, Teheran. The Chinese naturally shot back. Pakistan and India went for each other; Tanzania and Kenya unveiled an unexpected nuclear capacity to settle their grievances; Brazil hit Buenos Aires with a half-dozen fusion bombs and broke the back of Argentine resistance, ending their three-year war at a single savage stroke. The hard-line Rejectionists—those Arab countries, such as Syria, Iraq, Algeria, and Saudi Arabia, that still rejected peace with Israel—tried for a knockout blow against their old enemy. But they only managed to hit a handful of targets in the Israeli Protectorates that stretched from newly conquered Libya through West Jordan to Lebanon. In return, Rejectionist leaders watched until their eyes melted as mushrooms sprouted above their ancient capitals.

Though few warheads were aimed at civilian targets by either of the major contenders, civilian targets were still hit. Oftentimes primary targets were located in or near cities. Just as often, the missiles simply missed their targets. But they still hit somewhere, each unleashing in an instant the hellish energy of a star's core. The United States's shiny new civil defense came apart at the seams. The Soviets' vaunted system had never existed except on paper. A nation that could not feed or shelter its populace before the holocaust could hardly be prepared to cope with the greatest catastrophe in the history of the human race. Not that anyone could.

One hundred ten million Americans died in the attack, one hundred thirty million Russians. Deaths in the rest of the world were simply incalculable.

And then the nightmare began in earnest. . . .

"Gentlemen," the young man with premature gray at his temples had said, "we have confirmation from NEACP-2. Our satellites have shown missiles launched from silos in Apatity, Vorkuta, Chokurdakh, and Cherskiy on a circumpolar trajectory." His voice sounded strangely dead in the soundproofed War Room. "The President has ordered immediate retaliation by all ICBM squadrons, missile submarines, and SAC bomber fleets."

"So this is it," Sam Sloan had said. His voice sounded peculiar to him. Maybe it was the noise-suppressing tiles of the dropped ceiling, the hum of the air conditioning, or maybe the simple fact that they were in a bunker deep beneath the White House.

He saw a furrow appear between the almost invisibly pale eyebrows of Lt. William McKay, who stood in front of an unoccupied computer console with his heavy forearms folded across his chest. Sloan knew what McKay was thinking: the ex-Marine disapproved of his wasting breath to state the obvious.

It was a curious group crowded into the maroon-carpeted chamber. In the light of specially designed low-glare panels, uniformed technicians sat at stations along the wall, manning computers, monitoring a world-spanning communications network especially shielded against the electromagnetic pulses produced by thermonuclear explosions. The head of the room was taken up by a wall-sized screen on which was displayed a computerized map of the Northern Hemisphere. Red and blue masses showed the positions of the Soviet armies that had thrust into Western Europe, and the positions of the NATO forces that had driven them back. These were unheeded now. Almost every eye in the room was watching the winking red dots of confirmed Soviet missile launches. Red numerals appeared at the upper right corner, one set counting down the time to the predicted arrival-on-target of the land-based missiles, the second showing destination times of those launched by submarine. Neither number was large.

Tall, slender, and theatrically handsome, Vice President
Jeffrey MacGregor paced back and forth in front of the map,
ignoring it, one hand pressed to an earplug. His broad, high-
cheekboned face was pale, set in grim lines. At thirty-eight, he
was remarkably young for his post, but the news he had just
relayed to the other men in the War Room had seemed to age
him ten years.

A table topped in Formica stained to resemble walnut occupied the center of the room, surrounded by swivel-mounted
chairs. An elderly, desiccated man with a wattled neck, a
Roman ax-blade nose, and shockingly white hair sat at the far
end from MacGregor, thin lips pursed into a line, as though he
disapproved of the way the young Vice President had broken
the news. Lean liver-spotted fingers tapped a knee covered by
a shiny black robe.

Sam Sloan sat tensely at the table on Chief Justice Desmond
Shaneyfelt's left. Sloan was a handsome man, in his early
thirties, tall and lanky, with a down-home oblong face, brown
eyes, dark brown hair. Casey Wilson lounged in the chair
across from him, hands behind a head of sun-bleached blond
hair. He looked like a tanned teenager, fresh-faced, green-
eyed, eager; in fact he was America's top-scoring air ace since
the Korean War. He wore a dress uniform that didn't quite fit
his skinny frame, a gray-green unlike any U.S. military garb
Sloan had seen before two years ago. Sam Sloan wore one just
like it, though better fitting. So did Billy McKay, big and bull-
chested, with piercing blue eyes and close-cropped curly blond
hair. The fourth man wearing the unusual uniform was the
square-jawed, taciturn Rogers, a five-foot-eight cinder block
of a man with thinning sandy brown hair, who stood behind
Sloan. Immobile and unspeaking, Rogers seemed to be totally
unmoved by the events unfolding before his gunmetal-gray
eyes.

It was a strange uniform for Sloan, an Annapolis graduate
who held the rank of Commander in the U.S. Navy. But this
was a strange assignment for a man who had been a line
officer aboard a cruiser in the Libyan war zone a scant
twenty-five months before. Samuel Sloan, William McKay,
Thomas Rogers, and Kenneth C. "Casey" Wilson were the
four members of an elite military unit, the Guardians, formed
outside the normal chain of command and trained to hair-

trigger tautness to perform one very special task: to escort the President of the United States to safety in the event of nuclear war.

Justice Shaneyfelt sucked breath in sharply between his dentures. One by one, blinking blue lights were winking into existence in Montana, the Dakotas, Nebraska, Kansas, and Missouri. "Titan missile launchings confirmed," murmured a narrow-chested young tech in a pale-blue Air Force shirt. MacGregor stopped and glanced up at the screen, then resumed his pacing.

The time might almost be at hand for the Guardians to swing into action.

Sloan had felt a bead of sweat crawling down from his hairline as he watched the red numbers tick away. Were they ticking away his life?

He remembered another time he had waited for death to come calling. Sweltering in the auxiliary bridge of the *Winston-Salem*, listening to reports from the radarmen tracking the flight of four SS-N-11 missiles launched from Libyan Osa II missile boats in the Gulf of Sidra. Antimissile gunfire had taken out two of the ship killers. Then Sloan had been hurled against a bulkhead as the other missiles struck the cruiser. One holed the port bow above the waterline. The other hit the front of the superstructure and blasted *Winston-Salem*'s bridge into oblivion—and Sloan into command of the warship. That time there had been the crash of the cruiser's guns, the rattle of her antiaircraft fire, men shouting above the rhythmic pulse of her engines, the hot smell of sweat and oil and gun smoke.

Here there had been none of that. There was only the incessant murmur of the communications techs, the whisper of the air conditioning. The War Room reminded Sloan of nothing so much as a room in a Holiday Inn. It was all so unreal, remote, as if the world they'd known wasn't ending above their heads.

"Sir, we have satellite projections for Soviet missile trajectories." The voice was eerily calm, at one with the strange detachment of the scene. Did the others feel the strangeness of it? McKay, maybe, but he'd never show it. Casey Wilson was patting an up-tempo drumbeat on one thigh, but otherwise appeared to be his usual laid-back, happy-go-lucky self. Rogers

. . . as always, Rogers was quiet and unreadable.

"Put them on the screen." MacGregor had finally stopped his pacing and turned to gaze up at the screen as red arcs sprang into life.

"Jesus," a technician muttered. "They're coming in right on top of us!"

Sloan had an instant to think *No, most are going into the central states, the Missile Belt. We're only getting a few. . . .*

"Andrews Air Force Base reports radar returns from bogeys, azimuth three fifty-six, three fifty-seven, and three fifty-nine," a voice said. "Distance—"

From nowhere, everywhere it came: a rumble, subliminally low, building through basso to a jarring roar that Sloan felt in the core of his bones. "Where did it hit?" MacGregor asked in a wire-taut voice.

An Army tech read green numbers from a screen. "Seismic analysis of shock wave indicates one megaton explosion in air, hypocenter bearing thirty degrees, distance fifteen point six kilometers."

"So much for the University of Maryland," somebody said.

Chatter broke out on all sides: "Omaha reports strikes to northeast—"

"—fireball over Travis—"

"Grissom reports near miss—"

"Plattsburgh not responding—"

"Fort Ritchie no longer responds."

The first demonic rumbling had scarcely subsided when it began again. "Hypocenter bearing two ninety-nine; seven point one kilometers."

Sloan rubbed his chin and tried to visualize the map of metropolitan Washington they'd had to memorize during training. *That'd be about where the Washington Memorial Parkway meets the Chain Bridge Road.* A moment later someone called out a strike in Alexandria City, across the Potomac to the south-southwest, a hair over nine kilometers away. He thought of the Secret Service men on duty upstairs, riding the storm out with nothing but the walls of the White House to shield them, and winced.

He glanced at Shaneyfelt. The Chief Justice sat as if turned to stone, his thin cheeks an unhealthy ashen gray.

"—of a water strike in Mississippi River near Cairo."

"—above Newark. Oh, Christ, the people, the *people*!"

The former Naval officer winced in sympathy with the agony in the communications man's voice. Then he was thrown out of his chair. The carpeted concrete floor danced and jittered beneath him. *Earthquake?* he wondered wildly.

McKay had lurched back against the blank console. "What the fuck was *that*?" he exclaimed. "Beg pardon, Mr. Vice President."

"That's all right." MacGregor had staggered against the wall screen, barely keeping his balance. "What *was* it?"

"Ground burst," said the level voice of the man at the seismographic computer. "Two megatons, bearing sixty-three degrees, range seventeen point three kilometers—dear God, that's Andrews!"

Sloan got to his knees. A steady vibration hummed beneath them, scarcely perceptible, but there. "Virginia's taking a beating," someone said. Sloan clambered back into the chair.

"We've been lucky so far," he said.

"Yeah," McKay grunted. "Don't the Russians have a city-busting job with Sixteen hundred Pennsylvania Avenue painted on the nose cone?"

"My God!" croaked Justice Shaneyfelt. "How can you talk about it like that?"

McKay shrugged..

"Reports coming in from Western Europe," a technician murmured. "Hamburg hit, Leeds in England, repeated strikes along the Rhine and the Plateau d'Albion in France."

"There go our IRBM's and short-haul jobs," another remarked. Western Europe's intermediate-range ballistic missiles deployed near the Alps and the short-range Plutons in the Rhine valley had been poised to sow a swath of destruction across West Germany, interdicting the Soviets' line of advance toward France.

"NEACP-2 reporting." Several of the E-4B "flying bunkers" were aloft as decoys. Number Two was the President's plane. One of the techs in the War Room was in constant communication with it. "They're having trouble with satellite reception, but they've got a visual of strike patterns near Moscow, Murmansk, and missile bases in the Urals and eastern Siberia. Russia's taking it hard."

"Omaha no longer responding."

The roaring started low and built slowly. It never reached the crescendo of the Andrews explosion, but it went on and on until Sloan felt like screaming aloud. "That's a hell of a big one," said the seismograph technician.

"Ground burst. Range, seventy-eight klicks. Bearing two seventy-eight. Size—no, that can't be." The tech pressed buttons rapidly. "The computer says twenty-five megatons, sir." He sounded apologetic.

Casey Wilson put back his blond head and laughed. Everybody stared at him. "That was ours—the big SS-18 with our name on it," he said. "Oh, wow. Their missile command doesn't shoot any better than their MiG drivers do."

"We ain't going to Mount Weather." It was the first time the compact Rogers had spoken. Heads nodded. Buried beneath a mountain in the Blue Ridge range was a vast complex meant to serve as an alternate White House and government center in case of nuclear attack. But the multimegaton warhead had grounded too close to Mount Weather for even the heavily fortified facility to survive.

"Where's the wind coming from?" McKay asked.

"North-northwest, sir."

He nodded. "Good. We should be squared away where the fallout is concerned. It'll pass us to the south."

"Unless the wind backs a point," Sloan said. "That'd bring it right down on top of us."

They listened for the next two hours to increasingly fragmented reports of the course of the Third World War. By the time satellite communications were lost for good, it was apparent that the Union of Soviet Socialist Republics would not be a world power for years to come.

But neither will the U.S., Sloan thought. The concept gave him an empty pang; he felt strangely vulnerable.

Then they had listened to what remained of police, fire, and National Guard communications in the area. The picture they received was fragmentary but all too clear. Fires raged uncontrollably throughout the area outlined by the Beltway. The routes in and out of Washington that weren't choked with rubble were jammed with abandoned cars; the exodus of those fleeing the city had run headlong into the steady flow of white-collar workers driving to their jobs just about the time the missiles started falling. Police and rescue personnel were hopelessly swamped. Surviving hospitals already overflowed with casualties. Channel after channel throbbed with the agonized sobbing of ambulance crews, cops, firemen overwhelmed by the horror they could do nothing to hold back.

"Sir!" A voice broke through the erratic flow of grimness. White faces turned. It was the Air Force man in charge of keeping the comm link open between the President's plane and the White House, and his voice had lost its veneer of calm. "I've lost them! NEACP-2 isn't responding."

A chill filled the room that had nothing to do with the softly droning air conditioner. "Try to raise them," MacGregor said. His dark eyes were bleak.

"I'm trying, sir. Nothing." He worked buttons in a controlled frenzy, murmuring softly to the microphone clipped to his collar. "None of the stations we've still got contact with can raise it either." He shook his head. His eyes were the eyes of a deer pinned in the glare of a poacher's searchlight. "They were feeding me data right along. Then suddenly they were just—gone."

"There—there must be a mistake!" Shaneyfelt burst out. "Try again, young man."

The man spoke into his throat mike once more. A moment later he looked up. He had to clear his throat before he could speak. "Negative, sir. Nothing."

Shaneyfelt went white and slumped in his chair. MacGregor took two steps and leaned forward, clinging to the back of the chair at the head of the table with both hands, like a drowning man clutching a piece of driftwood. His head hung down. A single drop of moisture fell to the blue upholstered seat of the chair.

Fighting to draw breath past the tightness in his throat, Sloan felt himself getting to his feet. McKay already stood to rigid attention. In a moment the other Guardians had joined him, facing MacGregor. As one man, they raised hands to brows in a crisp salute.

"Mr. President," McKay said in a husky voice, "we're waiting for your orders."

CHAPTER
THREE

Outside, McKay saw orange flame envelope the right-hand guardhouse at the western gate. A guard ran out, wrapped in flame, screaming, hands pressed to his face. The black Secret Service agent aimed the scoped G-3 and put a round through the tortured man's head as two more Molotov cocktails burst against the guardhouse on the left. The crowd flowed against the gate. It bulged inward, and McKay heard the cries of those in front as those behind crushed them against the ironwork. He poured fire into the mob at the gate. Copper-jacketed bullets lanced through the bodies at the gate like hot knives through butter, driving into the people in back of them. But the inexorable pressure never slackened.

With a squeal of rending metal, the heavy chain securing the gate burst apart.

The mob poured in like water through a ruptured dam. "Tom," McKay said urgently into his throat mike. "Aren't they finished yet?" *If only MacGregor hadn't insisted on coming aboveground to be sworn in.* But MacGregor said it wasn't appropriate for the President of the United States to take his oath of office cowering in a hole in the ground.

"I think so," Rogers replied.

"Hustle 'em the hell downstairs. I'll hold here as long as I can."

"Roger. We're moving now."

Almost two hours had passed since communication with NEACP-2 had been lost. Just forty-five minutes ago, the War Room computers had estimated a 95 percent probability that no more warheads were incoming. That had been the Guardians' signal to move. While a reserve element of Secret Service agents had gone upstairs to join their comrades who had had the unenviable assignment of staying aboveground during the attack, the four Guardians had slipped into a special secret underground garage that held the escape vehicles.

They changed from dress uniforms into urban combat fatigues camouflaged to break up their silhouettes against buildings, sidewalks and rubble. They had checked and slung their primary weapons and loaded their packs into Mobile One, the V-450 armored car in which they and the new President would ride. Then, leaving Wilson behind in the vehicle, which he would drive on the breakout, they escorted MacGregor and Shaneyfelt upstairs for the swearing-in.

The West Wing was a ruin where a handful of Secret Service men huddled under sporadic fire from the old EOB. With the Oval Office no more than a memory, MacGregor and Shaneyfelt went to the Blue Room. There—amidst fallen statues and glass blown out from the bay windows, choking on smoke from the still-smoldering blue-and-gold curtains, trying hard not to notice the ugly purple stains where the body of a Secret Service man, almost decapitated by flying glass, had lain moments before—MacGregor had prepared to speak the words that would make him President. Keyed up, too nervous to stand still, McKay left Rogers and Sloan with Clete Parkinson, the black ex-football player who commanded the White House Secret Service detachment. McKay wanted to check on the situation outdoors.

Which, he had found, was rapidly going to hell.

The mob came on the run, flowing to left and right of the lifeless fountain in the center of the lawn, dodging through the blighted trees. They waved tire irons, lengths of pipe, sticks—anything that would serve as a weapon. The eastern gatehouses had been overrun. From the corner of his eye McKay saw a guard in a short-sleeved shirt dragged out and brained with a head-sized chunk of rubble. A half-second later a young woman stepped out of the guardhouse holding an M-16A1E1. She dropped to one knee, shouldered the long black rifle, and squeezed off a round with professional aplomb.

A Secret Service man behind the middle of the wall dropped his Mini-Uzi machine pistol and the clip he had been trying to feed into it and clapped his hands to his throat, which spurted blood from front and back. As he fell, McKay hauled the M-60 around and blew the woman apart. *Is there terrorist cadre planted in this mob?* he wondered. It was unusual for even trained troops to have the discipline to fire a single shot from an automatic weapon. *No broad from the secretaries' pool oughta be able to shoot like that.*

"Billy." Young Casey Wilson's voice spoke in his ear. "The wind's changed. It's coming from the northwest now. And it's freshened to fifteen, sixteen klicks per hour."

"Far fucking out," McKay answered, realizing that meant the cloud of fallout from the titanic Mount Weather grounder would shortly be laying its lethal shadow across Washington, D.C. "The bad guys are almost here. I'm on my way."

"Roger that. We'll have the motor running."

Small-arms fire was spattering the Portico now like a summer shower. McKay turned to the blue-jawed agent on his left. The man—his name was Loretto—had his Uzi switched to single shot and was coolly picking off the charging attackers, one bullet to a customer. It was almost as if he were unaware that he and his small detachment were dead men.

"We're pulling out." McKay's voice was a croak, and not just from the feathery tendrils of teargas the wind was blowing against the blistered facade of the White House. The idea of hauling ass and leaving the Secret Service men to certain death hurt like a gut shot. But it was his duty, just as it was Loretto's duty to stay behind. "Good luck," McKay told him.

Loretto's expression showed he knew how empty the wish was. "Just get the old man out safe," he said, and turned back to the wall.

An instant later Loretto's head snapped back. A bullet had struck above his right eye. A patch of skull flipped off in a shower of blood and clots of brain, and his body collapsed.

Cursing, McKay rose to his feet. The front-runners of the mob were fifteen feet away. He sprayed them with bullets, blazing away from the hip as though the M-60 were a submachine gun. Eight of them went down, ten. With the courage of the doomed, those behind trampled the writhing bodies and stormed the Portico.

Tasting bile, McKay turned and ran.

The entrance hall was empty. Gleaming white walls echoed to the sound of his boots. In front of him the American flag and the presidential banner that had flanked the entrance to the Blue Room lay on the floor. "McKay," a voice called from his left.

He wheeled, bringing up the Maremont. Sam Sloan stood at the landing of the main stairway, beyond a door at the east end of the foyer. His Galil assault rifle with grenade launcher attached below the barrel was hung around his neck on an Israeli-style long sling. "The others are on their way to the garage," he said. "The mob's coming in from the Ellipse now too."

McKay nodded. He started forward. The big glass-and-brass cylinder of an electric candelabrum had crashed down in the middle of the hall's checkerboard floor. An orgasm of firing erupted outside as McKay veered around it.

"Look out!" Sloan shouted, fumbling to bring up his Galil. McKay wheeled around to see a shirt-sleeved man come through the door, pointing an Uzi at him.

The Maremont roared, deafeningly loud in the confines of the hall. Red holes bloomed on the man's white shirtfront, climbing his chest like a vine. He fell backward, arms flinging the machine pistol alway from him in a terminal spasm. A barefoot blond woman burst through the door and was cut down in a shower of plaster chips as McKay held down the trigger of the M-60. A young man behind her tried furiously to backpedal. A round caught him in the right arm and spun him squarely into the bullet spray. The impacts hammered him into the wall. Dark eyes stared wildly at McKay through hair that had fallen into the young man's face. He opened his mouth to speak, coughed up pink froth, and slid slowly down, leaving a scarlet smear of blood on the white plaster wall.

McKay turned and followed Sloan down the stairs to the ground floor, then left past the library to a doorway where a Secret Service man stood, Uzi in hand, waving furiously for them to hurry. Sloan raced through and pounded down the stairs. McKay was almost at his heels, the Maremont bouncing on its sling. When they reached the end of the lower-floor corridor, McKay hauled a big grenade from his belt, pulled out the pin, and bowled the grenade back down the corridor as shouts and footfalls resounded down the main staircase.

At the end of the hall, an agent slammed the metal door shut as McKay passed. From a concealed panel in the cement wall beside the door, the agent threw a knife switch and blue sparks crackled from the metal door as the powerful flux from hidden electromagnets arc-welded it immovably to its frame. That action sealed the fate of any Secret Service survivors on the floors above, but the agent never hesitated. He was doing his job, as his comrades were doing theirs.

The odds were good he wouldn't outlive them by much.

The grenade burst with a muffled bang. Already on the landing below, Sloan stopped and looked back, his square face going white at the maniacal screaming that came through the thick metal. "Willy Peter," McKay said. "That'll give the bastards something to think about."

McKay pushed past him and ran down the stairs, past the bunkers and on to the underground garage on the level below. For a moment more, Sloan stood there, listening against his will to the shrieks of people locked in the searing embrace of white phosphorus. Then he and the Secret Service man followed McKay on down.

Three vehicles waited, squat and dark in the glare of the tungsten-halogen lights overhead. The growl of their engines filled the subterranean garage. They were V-450 Super Commandos, fast four-wheeled armored personnel carriers built by Cadillac Gage. Updated versions of the old V-150 Commando, they could provide protection from chemical weapons and radiation and offered a number of other improvements in range, versatility, and electronics. They had been privately developed, and weren't in use yet by any military service. These belonged to a specially purchased lot, and were painted an anonymous olive-drab green with no markings of any sort. Two of them sported low lozenge-shaped turrets from which sprouted the muzzles of an M-60 and a Browning M-2HB .50-caliber machine gun, mounted side by side. The turret of the third—Mobile One—was similar except for weaponry. A thick stub of a barrel protruded from its front next to a coaxial M-2. It went with the vehicles' main weapon, an M-19 automatic grenade launcher.

Sloan was clambering into the side door of Mobile One. The

driver's hatch was popped, and Wilson's tow head stuck out. The boyish ex-Air Force officer was wearing a cap with an old Rolling Stones patch. Tom Rogers sat halfway out of the turret, as solid and immovable as a statue.

Casey Wilson grinned. "We've been waiting on you."

"Get that thing buttoned up and let's *move!*" McKay yelled.

Wilson and Rogers disappeared into the depths of the 450, pulling their hatches to after them. "Lieutenant McKay," a voice said. He turned. It was Parkinson, approaching with the agent who had met him at the stairs.

McKay made himself stand calmly and wait for the black Secret Service agent-in-chief to come up to him, though his every nerve was screaming for them to be under way. He and Parkinson didn't get along any too well. He respected the man, no question. Parkinson was ex-Special Forces as well as a former linebacker for the Rams; he'd been on missions in Africa and the Mideast and had been wounded as an A-team leader in Brazil. McKay figured the problem was just that he and Parkinson were both strong personalities, dominant male types, and just naturally had to butt heads, like the rams he'd seen as a boy in those nature movies they used to show on TV.

But he knew there was more to it than that.

"We're riding with you," Parkinson announced in a voice pitched oddly high to be emerging from a chest so huge. Toe to toe with McKay, the agent stood an inch taller than the Guardian leader's six-three and was even bigger around the shoulders.

"There's going to be five of us in Mobile One," McKay said. "It's getting a bit crowded."

Parkinson frowned. "They're built for a crew of twelve."

"Not with that big forty mike-mike installed. And we've got a lot of cargo. Rucks, weapons, food, all our special electronic gear." He forced himself to speak levelly, though he thought it was crazy to stand here arguing when every second was vital.

"Dammit, it's *our* job to protect the President." Parkinson was almost shouting.

That was the crux of it, out in the open now. Parkinson resented the Guardians. He thought they were horning in on his territory, that their very existence was a reflection on the competence of the Secret Service. McKay looked from the huge man to the agent who stood beside him.

"All right. One of you can ride with us."

Parkinson's lips compressed. "Very well. Hayes, you go with them. I'll be in the lead car." He turned and walked quickly to one of the other 450's.

McKay jerked his head at the wiry redheaded Hayes. "Get in. We've wasted enough time."

They piled into Mobile One. The President was in back among the stowed rucksacks, struggling into a bulky Hardcorps 4 body armor vest with help from Sloan. He finally got it over his head and settled into place as McKay slammed the door. "I don't like to complain, Lieutenant McKay," MacGregor said tentatively, "but do I have to wear this thing? It weighs a ton, and it's awfully hot. I thought the car's armor would be enough protection."

Sloan was in the radioman's seat next to Wilson, donning a headset. McKay pulled down a seat in front of the engine compartment that occupied the left rear corner of the vehicle and sat. He slipped his M-60 into clips set into the hull. "Sorry, Mr. President. The hull's good protection, but if we take hits from a high-powered weapon—a machine gun, say, or even a deer rifle—there's danger of spalling."

"Spalling?"

"Momentum from bullet impacts can knock loose bolt heads or even chunks of hull metal inside the car," Sloan explained. "They can be lethal."

MacGregor nodded. "But why do I have to wear such a big vest? You all have smaller ones."

"We have to be able to maneuver fast on the outside, Mr. President," McKay said. "Can't be weighed down with all those K-47 plates. But all you have to do is stay safe. That number four's your best bet for that."

MacGregor nodded and settled back. Casey joyously kicked the accelerator, gunning the engine explosively, ready to be off. McKay pulled on a headset, tapped the mike to test it. "Mobile One ready. Sound off."

"Mobile Two ready," came Parkinson's voice, tight with suppressed anger. Mobile Three, Justice Shaneyfelt's vehicle, acknowledged a beat later.

"Let's roll."

•　　•　　•

"Hank," the tech in Army green called from the door of the nearly abandoned War Room. "We're almost ready to go. Come *on!*"

The narrow-chested Air Force man waved him away. "I have to clear the board. SOP."

The Army tech made a face. "Are you out of your fucking mind? This is the end of the world, man. Screw standard operating procedure."

Hank's rabbit face set stubbornly. "I have my orders and I intend to follow them." He glanced at his friend. "Who knows, Jerry? We may be back soon."

Jerry shook his head in exasperation. "I'll try to make 'em hold the bus."

He disappeared to join the rest of the technicians who had been operating the War Room's computer and communications equipment. They were in a second subterranean garage where their own escape vehicle waited. Their job was done; all that remained was for them to wait until the President's caravan got clear and then they'd make their own break.

Hank's fingers flew across the console. He was smiling under his mouse-brown mustache. Thinking of the ten pounds of gold coins stashed in the bag in his locker. A hundred-sixty-grand worth, before the balloon went up. Who knew what it was worth now?

Maybe I'll buy me some hot teenaged bitch with big tits, he thought. *I always wondered—*

"This is Stronghold." The words were precise, crisp, and cold as chilled metal. There was almost no static, no distance attenuation, though Hank Morheim knew the speaker was very far away indeed. And why shouldn't it be clear? He was plugged into the same network the American armed forces and intelligence services were.

"This is Nest calling," Hank said. His heart pulsed in his throat.

"One moment."

Half a world away, a telephone rang. A heavily laden chair swiveled ponderously from a vast window opening on a scene of alpine splendor blissfully untroubled by the end of the world. A huge hand enfolded the gilded handset. The fingers were spatulate and broad, peasant's fingers, yet smooth, uncallused. A thick gold band encircled the forefinger.

The heavy hand lifted the receiver. "Yes?"

A shiver ran through Hank's shoulders and back. He knew the sound of that rich bass rumble, though he had no inkling to whom it belonged—other than that he was the man to whom Hank had sold his loyalty for considerably more than thirty pieces of silver. "This is Nest," Hank said. "The Eagle has flown. Mount Weather denied, likewise Raven Rock emergency command facility. Eagle's destination unknown."

"We have that information. You have done well." The words were a massive caress. "There may be a place for you in the new order."

"I—thank you." Hank felt a hot flush of pleasure. It was good to be in with a winner. It made him feel strong. "Nest out."

Across the ocean, the strong hand still held the telephone receiver. In a moment the cold voice that had first answered Hank's call came on the line. "Master."

"Get me Langley."

CHAPTER
FOUR

Parkinson's V-450 drove onto a concrete ramp sloping gently upward. Wilson pulled Mobile One in behind it, and the final vehicle mounted the incline as heavy steel-and-concrete blast doors drew slowly aside to reveal the weird roiling yellow sky. Casey craned his neck forward. "Will you look at *that*." His jaw hung slightly open. He had remained so calm, almost carefree, in the bunker. Sloan wondered if it had taken the sight of what had happened to the sky to make it all real to the young fighter pilot. Parkinson's driver hit the gas and Mobile Two leaped out into the jaundiced sunlight.

Wilson stayed where he was, noisily idling the V-8 diesel as the first vehicle raced out of sight over the lip of the ramp and across the drive onto the southern lawn. In a moment the men in Mobile One clearly heard the snarl of the M-60 cutting across the slow hammer of a .50 caliber. "What've you got, Mobile Two?" McKay asked.

"Scum bags all over the south lawn," Parkinson told him. Parkinson had also spent five years as a Dallas policeman, both as a patrolman and on the SWAT team. His police experiences had left their mark on his vocabulary. "We'll clear 'em off in a minute."

Shouts and screams wafted down to Mobile One as the guns

continued to pound. The crowd noise turned from insensate fury to wailing high-pitched panic, then began to recede. "This is Two," Parkinson's voice crackled in the headset. "Got 'em on the run."

"Roger," McKay said. "Casey, hit it."

The 450 bounded ahead. It bounced over the top like Steve McQueen bombing over Telegraph Hill and hit the curving drive at a run, heeling over hard as Casey cranked the wheel left. The turret motor whined as Rogers traversed right. "I see 'em," his voice came over the intercom. "Nothin' but assholes and elbows."

"Stop her here, Casey." McKay got out of his seat and came forward to peer over Sloan's shoulder through the view slit as the vehicle bucked to a stop. The Washington Monument had broken off a third of the way up and lay pointing toward them like a gray stone finger, mute and accusing. The dome of the Jefferson Memorial had cracked like a marble eggshell. The waters of the Tidal Basin mirrored the towering cloud of the firestorm stalking through the southwest quadrant like Godzilla in a Japanese movie: with fire in its belly, red-shot black against a sky filled with rushing puke-colored clouds piled high and tumbling over one another.

Closer in, McKay saw feathery plumes of water down where the Anacostia and the Washington channel joined the putrid course of the Potomac. "They must have fireboats working," Sloan commented. "That's the Naval Station."

"Pretty hard-core," said McKay.

Mobile Two was planted in the middle of the lawn, scattering rounds after a thoroughly routed mob. The old mystique of armor, McKay reflected. There were enough rioters out there to tip the goddamn V-450 over and pound it open with rocks. As prodigious as the power of its two guns was, there were too many people too far gone in killing frenzy for that to stop them. But the apparition of a lumbering dinosaur with an invincible steel hide seldom failed to fill the human heart with terror.

"Need to clear my guns, Billy," Rogers said. "Shall I fire 'em up?"

"Don't grease 'em. They're headed in the right direction. Give 'em a little something to keep 'em moving." Mobile Three had emerged from the garage now, and at its signal the concealed blast doors were sliding back into place. The third vehicle pulled around right and onto the lawn in front of the smoldering remnants of the Rose Garden so the three turrets could cover the maximum frontage. McKay noted with approval that the Secret Service driver avoided the trap of becoming the third point of a neat triangle. No point in providing an easy geometric target, just in case there were bad guys with anti-tank weapons out there.

If the shithammer falls, Crenna had told them, everybody's *your enemy unless proven otherwise. That includes police, National Guard, regular armed forces, civilian governments. You just don't know who's been waiting to set himself up as a backyard Ayatollah*. The odds were a thousand to one against somebody lurking in the cherry trees of the Monument grounds, aiming the optical sight of a TOW antitank missile at the South Portico. But the Guardians had not been formed to take chances with the President's life—no matter what the odds.

The steel hull of Mobile One vibrated to the slow pounding of the M-2. The turf at the heels of the fleeing mob suddenly exploded in huge gouts. McKay grinned approvingly. He was a leatherneck, a foot soldier by training and inclination, and the idea of riding around in a big tin can waiting for some motherfucker with a throwaway rocket to fry his ass didn't have much appeal. But there was no way the President of the United States was going to hump it out of the stricken capital on foot. So they were stuck with the car. But there were compensations.

One of which was that Mobile One had the firepower of a whole infantry company.

The effect of the .50 was awesome. But it was nothing compared to what happened next. The mob had already spilled past the fountain and was streaming across E Street. Then came four thuds, dull and slow.

A wall of dirt and white smoke thirty meters wide shot up across the south end of the lawn as two armor-piercing HEDP and two WP grenades from One's 40 mm automatic launcher went off. Casey whistled appreciatively. "That M-19 sure can rock and roll."

"All squared away," Rogers said laconically.

"Let's go. Parkinson?"

"I read you."

"Lead off. Head out the gate onto State Place and cut south

of the Executive Office Building to Seventeenth, then see if we can jog over to Eighteenth. That might give us the best shot north.''

"Roger.'' The 450 turned right and drove across the lawn, its wheels churning up the pampered turf, till it reached the paved drive curving to the south. McKay let them get fifty yards ahead, then nodded to Casey. Mobile One rolled out.

McKay braced himself and stayed in a crouch behind Sloan. "Mobile Three, follow us at about thirty meters.'' It wasn't much interval, but McKay didn't want the three cars strung out over half of Foggy Bottom. They weren't worried about barrage artillery anyway. *May be the only goddamn thing we're* not *worried about.*

"Mobile One.'' It was Parkinson again. His car had just nosed through the gate onto State. "We're getting some police traffic. The interference is terrific, but it sounds like they've got a riot up around Dupont Circle.''

"Head north on Eighteenth anyway. If we have to we can cut around by Scott Circle.''

"Roger.'' A pause while static did its snap-crackle-pop dance in McKay's ears. The vehicle radios were the latest word in communications technology. They were not only shielded from electromagnetic interference and scrambled six ways from Sunday, but they had computerized filters up the waz. If this much shit was coming past their filters, it was a miracle the police signal was getting through at all. "Should we let the police know we're coming?''

"Negative.'' McKay didn't raise his voice, but the word rapped out like a blow.

"But if we could get some information on routes out, maybe an escort—''

"I said no. The closure on this mission is absolute. *Nobody* knows who we are.''

Casey glanced over, not smiling for once. That meant that if anyone tried to slow them down—even an Army roadblock—their mission was to blast through. It took a special kind of man to be a Guardian. You even had to be prepared to fire on your own side: the mission had absolute priority.

But no one said you had to like it.

Parkinson wasn't convinced. "I still say—''

"You've got your orders,'' McKay said.

The agent fell silent. His car had reached the corner of State and Seventeenth and stopped, its turret swinging right. A moment later McKay saw pallid flame dart from the muzzles. He heard Rogers traversing his turret to cover West Executive. "Old White House took it hard," Rogers remarked.

McKay peered through the slit to his right. The executive mansion loomed above the trees. Rogers was right. The windows were gone; the West Wing and executive offices had collapsed. Several of the pillars of the portico had fallen down, and the Truman balcony and the Promenade hung down drunkenly like slack lips. *If I'd known all that was going to happen, I wouldn't have let MacGregor into the fucking Blue Room,* McKay thought.

"I wonder if I'll be back," MacGregor said, peering wistfully out a slit. "I wonder if any president will live there again."

"Our assignment's terminated when we get to Heartland, Mr. President," Casey said brashly. "Maybe then we can go to work trying to get you back here."

MacGregor looked at him in what McKay thought was a peculiar way. Suddenly Casey yelped. McKay looked out the forward slit to see figures running down the block at them. One raised a bottle with a blazing rag stuffed into it high over his head. The .50 cal. burped, and the man went down hard, knocked rolling by the ounce-and-a-half slugs. The others scattered, but not fast enough. The sudden splash of flaming gasoline caught two of them. They fled shrieking up the street until Rogers bowled them over with a short burst.

"We had a hangup on Seventeenth," Parkinson radioed. "It's clear now. We're driving on."

"Roger." Mobile One crossed the street. MacGregor peered at the mobs visible on the front lawn of the White House.

"Why?" he asked. "They came right up in the face of the Secret Service men's guns. What could make people do that?"

"Fear, Mr. President," Sloan said. "Fear and pain and anger."

They pulled around onto Seventeenth. McKay saw Parkinson's "hangup": a handful of bodies slumped on the front steps of the battered EOB. Long arms—rifles or shotguns—lay near several of them. Mobile Two, its turret slowly revolving, was at the far end of the block, waiting just out of reach of the orange flames bellying out of the Renwick Gallery.

"Here's Mobile Three," Sloan said. All three vehicles

started down the street at about twenty klicks an hour. Negotiating around abandoned cars, Mobile Two scouted a hundred meters or so ahead, the other two coming along behind.

They probed cautiously through blasted streets. Images of horror confronted them on every side: a portly matron lying in front of a blazing hotel in a sprawl of blood, her guts trailing back into the lobby from which she had dragged herself after being eviscerated by a flying sheet of polarized glass; burned-out cars with families sitting inside, charred into black effigies; a young woman crushed under a Step-van that had been tossed like a Tonka toy by the blast wave; a little girl in pigtails, lying on her back with black foam crusted on her mouth, her lungs burst by air overpressure. A bearded black man in T-shirt and torn jeans stood barefoot over her and wept into his hands.

An ambulance lay on its side like a dead insect, blankets of flame flapping over the box and cab. A black medical tech lay beside it. His head had been crushed in with a cinder block. And not by accident, if the stocky white woman in an identical pale green uniform lying a few meters away with a fire ax imbedded in her breastbone was any clue. Hayes gulped and turned green under his freckles. The others looked at one another grim faced. No one asked the obvious question, why someone would kill the very people who were working hard to help them. It wasn't the kind of question they liked to think they could answer.

The air conditioner whined. It was working well; the temperature was quite comfortable inside the vehicle. "I may sound ungrateful," MacGregor said. He sat hanging on to a strap, staring out at the corpse of the city. "But I thought it would look even worse. Like those pictures of Hiroshima."

"Washington's not built of wood and paper, sir," Casey said. "Hiroshima and Nagasaki were."

Sloan was fiddling with the radio, monitoring scraps of emergency-wavelength broadcasts. "Got a transmission from Capitol Hill," he said. "Got a mob there too. They've over-run the Capitol and the House and Senate office buildings, and they're breaking into the shelters to get at the Senators. Just hauling them out and slaughtering them."

"Mobile One, this is Mobile Two." McKay saw the lead car stopped several blocks ahead, at the corner of Eighteenth and

Jefferson Place. "I can see Dupont Circle. They're having a war up there."

"Okay. Go right on Rhode Island, over to Logan, and see what Thirteenth looks like."

"We could really give the cops a hand up there," Parkinson said.

"Do it."

"Roger."

Mobile Two moved out to the northeast. Mobile One followed, driving past old Henry Wadsworth Longfellow, where he lay toppled off his pedestal into Connecticut Avenue. He didn't look happy.

"We'd make better time if we popped the hatch and I could stick my head out, see where we're going, you know?" Casey said.

"No way," McKay said. "All we need is to take a stray round down the hatch."

"More than that," Sloan said, "it's already up to ten rads per hour out there."

"That's not much," Casey persisted.

McKay grunted. "Bullshit, it's not."

"It's getting worse," said Sloan. "And we don't need it inside." Casey colored at the rebuff but kept his eyes on the road.

They raced through Scott Circle. Two police cars were nose to nose across Massachusetts Avenue, with the stern visage of Daniel Webster staring down on them from one side and orange flames billowing out of the Philippine Embassy on the other. A pair of blackened mummies, who were once chess addicts, lay beside a cement chess table with a gray fused mass of plastic on top. The unfortunate Washington wood-pushers had been caught in the open and hadn't moved fast enough to get out of the thermal pulse of a one-megaton blast.

Cops in bulky vests holding shotguns and M-16's stood behind the barricading patrol cars, staring from behind the faceplates of their riot helmets as the convoy rolled by across the street they were blocking. "We ought to wave, at least," Casey murmured, but he kept on rolling.

At Logan Circle they bore north on Thirteenth. Impressionistic glances down side streets showed fire engines hosing futile jets of water into flaming buildings where there was still pressure; an ambulance, sirens yowling, careening in and out of trashed-out cars as refugees clung to the outside like baby opossums on their mother's back. The V-450's passed survivors trudging toward some hopeful shelter under the eyes of police and National Guardsmen, or roaming apparently at random, blank-faced and apathetic.

Soon they found themselves slowing down even more. They were entering the zone where the blast radii of the Washington Parkway Interchange explosion and the burst north of the University of Maryland overlapped. The destruction here was far worse: buildings slopped all over the streets, burned-out cars jutted upended from piles of rubble.

"Jesus!" Sloan reeled back in his seat, tearing at the headphones. The scream from the lead vehicle had almost taken his head off.

"What is it, Parkinson?" McKay asked, his own ears ringing.

"See for yourself." The ex-linebacker's voice shook like a leaf.

Mobile Two had halted at a side street. Casey nosed his V-450 up behind it and stopped. Looters streamed out of the embassy of some Third World nation half a block along, toting television sets, computer terminals, paintings in gilt frames, oblivious alike to the squat armored cars and a pair of police in short-sleeved shirts who stood by watching. But it wasn't the looting, or the indifference of the police, that had wrenched the cry from Parkinson's throat.

Down the side street came a procession of the damned, the walking dead—naked, reeling creatures with their skin hanging off them in shreds like old tattered clothing. Their eyeballs had melted and run like wax, and now flies clustered in black clots on the shiny trails that ran down their flayed cheeks. They stumbled blindly along, mewling to one another, clutching shoulders and limbs with stumps of fingers. A dozen, then two, all ages—women, children, men, blacks, whites, Chicanos, all rendered indistinguishable in a melting pot fueled by thermonuclear flame.

"Oh, God!" MacGregor buried his face in his hands. Agent Hayes retched, grabbed a hat from somebody's ruck, and vomited into it. The thick sick-sweet odor filled the compartment.

Soon the vehicles were working their way north as best they could, cutting back and forth as they sought a passage out of the city. The air conditioner struggled to overpower the combined smells of vomit, sweat, and oil, but it was a losing battle. The Guardians had two problems: how to get the President out of Washington, and where to go once they were clear. Police broadcasts they'd monitored on the much more powerful equipment of the War Room told them the Potomac and Anacostia bridges were either out or clogged with cars. So their best bet was to work their way north.

In the mountains northwest of D.C. lay two special underground bunkers meant to serve as alternate government centers in case of nuclear attack. But Mount Weather had been hit by the huge SS-18 missile. And Raven Rock, on the Maryland-Pennsylvania border, had been inundated with ground bursts. By the evidence, the Soviets had been more concerned to hit the hardened "secret" installations dotted throughout Virginia and into Maryland than the capital itself. Or perhaps most of the missiles meant for Washington had simply missed, and Virginia paid the price for bias.

Now the Guardians' ultimate destination lay under a bluff in north-central Iowa: Heartland Complex. To reach it, they would rendezvous with a C-130 cargo plane at a secret CIA airfield in southern Pennsylvania. If all went well, they would fly most of the way to Heartland instead of having to battle their way across half a continent devastated by thermonuclear war. Before they'd left the War Room, they had confirmed that the base remained intact and secure. So now they were headed north to Pennsylvania.

Parkinson's voice came back over McKay's headphones. "Road's blocked, too high for the four-fifties to climb."

McKay squinted ahead. The lead vehicle was stopped a few blocks down from Grant Circle. The buildings to both sides had simply toppled into each other, forming a barrier as high as the deck of the Commando vehicle at its lowest.

"Back up and try another street over."

"Roger."

The front car backed up and trundled down a cross street. Casey leaned forward, arms crossed on the steering wheel, tapping his fingers impatiently. This stop-and-go crawling ate at his nerves, McKay knew. Wilson was used to the thoroughbred feel of an F-16, the high speed and exquisite responsiveness. Casey drove the way he flew: to the max, pushing himself and his machine to the very limits, yet always in control. It made him an ideal driver for the unit under the most dire circumstances; in an ambush or chase situation, where the driver's skill and speed of reflexes made all the difference, Casey was in his element. But here in the streets of a shattered city, unable to move faster than a man could run, he obviously felt trapped.

It would only get worse. Parkinson reported back that all the streets ahead were blocked by rubble. "There are places where we could climb over," the agent reported. "But somebody'd have to scout ahead on foot, make sure we didn't bog down."

"The way those two missiles fell, we can't expect to find anything much better anywhere we look," Sloan said.

"Face it, McKay," Parkinson said. "We're going to have to get help."

"No."

"Lieutenant McKay?" It was an old man's voice, brittle with impatience.

"Who's this?"

"Chief Justice Shaneyfelt. Why this ridiculous insistence on our going it alone? We should try to contact the civil authorities. We could commandeer a bulldozer, clear ourselves a path."

"I'm sorry, Mr. Chief Justice. I have my orders. No communications with anybody except a security-cleared base area."

"I insist on talking to President MacGregor!"

McKay shrugged and pulled off the headset. "It's for you, Mr. President."

Stooped over, MacGregor walked forward and held one earpiece against his ear. "We'd better not hang around here too long," Sloan said, reading glowing numbers from the panel in front of him. "Radiation count's shooting up. Over eighteen rads an hour already, and the computer says it's going to get a hell of a lot worse. This thing's well shielded, but there's a limit to what we can take."

McKay straightened and unbuckled his belt. Laying it aside, he opened a compartment in the hull, took out a folded one-piece white garment, and began to pull it on. He was big, and found it difficult to dress in the cramped space.

"Lieutenant?" He glanced around to see the President holding out the headset. "The Chief Justice wanted me to order you to turn around and try to get in touch with the police or National Guard.''

McKay met his gaze calmly. "What did you tell him, sir?"

"That you're in charge."

McKay nodded. He strapped a gas mask over his face and pulled a hood up over his head. "What're you doing?" Sloan asked, a frown on his long rectangular face.

"Going outside." His voice was garbled by the mask, but the larynx mike picked it up, and the calculator-sized communicator in McKay's right front shirt pocket transmitted it clearly to the plugs in his teammates' ears. "Somebody's going to have to pick a way through the rubble."

"You're going outside?" MacGregor's look was incredulous. "In *that*?"

"It's the only way." He took everything off his belt but his sheathed Kabar knife, his combat-modified .45 in the full-flap Kevlar holster he wore when he was in his cammies, and two magazine holders. Then he restrapped the belt around his waist. No use carrying canteens, medical kit, or another gas mask outside. He wouldn't be drinking through the mask, nor applying Band-Aids, and the less stuff that had to be decontaminated before he got back in the vehicle, the better.

"But the fallout—it's incredibly dangerous! What if somebody attacks you?"

McKay shrugged. "It's my job, Mr. President," he said, pulling on a pair of heavy gauntlets. "Nobody lives forever. Sloan, give me a hand getting the diaphragm over the hatch."

CHAPTER
FIVE

Another typical military fuckup, Billy McKay had thought bitterly as he studied his teammates. It was nine o'clock that first morning at the Project Guardian training camp somewhere in Arizona, and the un-air-conditioned briefing room in the old barracks was already stifling with dry desert heat. *I should have expected it.*

Major Crenna, looking quite dapper for a man with Death for a face, sat behind a desk at the head of the classroom, outlining the Guardians' mission. By his side stood a small, stocky Indian in an Army uniform with sergeant's stripes on his sleeves. He seemed to be the Major's factotum. McKay had heard this song and dance before, and so he lounged back in an uncomfortable wooden chair that must have dated from the Spanish-American War and studied the men who had been picked as his teammates.

Sitting to the right of McKay, comfortably at ease with one leg crossed over the other, was a tall, lanky man in his late twenties with a square lived-in-looking face and a shock of dark brown hair and a brown mustache. McKay had seen the face before, in a grainy wire photo of a newspaper. It belonged to Commander Samuel Gibbons Sloan, late of the cruiser *Winston-Salem.* He had become an overnight sensation after his ship was attacked by Libyan missile boats while on maneuvers in the Gulf of Sidra. His superior officers had all been wiped out by a bridge strike, and he had been forced to take command and fight his way free of a series of surface and air attacks by Libyan forces. The *Winston-Salem* had eventually limped to safety under an umbrella of Tomcat fighters launched from the *Nimitz*. The incident had been part of a steady escalation of hostilities between Libya, the U.S., and an Israeli-dominated Egypt. In the weeks since McKay's interview with Major Crenna, the incident had led to an Egyptian-Israeli invasion of Libya that was still in progress. It had made Sloan a nine-days' wonder with the media, a modern American hero to inspire the folks back home. Sloan looked like Tom Selleck, and with the same easy, folksy awshucks air as the actor, he was a natural for the role of hero.

His behavior during the cruiser's fighting withdrawal had indicated a cool disposition and a quick mind under fire, as well as a certain tactical intelligence. They were characteristics far rarer than commonly believed, and McKay respected them. But he still had a large question in his mind as to just what Cdr. Sloan was *doing* here.

To McKay's left, a little apart from the others, sat a kid in an Air Force uniform, with dirty blond hair and a pair of mirror shades propped on his slender nose. He was tapping the flat of one hand on the seat next to him and appeared to be paying attention to anything in the world but Crenna's gravel-dry baritone. He looked like a surf bum, but McKay knew his real story, if again only by reputation. His name was Kenneth C. Wilson, and he was a twenty-six-year-old lieutenant who happened to be the top-scoring American ace since Korea.

His moment of fame had happened almost a year before. Wilson had been leader of a flight of F-16's, flying MiGCAP for a strike force of F-15B's attacking Aden, the capital and chief deep-water port of the ever-troublesome People's Democratic Republic of Yemen, which was both supporting guerrillas against the Saudis and prosecuting an open war of its own against its vast but underpopulated neighbor.

Wilson's had been a risky assignment. With the waning of Soviet influence in Africa, South Yemen had become both a major Soviet stronghold and a showcase for the Soviet bloc's armed might, such as it was. East German mercenaries commanded the country's armed forces, while battle-hardened

North Vietnamese pilots trained an air force purchased with Libyan oil money, and Soviet technicians and advisers did their best to keep the whole show rolling. Because Yemen, remote as it was, provided the Soviets with combat experience against a foe vastly more civilized than the rebellious hillmen of Afghanistan and the Muslim Soviet Socialist Republics, being an "adviser" in Yemen was a posting much in demand for the more fire-eating elements of the Soviet military.

Despite his relative youth, "Casey" Wilson had won his position as flight leader by way of two earlier kills involving MiG-21's. This day the MiG's were out in force to resist the American strike against the vital port of Aden. When the smoke cleared, young Casey had to ditch his bullet-riddled F-16 in the shark-infested waters of the Gulf of Aden, to be picked up by rescue choppers from a carrier task force in the Indian Ocean. But neither the loss of his plane nor the presence of the big delta-shaped dorsal fins of great whites cleaving the water just beyond range of his sonic shark-repeller bothered Casey overmuch, because he had flamed no fewer than five of the big swing-wing MiG-23's that had confronted the strike force.

It made him an immediate sensation. It was the biggest single-mission kill by an American pilot since the Second World War. As a bonus, Wilson became by two kills the top-scoring American pilot since Korea. An Air Force back-seater —copilot and radar operator of a two-seat Phantom fighter— named Steve Ritchie was credited with taking part in six kills in Vietnam, but no *pilot* had more than five.

McKay gathered that Wilson had been rotated home immediately after his record-smashing mission; he had been an asset too valuable to risk in further air-to-air combat. If Wilson had anything like a normal fighter pilot's mentality, however, the intervening months would have been torture. The desire to get back into action, any action, might well have motivated Wilson to volunteer for this assignment.

But once again, it didn't explain why he'd been accepted.

Finally, behind McKay's left shoulder sat Tom Rogers. Though his uniform was brand spanking new, you could almost see the place where the sergeant's chevrons had been. Like McKay, Rogers was a mustang; his promotion to lieutenant had apparently followed his acceptance of Major Crenna's offer to join the Guardians. Solid, stolid, sandy-haired Rogers had been on active duty with the U.S. Army Special Forces for almost half his thirty-three years. Like the others, he was known to McKay—but not from headline articles in *Stars & Stripes*. Rogers had spent his whole career in the shadow world of covert operations. McKay didn't know anything very concrete about him—the stories told about him were always vague, unsubstantiated rumors. Rogers had probably been too young to be involved in the well-publicized assassination by bomb of a high-ranked member of Khomeini's Revolutionary Council, an action commonly credited to the leftists opposition, but it was known he had worked in Iran both before and after Khomeini's death brought about the dissolution of the Shiite regime and the coming to power of the broader-based Islamic Front. And he had worked in Cambodia and Latin America, and possibly on missions within the U.S.S.R. itself.

There was no way to document any of this; it was probably at least half BS. But the common theme running through all the tales was that Tom Rogers was one of the best: a very quiet type, not a cowboy, not flashy in the least, but an utterly reliable man with a can-do attitude and the skills—and balls—to back it up. McKay had never seen his face before. But of all his fellow Guardians, Rogers was the one he was very pleased to see now.

When the briefing was over, McKay hung back, waiting in front of Crenna's desk as the others returned to their quarters. The Major sat back and watched him with a sardonic smile on his ruined face. "May I help you, Lieutenant?"

"Where do I go to get out of this outfit?" he asked. The poker-faced Indian Sergeant had shut the door and now stood beside Crenna's desk. McKay already knew Crenna well enough to realize the Sergeant was a permanent fixture of Crenna's office.

Crenna's expression didn't change. "I thought you were all hot to get in."

"That was before I knew what you were coming up with for the rest of the team." He did his best to keep his tone level.

Crenna raised his remaining eyebrow. "What's wrong with them? They're fine men, with the best possible records."

"I don't deny that for a minute, Major." McKay's tone was heating up despite his resolve to play this hand cool. "But, for God's sake! A jet-jockey and a line officer off a fuckin' *cruiser*!" He shook his head. "I don't believe this! The mission you lined out for me calls for maximum experience in land warfare, urban combat, and antiterrorism. Stuff this guy Rogers and I have been doing for years.''

"I gather your objections don't pertain to the Lieutenant," Crenna murmured.

"Shit, no! But, Major—" He wagged his head like an exasperated bull. "I'm sure Commander Sloan and Lieutenant Wilson are total heroes, a real Farragut and an Eddie fucking Rickenbacker to go with him. But being a Guardian is going to call for infantry skills, the kind of experience you get on the ground, in the streets. Knowing where an enemy will hide, how to spot a sniper, when and where to pop a grenade. It's not that they ain't good men, Major. But they're going to be helpless as babies when it comes down to protecting the President, to say nothing of keeping their own asses from getting shot off."

Major Crenna nodded slowly. "I understand your objections, Lieutenant. But I think you underestimate these men. They have shown themselves to be brilliant and adaptable, as well as outstanding in the roles for which they were initially trained. And they—like you—will receive literally the best training in the world. We have laid on experts in all fields that pertain to this assignment. Including"—the intact corner of his mouth quirked up—"you and Lieutenant Rogers."

McKay laid big hands on the edge of Crenna's desk. "But why *bother*? The Green Bean—uh, I mean the Berets must be full of guys who've already been trained in this stuff. The same with Force Recon and the SEAL's and Rangers. Why not go with them?"

"Can you fly an airplane, Lieutenant?"

"Well, no, but—"

"Casey Wilson is an expert pilot—one of the world's best, by any reckoning. And are you a mechanic? That young man can work wonders with any manner of internal-combustion engine, be it plane or car or boat. Can you?"

"Well, I had an old Mustang when I was a kid. . . ." He let his voice trail off. Crenna was visibly unimpressed.

"And electronics, Lieutenant? How much work have you done in that field? Don't bother; I know you've taken communications courses. And Lieutenant Commander Sloan is an electrical engineer. And an expert in computers, hardware and software both. Plus he can operate any surface vessel you care to put him in, from a kayak to an aircraft carrier.''

"That's all good and well, Major—"

"Please don't squeeze so hard, Lieutenant. You'll leave fingerprints on my desk."

McKay stopped, stared down at his whitened knuckles. With a long sigh, he forced the tension from his knotted muscles. "Okay, Major." He managed a grin. "I'll lighten up. But if we're to be an elite unit intended to get the President out of Washington in the middle of World War Three, what do we need all this other stuff for? It's going to come down to straight shoot-'em-up, bang-you're-dead work in the end."

"Are you sure?" McKay stared at him. "You underestimate the difficulty of your task. To get the President to safety you may have to resort to whatever transport you can beg, borrow, or steal—including, need I say, aircraft and boats. And a state-of-the-art knowledge of electronics and computers could make the difference between life and death. There's going to be more involved in this than snooping, pooping, and shooting."

McKay squeezed his eyes shut. "All right. I grant you that, Major. But still—couldn't you have found somebody in SF or one of the other special-services units who knows how to fly and to work on computers?"

Crenna sat back. The Indian stood by, watching disinterestedly with his coal-black eyes. "Possibly, Lieutenant, possibly." Crenna steepled his hands before him, an oddly prissy gesture for such a hard-bitten man. "But there were other considerations involved in putting this project together besides the training or technical capacities of the participants. It took a lot of doing to sell this concept at the necessary high levels. It was necessary to have one man from each service— Army, Marines, Air Force, and Navy. No, don't interrupt. I *know* there are special-services outfits in each branch that could provide what you'd consider more appropriate recruits, McKay. But it took a certain amount of glamor to sell this package. Glamor is what Sloan has, and young Wilson too. Even you, to an extent. Your getting blown up in Libya made the wire services. But the better part of your career is deep-cover, buried so deep no one could ever find it. And what has Tom Rogers done that you could show even a trusted member of a secret Senate oversight committee?

"The military has a lot of power in America these days.

Maybe just a touch too much. But it's still politics that makes the world go round, Lieutenant. We *need* a team like the Guardians to keep our nation's command intact at the time it's needed most. So we did what we had to to get them.''

McKay stared at the hardwood floor. *Politics.* Shit. He might have known.

"They're good men, McKay. The best. And your team will be the best.''

His head snapped up. "*My* team? But I thought—''

"As you point out, Commander Sloan lacks the proper experience to command a unit of this nature. The Guardians are totally outside the normal military chain of command, so the fact that he outranks you is far less important than your qualifications to lead the team.''

"Outranks me! Jesus, he's got the same pull as a light colonel! I'm just a crummy lieutenant, and a Marine at that. We're still the Navy's poor cousin, Major. I never met a Navy officer who thought a fucking jarhead could be trained to shit in a pot, much less command.''

Crenna smiled. "I believe you underestimate Commander Sloan. He's already agreed to this setup, as have all the men.'' The smile widened. "It seems Lieutenant Rogers is as impressed with your reputation as you are unimpressed with his.''

He stood. "And as to the Commander—he's just as aware of his limitations as you are. He doesn't feel he's competent to command this outfit. And he knows you are.''

"He ain't gonna like it, though.''

McKay had had little opportunity to test his gloomy prediction over the next few months. Crenna hadn't been shitting him when he said they'd get the best training in the world. At least, not if "best'' had anything to do with "most demanding.''

There were courses in *everything*. From the time the Guardians crawled out of their beds to go running across the desert in the dawn's early light, trying to keep pace with the indefatigable Sgt. Betzinez, Crenna's Apache aide, to the time they crept back into the rack, they were busy full time with the damnedest array of mind-expanding and ball-busting courses imaginable.

It turned out that while each man was to have his specialty, his area of expertise, he was also expected to have at least a grounding in the others' fields. McKay's head swirled with bytes, bauds, and semiconductors; he went hand-to-hand with resistance, capacitance, voltage, and amperage; he even learned how to get a light plane off the ground and then back *onto* the ground without bending it badly. He wasn't stupid; in fact he was a hell of a lot brighter than the average Joe Blow. But there were times, as he wrestled with an equation that Sloan and Wilson ripped off with the ease of a dirty limerick, when he wondered if he shouldn't just pack it in and ask to be sent back to the Med to shoot at Arabs and get blown out of helicopters.

Their professors were a bag as mixed as the classes they taught. Their drillmaster was none other than Betzinez, who amply displayed the famed cruelty of his Chiricahua forebears, running them through a routine of calisthenics and physical training that would disjoint a yogi, founder a pack mule, and make Arnold Schwarzenegger forsake pumping iron for a life of eating quiche and reading the works of Marcel Proust.

There was Major Moon Duk Soo, R.O.K.A., fifth-dan black belt in Tae Kwon Do, a perpetually smiling brick wall of a man who was almost as wide across the shoulders as he was tall. He stood seven inches less than McKay's six-three, must have weighed seventy pounds less, and could toss any two of the Guardians around without ever straining his Ultra-Brite smile. There was the equally affable Sgt. Lal Gurung, on loan from Her Majesty's Gurkha Rifles, who showed them how to take out sentries the way he'd done as a lad in the Falklands. Even Rogers and McKay, old hands at this sort of thing, found they had plenty to learn from the compact khaki-clad man.

From Silicon Valley came Dr. Janice Torres, who knew computers the way Einstein knew the theories of general and special relativity, and who could keep up with Sgt. Betzinez on those early-morning constitutionals when even former Olympic marathoner Sam Sloan was dragging in the dust. When she'd finished bending their minds out of shape, they might be turned over to Charlton "Buck" Chasko, former Marine turned investment counselor, a potbellied, bearded, balding man who was Jeff Cooper's successor as dean of American combat handgunning. Or they might listen to Captain Yitzhak (whether it was his first or last name, nobody knew), who lectured on desert and counterterrorist warfare. He was an ageless little man with a ginger goatee and the complexion of a Frye boot, who'd served with the Israeli army since the Sinai War of '56 and was also an internationally rated chess master.

His New York-born countryman Barry Cohen was in charge of giving the Guardians the word on sniping. A slender young man with an engaging manner who could have passed for Uri Geller, he had been born into the profession. His father had been one of the "specialists" involved in the cross-Suez Channel war of attrition of the early seventies. Exempted from military service by secret fiat of the Israeli Prime Minister, young Cohen hired his long gun to anyone who could meet his exorbitant fees—as long as the Mossad cleared them.

From the Khyber Pass and the endless war against the Soviets came "Jake Shaw"—Major Yakub Shah, more properly, six feet seven inches tall with a red-dyed beard and a nose like a talwar. He was a Pathan of the Mohmand tribe, and an international authority on guerrilla resistance and mountain warfare. Going a few rounds with him in knife fighting—simulated by wearing goggles and using small blades capable only of leaving scratches—McKay was always left looking like a road map of New Jersey.

To let them know just what to expect if the hammer fell, they had lectures from Dr. Jeff LeWinter, a biochemist and at thirty one of the leading experts on the long- and short-term effects of N-weapons and warfare. Less appropriate, to McKay's way of thinking, were the classes they had to take on jungle warfare. But there was no arguing with the choice of instructors. Colonel Phoc Tri was an old comrade-in-arms of Tom Rogers, having served with him off and on against the North Vietnamese in Cambodia in the late seventies and early eighties. At thirteen, the Colonel had been in on the fall of Phnom Penh, though not from the side of the angels. Which wasn't surprising, since the Colonel was, and always had been, a member in good standing of the Khmer Rouge. His presence was somewhat controversial. But McKay had served with Soviet agents in Iran, so he wasn't in a position to complain.

From all over the world they came, specialists in communications, field medicine, every kind of warfare conceivable. Gradually, their roles in the team came into focus. McKay was the natural leader, confident and decisive but not afraid to ask advice when he was out of his territory. In a patrol situation he'd take point, and he carried the scaled-down but still beefy Maremont light M-60.

Sam Sloan, of course, handled electronics, commo, and computer work. He learned to handle patrolling fairly well, though McKay worried about how he'd stand up when the shit started to fly. There was no way to simulate real live life-or-death battle. The fact that Sloan had stood up under fire before was a good sign, but fighting on a cruiser under attack by missile boats and aircraft was a world away from hunkering behind a bush with AK rounds cracking by your ears. Sloan would never be great shakes as a marksman, but he showed a surprising affinity for the M-203 40 mm grenade launcher. On the ground he was a dedicated rifle grenadier.

Casey Wilson was the sniper and marksman. He was a phenomenal shot, far better than McKay, who was rated Expert by exacting Marine standards. He loved high-tech gimmicks, yet the weapon he chose was in most particulars old hat: a bolt-action M-40 with synthetic stock and a bipod. There were any number of nifty semiauto sniper's weapons available, from the Army's old standard M-21—a converted M-14—to an immense creature made by Walther that looked like a bench-rest rifle and cost as much as a luxury car. Yet Casey took the prosaic bolt gun as the most accurate available. Of course he had a real *Star Wars*-style telescopic sight to go with it, with automatic ranging and "starlight" capabilities.

Casey was a strange creature. He was either being as hyper as a wirehaired terrier, or so laid back you were tempted to check his pulse. If you got him into a vehicle, he was wired, practically vibrating behind the wheel—until he actually started to roll. Then he turned into another person entirely, a calm, in-control Chuck Yeager clone. In the field he'd crouch down behind the crestline of a hill for hours in exercises, waiting for the proper shot at a thousand-meter target. But in unarmed combat drill he was the only one of the teammates McKay was actually afraid of. He simply went berserk. He'd try anything, matching a neophyte's propensity for trying any fool trick out of sheer ignorance to the steel-cable muscles and tripwire reflexes of a fighter pilot. McKay learned that at first Casey'd been too aggressive even for a fighter pilot, which on the whole was like being too aggressive to be a bobcat, and had flunked out of air-combat school. He'd taken up t'ai ch'i and meditation to calm himself down. It worked, but he'd ended up something of a space cadet, almost as flaky as a SEAL. And *they* were the weirdest people McKay knew.

As the team's driver and mechanic, Casey was an asset to them, but McKay again feared his lack of experience on the ground.

Finally there was Rogers. Rogers was turret gunner in the V-450 Super Commando that was chosen to be the Guardians' main vehicle, with Sloan to take his place if hard-core scouting and recon work was called for. He was the group medic, and his tool for social occasions was a plain assault rifle. He was the group's utility outfielder. There just wasn't much he couldn't do.

Doubts about his team weren't all that worried Billy McKay when exhaustion and the demanding rounds of training left him time and energy to think. Or even in the months beyond, after the training had been completed and the Guardians were posted to the presidential detail. Because their training had been vastly wider in scope than anything which even the most elite bodyguards could require. Over and over, he found himself asking the question, *Just what in hell is our real mission?*

CHAPTER
SIX

"For Christ's sake," Parkinson's voice grated in McKay's earplug. "Can't we make any better time?"

"You want to come out here and help me direct traffic?" McKay rumbled. Parkinson didn't answer.

Shit, McKay thought, *why'd I waste breath on a silly-ass response like that?* The tension was getting to him. That was bad. He could afford no false moves now.

It had been a hard grind, scrambling up mounds of debris, block after block of fallen stone, bricks, pieces of girder, treacherous with hidden holes to trap and break an ankle, or big chunks that could twist unexpectedly to crush a foot. McKay scouted an entire block at a time; no point in bringing the cars halfway and then having to turn back. Then he would take the cars through, slowly, guiding Parkinson's driver with his free hand, the other two 450's following close behind.

Overhead the sky had darkened, congealed. The clouds had gone a deeper, rancid yellow with lots of brown and gray in it. It reminded McKay of that hot mustard he used to like on the bologna sandwiches his mother made for him when he was young. It would make the tears start in his eyes. That's what the sky looked like now. Hot mustard.

It was a real, bona fide race against time. Particles of dust had been sucked up into the cloud that blossomed from the Mount Weather groundburst, and the dust had been rendered radioactive. Unstable elements inside the minute particles decayed constantly, releasing ionizing radiation in three forms: alpha and beta particles and gamma rays. Alpha particles—the nuclei of helium atoms, two protons and two neutrons apiece—didn't do much unless you breathed or swallowed them; beta particles were plain old garden-variety electrons and could cause burns if they came in contact with flesh, but they weren't a whole lot worse than alphas. It was the third, the highly penetrative gamma rays, that posed the real threat. Even the protective armor of the Super Commandos could only cut down a certain amount on the short-wave radiation emitted from the fallout particles—and McKay's funny suit far less.

So now it all came down to a race against the wind inexorably blowing the lethal dust cloud from Mount Weather toward Washington. The rad meter strapped to McKay's left wrist was like a referee's stopwatch for this particular race. If he and his team didn't beat the slowly climbing red numbers, they were dead.

The Remington was as heavy as lead in his hands as he trudged back along mounds of wreckage to the intersection where the vehicles waited. With the uncertain footing, it wasn't exactly safe to carry the gun cocked, but he was damned if he'd sling the riot gun. If he needed it at all, he'd need it *now*.

Each of them had a primary weapon: McKay the M-60; Casey Wilson a fine-tuned M-40 sniper's rifle with the latest high-tech electronic scope; Sloan the Galil short-assault rifle with the M-203 grenade launcher; Tom Rogers a plain Galil SAR. But each had a backup weapon, like McKay's present 12-gauge Remington 1100 autoloader shotgun, for special situations like this.

"Lieutenant McKay?"

McKay was working his way across a pile of jumbled blocks toward the corner of a side street he'd just scoped out. It sucked, but it was the best route he could find. He didn't want to leave the vehicles stacked up on Thirteenth waiting for someone to drop a Molotov on them—especially with the rad count climbing like an F-15 with the stick all the way back. It took him a moment to recognize the voice of the Secret Service agent commanding Mobile Three.

He blinked sweat out of his eyes. The radiation suit was rubberized and incredibly hot, and the sweat just stayed. "What do you have, Jimenez?"

"Looters, down at the far end of the block. Thought you'd want to be alert." Mobile Three was sitting at the intersection a block south of where McKay was.

"Thanks." The air echoed in McKay's ears as it pumped in and out of his big chest. The sound wouldn't make it any easier to hear any assholes who might be snooping and pooping through the rubble getting ready to jump him. On the other hand, his Guardian training had included filmstrips showing the effects of exposure to high levels of radiation. He wasn't any too eager to die of convulsions or the bloody shits, so he'd stay in his suit like a good little soldier boy.

"Jimenez," he heard Parkinson say, "clear those assholes out."

"Negative, Jimenez!" McKay shouted. "Jesus, Parkinson, give me a break!"

"Just why the hell not, McKay? We can't just sit here and watch law and order break down around us."

"Haven't you gotten it through your head it's *already* broken down? You're not a cop anymore." He shook his head as if the agent-in-charge could see him. "We don't need to announce our presence to everybody inside of a mile of us."

"Maybe the sound of machine guns would keep people clear of us, McKay," Sloan said.

"You want to bet the President's life on that? It might just bring somebody around with a LAW and a motherfucker of a grudge against the world in general." *Jesus,* he thought. *Navy types.* He hoped he was not going to have a large-scale personality conflict with Sloan. Parkinson was already more than he wanted to deal with. "Now cut the shit. Parkinson, bring Two around the corner. Casey, follow him up. There's not room for all three of you, so Jimenez, you close up to the corner and wait until we get Mobile Two over the hump."

The lead car nosed around onto the side street. Holding the Remington ready in one hand, McKay waved Parkinson's driver forward with the other. The street had been lined with small shops and office buildings, none more than four stories tall. It lay roughly at the midpoint between the hypocenters of the Chain Bridge Road overpass blast and the one near the University of Maryland. Building fronts on both sides of the street had been weakened by the first blast and dropped by the second. Supported by steel structural members, the buildings themselves mostly survived, gaping like huge idiot maws at the strange procession crawling over the detritus, one bulky white mannequin guiding three squat drab-green beetles through the humid unquiet air.

Where the V-450's had to start mounting the rubble, a four-story structure had gone, sloping from the north and leaving the southern side of the street almost clear. McKay had figured a route skirting the first mound, then over a metal-high heap distributed almost evenly over the asphalt except for where it covered abandoned cars and vans in great humps. Then they were to slalom around a few random piles at the east end to reach Twelfth. He wished he had a steel rod to probe down into the wreckage to make sure there were no pockets that would cave in like tank traps beneath the ten-ton armored cars. He didn't waste a lot of time fretting about it, though. Billy McKay never troubled himself much over what he could have known or should have known. He just made do with what he did know, and got the hell on with it.

At his back a brick facade had been peeled off to reveal the Formica tables and colorful plastic chairs of a Burger King. A few early morning customers had been caught by the airburst to the northeast. Between the glass blasted inward in huge jagged sheets and the flash of the hydrogen warhead, McKay figured it would be hard to tell the victims from their hamburgers—not that he looked too closely. The plastic strips bearing letters and numbers announcing the prices of Whoppers, milkshakes, soydogs, and fries had melted into colorful snail trails, and the chairs had run like birthday candles.

Across the way he could see the steel gleam of a dentist's chair in what had been a storefront dental clinic, and next to it the jumbled remains of a computer store. A little way farther down on his side of the street, a pharmacy had miraculously survived with no apparent damage beyond gutted windows.

Mobile Two groaned up onto the first obstruction. McKay held his breath as its wheels sank a handsbreadth into the debris, and he let it out slowly when they went no deeper. "Billy," he heard Casey say from Mobile One, which sat revving its engines impatiently just behind the lead car. "What's this stuff all over the street?"

"Looks like they had 'em a ticker-tape parade," Rogers remarked.

The hummocks of rubble were dusted with paper rectangles like outsized snowflakes. Grinning inside his mask, McKay stooped and picked one up. He held it up in front of the view slit of Parkinson's driver. "Fuck me to tears!" the driver exclaimed. "It's a naked broad."

McKay flipped it around for a look. It was an eight-by-ten glossy of a leggy young black woman with a top hat and a pair of sequined spike-heel shoes and nothing between except a smile of surpassing toothiness and various terrain features. "Streets're full of the damned things," he said. "Pictures of naked women—some of 'em a lot less tame than this one. I think there was a modeling agency up above the damned Burger King."

"Too bad we don't have time to dig out their address files," Jimenez remarked dryly.

"Can we cut the shit, McKay?" Parkinson demanded. "You're the one who was in such a hurry."

"We're all in a hurry, Parkinson. Not even those Super Commandos'll keep the gamma rays out completely." He flipped the photo away. It fluttered down like a bird with a broken wing to light on a cinder block. The model smiled glossily up at him. *Wonder what she's doin' now*, McKay thought. *If anything.* He had a flash of a mummy, twisted and blackened in its final agony, beaming hideously at him with those expensively capped teeth. A sharp chill ran down his spine like a trickle of ice water. *Colonel Donoghue was right,* he told himself, recalling his unit commander in the Med. *You got too damn much imagination.*

"Okay, Turpin," he said to Parkinson's driver. "Enough of this. Put her in gear and let's get gone."

The thermonuclear storm had passed; the basaltic rocks of the Kolymskoye Nagorye had been fused to green-black glass across an extent of several thousand hectares by ground bursts. The SS-19 missile silos dug deep into the highland plain were buried, tombs for men and the great silvery birds, artifacts of technological civilization, that would never fly to seed brief miniature stars half a world away. Of two dozen missiles, all but eight remained in their wombs, aborted by malfunction or the enemy's own silver birds.

But one of the hell-birds had neither been killed nor irretrievably trapped. The malfunction that kept it in its steel-and-concrete shell had been external, a broken circuit in the rocket-fuel ignition console. By the time sweating technicians in brown coveralls had located the problem, the One-Day War had passed several hours into history. So had the Union of Soviet Socialist Republics.

If the laboring Strategic Rocket Force techs thought at all of the dying of their motherland, it only fueled their determination—as indeed did the certainty of their own deaths. If a Russian could not win, he could at least console himself by insuring no one else would reap the victory. And to die in one proverbial blaze of glory was a dream that dwelled deep in the Russian psyche. This was the mentality that goaded the Politburo to launch its doomed war. It was the goad that drove the technicians to repair this final instrument of vengeance and launch the final blow of a dying giant, like a stricken dinosaur lashing out one last time with its spiked tail as news of its brain's death finally reached its limbs. For they were dead men, dead as half their countryfolk. The supplies intended to keep them alive for weeks while the fallout outside dropped to survivable levels were doubtless piled in bunkers beneath Black Sea dachas *owned by the* nachalstvo, *the New Class that was the U.S.S.R.'s aristocracy*. So they toiled single-mindedly, as ones already dead.

As the afternoon shadows of surrounding peaks lengthened across the moonscape of black-green glass, an explosive charge blew a massive concrete plug out of a tube sunk into the earth. An orange glow spilled out as though a vent had been opened into Hell. Slowly, the bird was born of fire, riding upward on a pillar of flame. High it rose, untroubled by the baked blackness of the plain below, high, high, until it drifted alone on a sea of stars above an earth whose wounds were hidden by white bandages of cloud. In answer to the imperative built into it like the homing instinct of a flesh-and-blood bird, the gleaming alloy Phoenix tipped to the north and soared onward to its own destiny above the heart of an enemy capital. . . .

A hand swaddled in the thick glove of a rad suit gestured.

"Come on, Turpin, you got it," McKay said. With a growl, the V-450 started lumbering up the meter-high slope of the rubble mass that covered the street. Meanwhile, a half-block behind, the turret of Mobile One poked up over the top of the first big heap. Wilson was waiting for Mobile Two to negotiate the street successfully before going ahead. Mobile Three, with Chief Justice Shaneyfelt fuming inside, still idled its engine out on Thirteenth.

"Billy!"

Rogers' cry rang in his ears as McKay wheeled, bringing up the shotgun. Three men were coming out of the drugstore at a heavy run, slogging through the debris as though through surf. McKay's brain registered weapons in their hands, and then he jerked the shotgun's trigger.

In the lead was a husky dirty-blond man with a two days' growth of reddish beard and a grimy rag tied around his forehead. The charge of No. 4 buckshot caught him over the name stenciled in black on the left-hand pocket of his Army jacket. He spun around in a red mist and fell, a hand ax falling from his hand.

Behind him was a potbellied Hispanic-looking man, also in tattered Army jacket, with a saw-backed Randle knife in his hand. Off balance from the recoil of the first shot, McKay put a foot back to steady himself. It pushed through a piece of wallboard and sank in to the shin. Waving his left hand in a desperate attempt to keep from falling and snapping his leg, McKay triggered another blast. The knife wielder's face exploded.

The third man had no jacket, only an olive-drab T-shirt and a crowbar. He was just outside the Rexall, five or six meters from McKay. He cocked the crowbar back and threw it.

The tire iron slammed hard across McKay's right wrist and forearm. The Remington thudded into the rubble.

A wild babble had broken loose in McKay's earplug. His view blocked by a mound of rubble, Wilson wanted to know what was going on. Parkinson was shouting to his gunner, and Justice Shaneyfelt was being loudly outraged. McKay had no time to worry about the lack of radio discipline as the third man launched himself in a flying leap at the trapped Guardian.

With no chance to go for the .45 holstered at his waist, McKay braced himself as best he could. The man was about his height though nowhere near as heavy, and the muscles of his arms were like wound cable. Like the other two, he was in his early twenties; as the country's economy had worsened through the eighties and early nineties, street gangs were no longer the preserve of adolescents. Groups of all-too-adult "Runners" began to prowl urban avenues in search of human prey.

McKay caught him, grappled him, pivoted on a hip, and swung the man past him. As the man landed heavily, McKay felt his right knee torque painfully. The leg gave. He dropped to his other knee. His right hand still felt numb and clumsy from the blow with the tire iron. He fumbled for the .45 with his left hand.

Scarcely three meters from his head, Mobile Two's .50-cal. roared. It was a shattering sound, absolutely indescribable, striking him like a hammer. Even as he drew the big Colt automatic, McKay ducked instinctively. There were few men as tough as Billy McKay, but to be standing in line with the muzzle blast of a Browning M-2 .50-caliber machine gun and not flinch would have taken a superhero straight out of Marvel Comics.

The front of the drugstore disappeared behind a cloud of cement dust. Another looter had popped up in the doorway, aiming a small black revolver at Billy McKay's broad back. Mason, the gunner in Parkinson's 450, had been forced to fire a burst right over the ex-Marine's head.

Out of the line of the stunning muzzle blast, the third man picked himself up and hurled himself on McKay again. The .45 was partway out of its holster. The man grabbed McKay's thick wrist with one hand and the gun with the other and twisted as McKay clubbed at the side of his head with his right hand. The man was wiry and not much shorter than McKay. He managed to wrest the automatic away before McKay smashed his nose with a flailing fist. The pistol fell.

The Runner kicked it away and whipped a switchblade from the pocket of his old-issue fatigue pants. The feeling had returned to McKay's right hand, and he drew his big Kabar knife with it.

He faced his opponent, the knife held by his side, his left arm raised to defend. It struck him that the knife-fighting tactics he'd learned in Guardian training just might not fully apply here. Normally you had to be willing to take a few slices on your left arm to get some good cutting done with your right. McKay wasn't squeamish about getting his arm nicked, but he didn't like to think what would happen if the integrity of his fallout suit was breached. The rad meter on his wrist made the irony all too clear. He was going hand-to-hand with a dead man.

The man circled. He kept feinting with the switchblade, tracing wide arabesques in the air that told McKay he didn't really know what he was doing. Just a punk, used to using a shiv to intimidate the citizens or carve up other, equally inexpert punks. Not that Billy McKay, one-time barroom brawler, close-combat instructor at Parris Island, street fighter, and all-around trained killer, was making such a great showing. Of course, he wasn't accustomed to fighting in a bulky rad suit that gave him both the appearance and the agility of a dancing bear, nor did it help that this bear had one foot in a trap plus a weakened knee. But those were just excuses.

And excuses weren't much use to a dead man.

"I'll cut you, asshole," the man said through gritted teeth. His face was lean and tan where sweat had eroded through the grime on his bony features. His hair was black and short, with a red handkerchief knotted about his forehead. He wore a black T-shirt with a gold Harley Davidson eagle on it and fatigue pants.

McKay could have told him a few things but preferred to save his breath. "McKay," Sloan's voice said in his ears. "I'm coming out."

"Bullshit, you are." A quick flash of nicotine-yellowed teeth told him his antagonist thought he was talking to him.

"Don't have a choice, McKay," Parkinson said. "Even if that fucker lets us get a clear shot at him, our MG muzzles won't depress that far."

"No!" McKay grunted. The Runner darted to his right, closing. McKay tried to wheel, was brought up by his trapped foot, slashed wildly. The Runner cursed and danced back, blood starting from a line on his forearm. A lucky slash for McKay. "Can't afford to risk contaminating the vehicle. Can't waste time either. I don't polish this asshole off in another minute, drive the hell over both of us and get out of here."

His antagonist's dark eyes had widened. "Take me with you. You don't, we're both dead men." The man's voice was hoarse, jagged as the broken glass that glittered like diamonds in the rubble all around. "Fallout's gotta be coming."

"Come a little closer," McKay said huskily, "and I'll show you what a dead man looks like."

The man laughed. He dodged left, then lunged straight for McKay. McKay caught his knife wrist, drove his own blade upward. The man made no attempt to parry the blow. McKay felt it bite flesh, then a jarring impact as it grated against bone. The man grunted softly—and then his cable-strong fingers closed on McKay's mask.

Reflexively McKay released the hilt of his Kabar and snatched the Runner's left wrist. The other man pressed his pain-twisted face close to McKay's. "How much longer can you stand it, government man?"

It was an impasse. If McKay tried to tear the clawed hand from him, his mask would go with it—and McKay would start breathing fallout. Maybe not much. But he couldn't risk much. Once inside his lungs, even the relatively harmless alpha emitters would cause him damage. The life of the President of the United States would be resting on his shoulders and there would be no hope of hospital treatment for Christ knew how long. If he had both hands he could break the grip, but he didn't like the idea of getting the switchblade in his belly much more than getting a lung full of powdered death.

He began to clamp down with his left hand. Hard. He saw the other man's eyes start from their sockets, felt the bones of the wrist beginning to compress in his grip. "Th-think you can take me like that, pig man?" the Runner snarled through clenched teeth. He began to struggle with a madman's strength, fighting to rip the life-preserving mask from Mc-Kay's face.

Abruptly, he let go. His mouth opened, a pink cavern before McKay's eyes—

And then the scene went white.

CHAPTER
SEVEN

With a desperate heave of his huge shoulders, McKay threw the Runner away from him. He risked losing the mask, but that problem had just become almost academic. He'd never seen a flash like that before, but he knew what it was.

The street was bathed in a hideous stark whiteness that washed out all color, all contrast. McKay's mask stayed in place. Through the polarized lenses he saw the Runner staggering away from him, holding both hands over his face. With a strange exaggerated clarity, McKay saw the hairs on the Runner's arms curl and crisp, saw black smoke begin to trail upward from the black T-shirt. Then he turned and threw himself facedown.

He had felt it on the back of his neck and head, the light of false, thermonuclear dawn. The fact that he was still alive encouraged him. He was outside the radius of total destruction, the embrace of the fifty-million-degree fireball. His mouth was dry and tasted of metal. He didn't feel the heat anymore, only a strange prickling. The buildings that still stood were shielding him from the direct glow of the blast. *Now if the fuckin' building doesn't come down on me . . .*

The earth convulsed beneath him. His gloved fingers dug at the rubble, and he pressed his masked face down as far as he could. He felt chunks of rubble rain down on his back and legs, could only hope none of them was big enough to do him harm. The sound that came with the shock wave was indescribable. The auditory center of his brain could not deal with the vast, horrendous, all-encompassing noise. Afterward McKay could not have told what kind of sound the hydrogen warhead made, or even if it made one.

The final messenger of Soviet vengeance had exploded a few hundred meters north of the Capitol, above the Commodore Hotel hard by Union Station, vaporizing rioters, Senators, and congresspersons alike. Channeled by the buildings that still lined the streets, blast waves emanated from the hypocenter of the explosion, reaching farther than they would have across open land. One of these rocketed down Thirteenth Street, picked up Mobile Three, and flipped it end over end along the block. The V-450 bounced nose and tail for fifty meters, caromed off an abandoned sedan, and exploded.

Mobil One and Two were shielded from the full fury of the explosion. So was McKay. He felt a remnant of the blast wave that blew Shaneyfelt's vehicle away as the wave bled down McKay's tributary street. A moment later and the air was sucked from his lungs. The shock wave had literally forced the air away, causing a temporary vacuum. McKay fought down the panic that boiled up within him, and then blacked out.

"Billy." The voice came from far away. He stirred. He was comfortable where he was, and up beyond the walls of the pit of sleep he sensed pain and fear and turmoil awaiting him. "Billy, for God's sake, are you all right?"

It was the voice of Sam Sloan, fuzzed with static from the play of unimaginable energies in the dark mushroom that filled the southern sky. A hint of panic edged the words. *Bad sign,* McKay thought. *Can't have Guardians losing control when things go wrong. Little things like H-bombs going off overhead.*

He shook himself. Suddenly he was back in possession of his senses—and his memories. His body ached, his left knee was a crimson splash of agony against the dull general pain. He rolled over and pulled himself up to a sitting position. "I'm all right," he croaked. He felt as if his body had been scooped out like a cantaloupe. "I think. What about the President?"

"We're all okay in Mobile One and Two. We were shielded by the buildings."

He glanced at the figure writhing on the debris across the street from him. Quickly he looked away and began to work his trapped foot free. Now that he had the leisure to concentrate on it, he was able to slip it loose fairly easily. "What about Three?"

A pause. "Casey's backed us down to the corner to have a look, McKay." Sloan's voice was all business now—back to calling his unit leader by his surname. "Three's turned turtle and is on fire."

"Shouldn't've risked it."

"I ordered them to check out Three, Lieutenant," another, weary voice said. "I felt responsible for the Chief Justice's welfare."

McKay frowned and pulled his leg out. He felt along it. Nothing seemed broken. "And I'm responsible for your welfare, Mr. President."

"I'm sorry," MacGregor said contritely. "Shouldn't we be doing something for those men?"

Gingerly, McKay got to his feet. His Remington lay nearby. He picked it up and slung it over his shoulder. If there were any more Runners stalking him now, they were welcome to him. They were a lot harder core than he was.

"No way," he said, and walked over to recover his .45. He limped a little. His knee felt doubtful, but it was holding his weight okay.

"What do you mean?" It was Parkinson, and he was pissed. "McKay, those are my men in that car!"

"Yeah, along with the Chief Justice of the United States. And they're all crispy critters by now."

"But we have to make sure! Somebody might be alive. Damn you, McKay, *I'm not running out on my men!*"

McKay straightened, .45 in hand. Mobile Two had run in against the south side of the street when the warhead detonated. Cool-headed, at least as far as action was concerned, Parkinson had ordered the MG turret to traverse to cover the street. Now McKay was practically looking down the twin muzzles, and it gave him a strange tingling sensation, like what he'd felt when the fireball had known its brief hellish life. Would Parkinson actually have his gunner fire him up? Secret Service men were trained to hair-trigger obedience to orders, but Parkinson was not exactly accustomed to taking orders from Billy McKay. And even more deeply ingrained in Parkinson than obedience was the imperative of the Special Forces team leader: you don't leave your men behind.

Shit, McKay thought. *They were my men too.* "We're all expendable in this, Parkinson. And those men have been expended. Now get moving."

There was another pause, and then Mobile Two's engine whined and the car started forward. McKay stood watching stonily as it went by and waddled into the clear on Fourteenth. Mobile One followed. McKay could almost taste the young ex-pilot's impatience as he gingerly followed the lead vehicle's tracks across the mounds of rubble.

When it was past, he unslung the Remington, brought it to his shoulder, fired three shells. The blackened, hairless figure thrashed briefly and lay still. McKay watched a moment, then turned and trudged along the tracks left by the heavy armored cars.

On a hunch, McKay worked the reduced convoy west, toward Rock Creek Park. In the late eighties it had been expanded, and the few streets that crossed it, including the parkway which had followed the course of the creek, had been blocked off or rerouted through tunnels beneath the park to increase the illusion of an inner-city wildlife preserve clear up through the Maryland suburbs north of the District of Columbia. If the trees weren't ablaze, the park should give them a passage to the north that would be relatively free of the rubble and derelict vehicles that choked the streets.

Thanks to a relatively wet summer, the trees hadn't burned, except in a few places at the edges. The two armored cars humped over the curb and rolled into the park near the entrance to the Military Road tunnel, making for Rock Creek. Along the artificially contained course of the river, it was hard to tell anything at all had happened to the concrete, steel, and Mylarized glass world beyond the park, except that the leaves of the trees had a withered, dead look.

McKay had ridden the last few blocks on the rear deck of Mobile Two, and when they reached the park he climbed back into his own V-450. The diaphragm, a big plastic envelope, was still in place over the right-hand door. Inside, McKay shut the door, then began the cumbersome process of stripping off his rad suit and cleansing himself and his gear of radioactive dust with aerosols and a vacuum hose powered off the big diesel.

They ran north, cruising the verdant banks, bumping over the rocks of the streambed, sometimes running in water up to the hubs.

"It all seems so surreal," MacGregor remarked, watching out the view slits. "The park seems so calm, undisturbed. But when I get a glimpse of the city through the trees, it looks like something from Dante's *Inferno*. Like a Doré engraving."

McKay shrugged. He didn't entirely get the President's reference. He felt redheaded Agent Hayes's eyes hot upon him. McKay looked across the compartment at him and smiled. Hayes glowered and looked away. Like Parkinson, the youthful agent seemed to blame McKay for the loss of the crew of Mobile Three.

"There's so much happening I don't understand," MacGregor went on. He clung to a strap let into the hull by his seat. The V-450 lurched and pitched like a ship in a heavy sea as Casey Wilson maneuvered it up onto the bank. "Why did those men attack the vehicles? What could they do with knives and crowbars against armored cars?"

"More than you think, Mr. President," McKay said. "These things aren't invulnerable. You get close enough, the people inside can't shoot at you without opening something up, and then it's a whole new ball game if you've got the balls and brains." He shook his head. "Shit, they almost pulled it off."

"But what did they want? To hijack our vehicles?"

"May've had that in mind. That wouldn't have worked too well, but they didn't have time to think things through." He remembered the hate and self-abandonment that had burned in the Runner's black eyes. *He nearly took me. He was just a punk, but he damn near aced me. And all 'cause he had nothing more to lose.*

"They might just have wanted to kill us, Mr. President. I think they knew they were dead. Maybe they just couldn't take the thought of us rolling on through in comfort while the fallout ate 'em out from inside."

MacGregor's eyes held his for a minute, then flicked away.

McKay had the uncomfortable sensation he was talking too much. He subsided into a stony silence, with his arms folded across his chest.

Normally a June afternoon would find the park thronged with picnickers, hikers, horseback riders, and nature lovers. Today it was mostly deserted. Even though the government's "relocation program"—a nice way of saying evacuation—had come promptly unglued with the first explosion, the overriding urge most people in the Washington metroplex felt was to get the hell out. Some realized the fallout was coming. Most simply understood that the stricken city was dying, with power out, water and sewers not flowing, and food unavailable at the supermarket for who knew how long. And law and order— Well, in Washington, D.C., and increasingly in the lily-white suburbs on its fringes, law and order had been growing increasingly fragile over the last few years. But now the last constraints were off. Bad as even Washington's inner city had been before, things were now immeasurably worse.

They did pass groups of people from time to time, though, as the refugees picked their way north. Mostly they were dazed, wandering aimlessly through the woods or clumped in clearings alongside the banks of the yellow-brown creek. Once McKay glimpsed a crowd of several hundred, clustered around a van with Red Cross markings while several men and women with Civil Defense arm bands moved around them like sheepdogs. The van appeared to be a field kitchen. The survivors were lined up for trays of hot food, or milled around listlessly, showing none of the animation of the mobs in Lafayette Park and Dupont Circle, to say nothing of the homicidal fury.

Sloan sat in the radioman's seat, monitoring whatever signals he could. There was less radio activity than there had been before. State-of-the-art electronic gear like that in the 450's was designed to resist nuclear-induced electromagnetic pulses that could nullify radio transmissions; older stuff, which comprised most of the emergency-net equipment, had special Faraday-cage shielding to protect it when nuclear explosions were expected, but the shielding had to be removed for the equipment to be used. So the unexpected final blast had wiped a lot of traffic off the air. What remained was even more hysterical than before.

"The roads out are worse than hopeless," Sloan reported.

"And that last bomb may have caused as many casualties as all the others put together."

MacGregor looked forward. His handsome face was furrowed, old. "Why?"

"A lot of people came out of their shelters when they thought it was all over." Sloan's mouth felt like parchment. "The blast caught them in the open."

The President said nothing. His devastated expression was eloquent enough.

Sloan heard the whine of servos as Rogers traversed the turret. Craning his neck to look out the view slit protected by heavy leaded glass, he wondered what Rogers was thinking. The laconic ex-Green Beret was a hard man to read. Though they had spent months together in the closest proximity, Sloan knew little more about his fellow Guardian than the day he'd met him.

Sloan watched a young couple hike along the side of the stream. They wore shorts, Pendleton shirts with the sleeves rolled up, hiking boots, and backpacks. "Smart," Casey murmured. "They're missin' all the traffic on the surface roads. And they got handkerchiefs on over their faces to filter the fallout."

Sloan glanced at his console and his throat tightened. "It won't do them any good."

"We could give them a lift on the deck," the President said. Sloan glanced back sharply, then understood. *A hundred people in distress are a statistic; two, a tragedy.* It was a paraphrase of some Nazi war criminal's statement at Nuremberg, Sloan recalled with a start. But it was sound psychology.

"We get started helping the helpless, Mr. President, where will we stop?" McKay rumbled.

Is he really that goddamned hard-core? Doesn't he have any *compassion?* Sloan wondered angrily. But the feeling passed at once. McKay was right. It sounded heartless, and God, how Sam Sloan hated to hear it. But it was the truth.

"It wouldn't help them anyway, Mr. President," he heard his own voice say. "They'd have taken too many rems by the time we could get clear of the cloud from Mount Weather."

They trundled by the young couple. The boy looked up curiously, his tanned young face showing no fear of the squat metal monsters. The girl simply walked on, hunched forward against the weight of her pack. *She knows,* Sloan thought in agony. *She knows.*

The V-450's crawled on around a bend, beneath a jutting shelf of what appeared to be rock but was instead a weathered-concrete extrusion of the bed of the creek itself, stained and molded like the artificial terrain in one of the bear pens at the National Zoological Park in the southern reaches of Rock Creek Park. A country boy himself, Sloan wondered about the people who had come to the park in the midst of disaster. *The urban environment isn't really for humans,* he thought. *In times of stress, it's just natural for them to seek the shelter of green places, wild places, whatever gives even the illusion of sheltering wilderness.*

Rock Creek Park led them past the Beltway clear up through Kensington before it petered out. For a time, the vehicles battled through a tangle of suburban streets choked with cars and refugees on foot. Turpin and Casey were both adept at squeezing the bulky 450's through tiny spaces between stalled and often abandoned cars, into alleys, across vacant lots, even through yards front and back. The armored cars made short work of cinder-block walls and had the power to push obstructing cars out of their path by brute force.

"Good thing we don't have to worry about the paint jobs on these mothers," Casey observed. He had Mobile One parked on somebody's lawn and sat hunched forward over the steering wheel, watching Two crunch between a Brazilian-made station wagon and a stalled garbage truck.

There came a tapping on the hull above MacGregor's right shoulder. McKay nearly jumped out of his skin. "What the fuck is that?" he roared.

"Somebody knocking, sounds like," Hayes murmured. His Mini-Uzi appeared in his hand. The Israeli-made machine pistol was what its name suggested, a miniaturized version of the famous submachine gun, easily small enough to fit in a shoulder holster and with a high enough rate of fire that it was virtually impossible to fire without eating an entire fifteen-round clip. That made McKay wonder about its utility, but the Secret Service had seemed wedded to the things.

"Rogers?" McKay barked into his throat mike. "Have you gone to sleep up in the goddamn turret?"

"Been keepin' an eye on the scene at the supermarket out

there." Two blocks away, a Safeway was being looted by a frantic crowd. Several green-and-white prowl cars from the local police force were on hand. Light bars winked and flashed to beat the band, and cops with flak jackets, riot helmets, plexiglass shields, and electrified batons stood by, but they seemed to be on hand mainly as referees. It would have taken barbed-wire rolls, Claymores, and machine gun emplacements to keep the panic-stricken suburbanites from cleaning the place out. Though what they were fighting for was a mystery, Sloan had remarked that this long after the bombing, there wasn't likely to be anything left on the shelves but detergent, charcoal starter, and Kitty Litter.

The rapping came again, diffident but definite. "Jesus Christ," McKay said. "Sloan, what's it like out there?"

"Background or a little hotter. Unless the wind backs again, we won't get fallout from the Mount Weather grounder this far north, and none of the other ground strikes we have a plot for pose us any threat."

McKay slid over to the President's side and slid open the armored visor of the view slit in the left-hand door. A middle-aged man stood outside. He was balding, with a sad, lined gray face. He was in shirt-sleeves and his baggy pants were held up by suspenders. Behind him, McKay could see the front porch of the house on whose lawn they were waiting, a white shoe box with green trim and pink plastic flamingos standing guard over a garden that had been filled in with brick-red gravel. McKay had the impression of a worried presence hovering behind the drawn-back drapes of a picture window that had had the immense good fortune not to be facing in the direction of any nearby detonations.

"Good God, it's a citizen," McKay said. "Ask him what he wants, Sloan, and turn the audio pickups on."

"Can I help you, sir?" Sloan's voice vibrated through the hull. The householder jumped back a step, eyes widening in fright.

"Tell him not to be afraid." Sloan relayed the information. The citizen didn't look reassured. "Now ask him again."

Sloan did. The man bit his lip and clung to his suspenders. "C-Could you please move your cars or whatever they are off my lawn? The tires are ruining my turf, and I think you've broken off some of my sprinkler heads."

"Fuck *me*," McKay said.

"Shouldn't you be trying to evacuate the area, sir?" Sloan asked. "You might take fallout here."

"Just get off my lawn. Please." He glanced back over his shoulder. "You're upsetting my wife terribly," he said, dropping his voice to a conspiratorial whisper.

"Parkinson's got the Estrêla station wagon out of the way," Casey reported. "Just as well he munched it, man. Those things get rancid mileage."

"Sir—" Sloan began.

"Just go. Please go."

"Do like the man says, Casey," McKay said. He rocked sideways as the 450 lurched into motion, gouging furrows across the householder's pampered lawn.

Hayes was staring at McKay. His squarish, soft-cornered face had gone pale beneath his freckles, giving his features a greenish cast. "My God," he murmured in disbelief. "Has everyone gone crazy?"

McKay scratched the short blond curls at the back of his head. He'd sweated heavily in the rad suit, and it had plastered his hair down. Now it had begun to itch. "Yeah," he said slowly as Casey maneuvered the vehicle through the space made by Parkinson's car. "Yeah, I guess maybe they have."

CHAPTER
EIGHT

They skirted Rockville to the east, and by the time they passed Gaithersburg they entered a region where suburbs and cement-covered industrial plots were interspersed with land that had been condemned, seized by the federal government, and returned to agricultural uses under the Emergency Farmland Reclamation Act of 1989. Much of it lay fallow. Despite extensive subsidization, most of the farmers who had "homesteaded" the land in uneconomically small plots had already folded, the land being taken over by banks or Montgomery County for nonpayment of property taxes. The weed-grown fields provided a convenient route for the V-450's, however.

For a few kilometers, they paralleled Interstate 270. Proximity to the highway, the main artery leading northwest from Washington, made McKay nervous. It was choked with refugees, as well as police, military, and various government personnel who might as easily try to exploit the chaos as contain it. Ugly as the former possibility was, McKay was cynical enough to keep it strongly in mind, even without the warnings Major Crenna had drilled into all four Guardians.

After a short time of following it, McKay decided to get across 270. The area west to the Blue Ridge Mountains wasn't exactly underpopulated, but it was a lot less densely crowded than the Hagerstown-Baltimore-Washington triangle. And that triangle was even more crowded now as refugees streamed out of Washington and Baltimore, the latter having taken at least two hits. However, the two armored cars could do no more than follow 270 until they found a way to get across the raging flood of humanity.

Two-seventy was a nightmare. It was packed solid with cars, buses, big semis, and every few hundred yards, burning vehicles sent orange sheets of flame and black snakes of smoke up into the sky. The only traffic that moved at all was motor-cycles working their way through the bumper-to-bumper jam as best they could, or the few enterprising off-road and four-wheel-drive vehicles moving beside the highway. Rogers and Mason, Parkinson's gunner, kept a careful eye on this intrepid mass of people, but none of them came very close. These refugees weren't Street Runners and were duly impressed by the guns jutting out of the two hunchbacked turrets.

For some reason—perhaps following the dictates of the long-defunct Shell Answer Man to stay with your car no matter what—a number of stranded drivers stuck grimly to their trapped vehicles, sitting hunched over the wheel inside as if to wait for the traffic jam to clear. They'd have a long wait, Sloan reflected. It would be days before it was cleared, maybe weeks or even months, depending on the vagaries of wind and radioactive dust.

Or maybe never, he thought.

Other motorists had climbed atop their cars and sat alone or in little dispirited knots as though trying to escape flood-waters, watching their fellow refugees stream past in an endless current.

The people on foot were the hardest to take. Thousands upon thousands of them—children, women, men, old, young, and in between—trudged through the slanting yellow light that filtered through the low-hanging clouds. Some toted pieces of luggage, suitcases, and handbags with a few miserable posses-sions stuffed into them. Others, more provident or fortunate, carried backpacks. The Guardians didn't see any of the beds and birdcages classically carried by refugees, but what they saw was disturbing enough.

There were the pathetic: children clutching teddy bears or huge glaring-pink stuffed animals or other toys as if for reas-surance, and one emphysematous old woman with legs like withered twigs beneath the hem of a faded dress, breathing through hoses run up into her nostrils, tottering along while her husband wheeled a portable oxygen tank alongside, looking worse off than she. And there were the bizarre: a beautiful blond teenaged girl in purple shorts and tube top, roller-skating blithely in and out of the crush of traffic with the headset of a pocket microcassette recorder over her ears; a stout middle-aged woman in a flower-print hat, pushing a shopping cart laden with well-stuffed grocery bags.

"Jesus," Casey murmured, pushing back his Rolling Stones cap to scratch his forehead. "Where'd she get that shit?"

"Probably looted from the last suburb we passed," Sloan said somberly.

Casey shook his head. "Never thought there'd be bag ladies after the holocaust. Crenna never mentioned *that* in our training."

Hayes stared at him in disbelief. The Secret Service agent wasn't much older than the ex-fighter jockey, and he seemed horrified by Casey's flippancy. MacGregor simply stared out the armor-glass view slit and said nothing.

Even laconic Rogers was apparently affected by the sight. "Remind you of anything, Billy?" he asked from the turret.

A ripple of pain passed briefly across McKay's rugged features and was gone. His blue eyes grew colder. "Yeah. Fucking Beirut, when I was just a kid with the peacekeeping force in Lebanon." He shook his head. "Just for starters." He'd seen similar processions of panicked refugees before, in the Mideast. But somehow, even after the training he had undergone for his current assignment, somehow it had never seemed real to him that he would see his own people reduced to streaming in blind masses along clogged roads, in search of sanctuary that no longer existed.

"Got some armed parties on foot up ahead of us," Parkinson's voice crackled over the intervehicle communications. The sound was cleaner here, without billions of high-energy particles floating around to screw up communications.

The whine of the turret servos answered him. "What do they look like?" McKay asked.

"Three or four guys in camouflage suits with long arms of some sort."

"Military?"

"Cammie clowns." Rogers' disgust came plainly through his words.

"I have a cousin like that," Casey said. "He's got, like, a

whole set of cammies and an HK-91 with a billion rounds of ammo, and he's just waiting for the world to blow up so he can use all that shit."

"He's got his goddamn chance now," McKay said. "Parkinson, keep an eye on the gun-shop commandos. They probably won't give us trouble, but . . ." He didn't need to complete the sentence.

"Some National Guard types were confiscating people's weapons a few klicks back, where we met up with the highway," Rogers reported. "Not just assault rifles, but everything. Pistols, shotguns, whole nine yards."

"Assholes," McKay said.

"I think it's a good idea," Sloan protested. "It'll keep them from causing trouble."

"And who'll protect them, the ay-lite National Guard?" McKay asked. He shook his head. "Shit."

Sloan turned around, obviously willing to argue the point. A look at McKay's face and he dropped his eyes and turned back to his console.

"Stream up ahead," Parkinson reported. "Goes under Two-seventy and looks big enough to cross."

"Got it on the map screen," Sloan reported. Mobile One's onboard computer contained a number of maps, including ones covering the Bos-Wash area extensively, and less detailed ones outlining several possible routes to Heartland, in case rendezvous with the CIA transport proved impossible. Needless to say, the device wasn't exactly standard equipment, even in a vehicle as advanced as the V-450 Super Commando.

The bridge over the stream was high and wide enough to permit the 450's passage. Mobile One stood off five hundred meters from the road, in the middle of a pasture that had been about two-thirds reclaimed from the blacktop and cement of a defunct factory, keeping carefully clear of the remaining buildings as well as the highway, while Mobile Two checked ahead to make sure the streambed would hold the heavy vehicles. To McKay's relief, Parkinson dished him up no shit about the risk of Two's bogging down hopelessly in sand or having someone drop a Coke bottle filled with gasoline on its rear deck from the overpass. Laying his bull neck on the line for the President was something Parkinson understood.

Two's wide low-ground-pressure tires sank several centimeters into the bed, but no more. It crawled under the bridge while the refugees flowed on overhead, most of them blind to the vehicle's passage. "We made it fine," Parkinson reported. "Bed's mostly gravel." He ordered his car to take up covering position on a brushy green ridge several hundred meters west of the highway, and provided overwatch for Mobile One while Wilson drove along the bank to the bridge and then nosed the 450 down into the streambed.

The big cars' maneuvers had finally attracted the attention of the dazed and listless refugees. People lined the railing of the bridge, pointing at the approaching V-450 and shouting. Restless, McKay stood up from his seat again and came forward to peer over Sloan's shoulder, holding the back of the seat against the lurching of the vehicle as it plowed through the shallow water.

"Should I clear 'em off, Billy?" Rogers asked from the turret. The motors whined as the gun muzzles traversed forward.

"My God, no!" MacGregor exclaimed. He half stood from his fold-down seat, fell back against the hull as one wheel lurched over a big rock, pulled himself up again, and shook off Hayes, who'd sprung to his side to steady him. "You can't shoot innocent people!"

"Lieutenant Rogers didn't mean that, Mr. President," McKay said. "He just wants to know if he should fire over their heads."

MacGregor stared hard at the ex-Marine. For a moment he seemed about to say something. McKay kept looking out through Sloan's view slit. Finally MacGregor sighed and let himself back into the seat.

"Hold your fire, Tom," McKay said. "Won't do any harm to have them look at us." Unnoticed behind him, the President relaxed. He'd been about to forbid Rogers to shoot, even to warn the refugees.

The water sloshed around the huge tires. The armored view slits darkened as the 450 crept into the shadow of the bridge, thrown out over the reclaimed field by the sun as it fell toward the mountains to the west. The watchers on the bridge waved frantically.

Monitoring the outside audio pickups on his headset, Sloan grimaced. "They want us to give them a lift."

Pain washed across MacGregor's face. The handsome features had paled and begun to sag from the continuous strain of nervous exhaustion. "I wish we could."

McKay's mouth drew into a taut line, and his eyes narrowed. "So do I, Mr. President. So do I."

They passed under one-half of the divided highway. Heads peered down at them, faceless silhouettes against the afternoon light. Casey steered the car around the bridge pilings and started for the bank.

"Look out!" came Rogers' cry. On both sides of the stream, people were spilling down the flanks of the bridge embankment, running for the lumbering vehicle with heedless, desperate energy.

"Don't shoot!" ripped from MacGregor's throat. The Super Commando slewed over heavily onto its side as Casey swerved to avoid the bank. The people splashed into the crawling chemical-greasy water. In an instant they surrounded the car, clutching with frantic hands as if to catch and hold it.

The crackle of an M-60 penetrated the hull, along with the more deliberate thud of a .50 caliber. Big chunks of black soil flew from the embankment. People scattered in all directions, leaving a matron in stretch pants writhing on the dirt, clutching at her knee. The yellow of the pants had suddenly gone scarlet. "Parkinson, hold your goddamn fire!" McKay shouted. "Casey, for Christ's sake keep moving!"

The driver's face was white beneath his California tan. "I might run somebody over."

"Do it. If they don't get out of the way—" McKay clutched the back of Sloan's chair and didn't finish the sentence.

The mud of the stream bottom sucked at the tires, slowing the vehicle down. The 450 rocked as people hauled themselves aboard. The blunt snout of the vehicle plowed a way through the screaming, splashing mass. Sloan saw a frenzied face appear in front of his view slit, a fat red moon of hysteria. The 450 surged ahead and the face disappeared from view. "Jesus," Sloan said. Casey turned whiter still but said nothing.

"I'm prepping a gas grenade, Billy." Rogers' voice was calm as always. "I'm going to pitch it out the top hatch."

"Roger that," McKay said. He was grateful for Rogers' seemingly impenetrable calm. Fists drummed on the hull and feet pounded on the deck overhead. A babble of voices came through the hull as the crowd fought for positions on the car.

A moment later he felt the slight shudder as Rogers undogged the hatch, rolled out the canister, and slammed the hatch to again. The crowd moaned as dense white smoke began to stream down past the view slits.

"Tear gas is water-soluble, McKay," Sloan said. "Is the stream going to absorb it all?"

"I sure as hell hope not."

"They're clearing out, Billy!" Casey's voice rang with relief. He gunned the engine and the 450 leaped forward. Choking, coughing, weeping, the crowd thinned away as the gas spread into a low fat cloud hunkering on the water's surface like living fog from a horror movie.

"Oh God, oh God, oh God." Hayes was sobbing a broken litany. McKay and MacGregor moved back to peer out the rear slits.

Thrashing through the water in the muddy wake churned up by the Super Commando's wheels, her face streaming tears, was a young housewife. Her pudgy, doughy legs pumped like pistons. Her chubby arms held out a baby in pink flannel, imploring the unyielding steel machine to take it along to a safety she knew in the depths of her she could never reach.

Farther and farther back she fell. Her mouth was a black hole as she screamed for them to save her baby. MacGregor buried his face in his hands. McKay stared back at the lonely, hopeless figure, his great hands knotted into fists. A single droplet rolled down one weathered cheek. Then the 450's diesel was pushing the car onto the low bank with a deep-throated growl, and the woman with child were left behind as the car sprinted across the green fields to where Parkinson's vehicle stood silent guard.

To McKay's relief, the maps were accurate. Too often he had gone into territory that was held by an enemy but supposedly well-known, only to find he was relying on hopelessly outmoded or geographically inaccurate maps. He knew no effort or expense had been spared to get the Guardians the best equipment and support possible. He also knew how frequently the government lavished both effort and expense on total fiascos.

But so far they had escaped the steely claws of a major snafu. Little-known county roads appeared on Sloan's screen like capillaries on a bloodshot eye. Within a few hundred yards of the clogged artery of Interstate 270 they found a modest strip of blacktop running toward the Blue Ridge range without a car in sight in either direction. The hordes fleeing the devastated cities simply didn't know where the little side roads were. They'd probably find them soon enough, but for now the two V-450's made good speed through rolling piedmont. They passed isolated farmhouses and steered wide of small towns, which now usually looked like junkyards and car lots because of the massive influx of refugees in cars and vans and trucks.

Several more times they had to make their way across major roads choked solid with cars. Each time, they had to find ways across as they had with 270. Each time they were confronted with new spectacles of horror created by a populace uprooted, terrified, and beyond hope. Once a pair of National Guardsmen tried to flag them down as they rolled along a flood-control channel beneath yet another traffic jam. Brutal exhaustion had taken its toll of Parkinson's scruples. When the Guardsmen tried to force the cars to stop, it was the Secret Service agent's turret guns that fired close over their helmeted heads and sent them scurrying back up the concrete embankment.

At length they passed Sharpsburg and began to twine upward into the green-clad Blue Ridge range. The sun had disappeared behind the mountains, leaving in the east a strange greenish sky penetrated by pillars of black smoke rising from Washington, Baltimore, and Philadelphia. Far in the northeast a lurid glow touched the low and heavy sky. From the scattered radio communications Sam Sloan had been able to monitor, the Guardians gathered that a huge liquid propane gas storage facility had ruptured, spreading a cloud of poison gas across an entire city. The gas had suddenly taken fire, and Trenton, New Jersey, which had escaped without feeling the bite of bombs, writhed in the grip of a firestorm such as the nuked cities were mostly spared.

On a lonely wooded slope, with a mountain bulking reassuringly between them and the smoldering ruin the One-Day War had left of the Eastern seaboard, the two vehicles nosed off a winding road onto a dirt track. They were soon creeping upward into the woods to find shelter as night laid a poultice across the ravaged land.

CHAPTER
NINE

It had all begun in a hospital room, many weeks before the briefing in the Arizona desert.

McKay lay in bed, wrapped in bandages and a haze of drugs. He twisted and moaned, locked in a restless dream of battle that turned into a pure hell of fire and noise and blackness. Gradually an image took form before his eyes: a face.

He recoiled from it. "Jesus. I must be havin' a hell of a nightmare to see a face like *that*."

A dry chuckle snatched him to full consciousness. He realized he'd spoken aloud and that the torn and tortured visage before his eyes was no nightmare.

"Shit, I'm sorry," he said huskily. Traffic sounds hooted, growled, and farted vaguely from the sun-bright streets of Haifa five stories below the noise dampened by the whisper-whine of the U.S. Navy hospital's overworked air-conditioning system. "I ain't usually such an asshole." Lips and tongue stumbled. McKay was unused to apologizing, as well as being doped to the eyeballs. At the blurred edge of his vision he saw a gold gleam of oakleaf on shoulderboard, and added, "Sir."

"I don't mind, son." The voice was dry and gravelly as a Libyan wadi. "Had to get used to this face a long time since.

And I don't have to look at it myself, except when I'm shaving. Pleased to make your acquaintance, Lieutenant. I'm Major Crenna.''

Both McKay's arms were swathed in bandages to the fingertips. An inflated splint immobilized his right arm, and wires led from electrodes sunk in the bone to an electrolytic healing unit that squatted along with all the other machinery next to the bed. He gestured weakly with pink fingertips. "Forgive me for not shakin' your hand, Major.''

Half a mouth smiled. "You've got a sense of humor. Good. You'll need it.''

A pale eyebrow arched under the bandages that encased McKay's skull. "For what?''

"A job I've come to offer you.''

McKay ran an eye over the man. Medium height, slim athletic build, spring-steel compact. Army uniform. Green beret with Twenty-third Group flashes. "If the Company sent you,'' he said, "forget it. I've done my time with SOG in Lebanon and North Africa.''

Again the half-smile. "I'm not affiliated with the CIA. Nor any other agency of the United States government. Nor the military.''

"Looking for mercs? I've still got fifteen months on this hitch—not that I'm interested.''

"No mercenary either,'' Major Crenna said. "I'm . . . official.'' He sat down on a straight-backed metal chair. "I've seen your file. You're quite a Marine. Bronze Star, four recommendations for the Silver, and if you hadn't been on covert ops, you'd have gotten a recommendation for a Medal of Honor for some of your exploits.'' He didn't use the common, and mistaken, practice of referring to the nation's highest military medal as "Congressional.''

"Don't forget the Purple Heart,'' McKay said sardonically through blistered lips.

"You've also got as many reprimands in your file as any man I've ever seen,'' the compact Major continued, "and have three times been recommended for court-martial.''

"Hell, Major, I was just a green kid fresh out of boot camp when I picked up those reprimands.''

"But not the three brushes with courts-martial. What were they? Once for assaulting another DI when you were at Parris Island, once for refusing an order, once for insubordination.

You lost your stripes twice, Lieutenant, and came close to being cashiered that third time.'' He shook his head. "Fortunate the court-martial board found Captain Corrick guilty of negligence.''

McKay shrugged, then winced. His body wasn't yet up to this kind of thing. "What's all this about anyway—Major?''

Crenna showed his teeth. They were perfect all the way across, even and white, as if whatever mishap had shredded the left half of his face into a mask of runneled scar tissue had left them untouched. His single gray eye was bright as burnished steel. "You must be recovering. Your insubordination's coming back strong.''

McKay said nothing. Crenna sat back and crossed his legs. He took out a pack of cigarettes. "Smoke?''

"Against hospital regs," McKay said. "I could be court-martialed.'' He reached over and accepted a Camel, then a light from an old-fashioned nondisposable steel lighter. He drew deeply and lay back, studying Crenna.

"I understand you have a few differences with our military policy overseas," the Major said. He lit his own cigarette.

McKay shrugged. "I'm just a fucking grunt. They tell me to saddle up and go, I saddle up and go.''

"But you don't stop thinking." It wasn't a question. "That's one of the reasons you're being considered for this assignment. A confidential, dangerous, and supremely challenging assignment. So feel free to tell me how you really feel. It won't go beyond this room.''

McKay settled back on the bed and drew on his cigarette. The new skin on his back was tightening, beginning to itch. That was the only place he'd have scarring, the doctors told him, on his back and a little on his right arm. He could live with that. He could live with the temporary low-level whole-body ache drugs could only blunt but not drive away. What he couldn't deal with was the damned itching under the splint and bandages.

"Okay," he said. "So I don't think everything we're doing overseas is so great. I think maybe if we'd mind our own business more, be concerned more with our own defenses and less with proppin' up every government that comes to us with a song-and-dance about how they're the only thing holdin' off the commies, we'd be a lot better off.'' His blue eyes stared up at the stained dropped acoustical tile of the ceiling. "My granddaddy served with General Stroup on Tarawa, where the General got his Medal of Honor. General Stroup always said the place for American soldiers was guarding American soil. Never seen anything in my time overseas to make me argue with that."

Crenna nodded slowly, jutting his sharp chin. "You love your country, Lieutenant?"

McKay's eyes probed him like ice needles. "I'm pretty fucked up here, Major," he said slowly and tautly, "and I'm wired up like a power plant, but I guess maybe I could still manage to get up and throw you down the stairs, Major."

Crenna gave him a ghastly skull's smile. "The fact I'm a superior officer wouldn't slow you down, would it?" McKay's expression answered him. He barked a short laugh. "Easy to see how you racked up all those reprimands. A person might have a harder time figuring out why you weren't cashiered."

He leaned forward. Smoke wreathed his ruined face. "Another person might, anyway. I *know* why you weren't. Because you're a damned good Marine. One of the best. Particularly scouting enemy-held beachheads when you were with Force Recon, and on those covert missions for the Studies and Observations Group, Southwest Asia Command."

McKay kept watching him steadily. This grotesquely scarred Green Beanie major knew quite a bit about him, including, no doubt, a good deal that wasn't on his service record. Not surprising, in and of itself. During his hitch with the deceptively named Studies and Observations Group in the Southern Med he'd worked alongside Green Berets as well as Army Rangers, SEAL's, and CIA cowboys, among others, any of whom might have been given access to his secret files if the powers that be decreed they had a need to know.

But he remained wary of this man who called himself Crenna. A lot of his associates in SOG-SWAC hadn't exactly played by the rules—that was what the Group was all about, after all. But some of them weren't exactly playing the game they were supposed to either. Some of them got into running drugs and contraband, some into extracurricular sanctions, and some actually dealt with the Arabs and commies. None of them were shy about using the covert methods in which they'd been trained. And all too many weren't playing with a full deck. This Major Crenna, if he knew the details of McKay's career in covert ops, was by definition not on the level.

Whether he was a good guy or a bad guy remained to be seen.

"So why'd you enlist, McKay? And why do you stay in?"

McKay chewed the inside of his mouth. No point in bullshitting this crazy major. Not that that was his style. "Didn't have a lot of choice about joining, Major."

"I knew that."

"As to why I stayed . . ." He shrugged, then held back a wince at the pangs that shot down his back. "Serving my country, I guess."

"But you didn't agree with what you were doing?"

"Not a lot of the time. But that, you know, that wasn't my decision. And I figured if the country really needed me, I might as well be in the service, be trained, so I could do some good if and when the shitstorm came." He took a deep drag, knocked ash onto the linoleum floor. "Also—shit. I like a good fight. Marine Corps's the only way I know how to do it legal." He grinned.

Crenna grinned back.

McKay let a smoke trail slip out between puffy lips white with zinc salve. "You said something about a job for me, Major. What did you have in mind?"

"I want you to become a member of a special team. Very elite, very secret. Handpicked by me. Four men. Each the best I can get."

"What's the mission?"

"Guarding the life of the President of the United States."

McKay stared at the Major across a half-dozen heartbeats. A traffic cop's whistle chirped from a million miles off. Then he busted up laughing. It hurt his cracked ribs and broken arm and strained ligaments and healing burns and every other goddamned thing, but he couldn't help himself. He laughed as he always did, loud and long from deep inside his barrel chest.

When he settled down, there were tears in his pale blue eyes. "I think the damn dope they have me on is making me goofy," he said. "Is it giving me hallucinations too, or did you say what I thought you did?"

"You heard me, Lieutenant." Crenna's tone was neutral, neither offended nor playing along. Just stating dry fact.

McKay worked his massive jaw around. "What's the Secret Service going to say about that?"

"They're not happy about it."

McKay's cheeks drew up, deepening the lines at the outer corners of his eyes. "That's about the same kind of fucked-up mission I'm used to over here. Trying to cooperate on a delicate assignment with people who resent us, don't want us around. That works real well, Major."

Crenna shook his head. "The Service is unhappy because they feel you—that is, our team—will be trespassing on their terrain. But the fact is, you won't."

"But protectin' the President's Secret Service turf."

" 'Protecting' was perhaps not the correct word to use. You and your fellow members of the team, which will be called 'the Guardians,' will be charged with escorting the President of the United States to safety in event of thermonuclear war."

McKay lay back and closed his eyes. Crenna stood. "I'll leave you now, give you some time to consider."

"Don't bother."

The Major paused. "You're not in?"

McKay laughed softly. "Oh no. I'm in. I'm in all the way."

William Kosciusko McKay was born in the Camelot year of 1962. Even in his grimy blue-collar Pittsburgh neighborhood expectations were rising. The future looked bright for the first of nine children. Not that his steelworker father, Thomas, had any real expectation of becoming rich. The country was simply caught up in the booming optimism of the New Frontier.

Camelot came crashing abruptly down, fading safely into the realm of myth before the moat could run low and reveal the toothy and scaled monsters that lived in it. In 1965 the first Marines went ashore in Southeast Asia to fight a war Kennedy and Johnson had sworn they'd never be involved in. One of the first casualties in that Marine advance force was Corporal Lawrence McKay, Tom McKay's younger brother.

The Marines were a tradition in the McKay family. Since the first McKays had arrived from Ireland in 1848, at least one male of each generation had joined the USMC. McKay's grandfather served in the Pacific in World War Two and later lost three toes of his left foot on the long, grisly subzero slog back from frozen Chosun in Korea. Grandpa's dad had been in Nicaragua, fighting the Sandinistas to make the country safe for Tacho Somoza I, and at Belleau Wood before that, to make the world safe for democracy. *His* dad had been in the

Spanish-American War and the Philippine insurrection, and so on.

Tom McKay had no strong feelings about the war in Indochina. McKays were never crusaders. They served their country, but they never wore their patriotism on their sleeves. In fact, a certain skepticism was another family tradition. One McKay faced Boxer lead at Peking alongside blue-clad Japanese troops; and two generations later another McKay was killing descendants of his grandfather's comrades-in-arms. The McKays realized that a lot of what they were called on to do was bullshit, but they believed in their country, right or wrong. When he finished high school, what Tom did was marry Marie Sokolowski, the pretty, plump, black-haired daughter of Polish immigrants who'd fled the communist regime after the war, and take a job in the steel mill, leaving Larry to carry on the family tradition in the Corps.

But when his kid brother came home in a plastic body bag, Tom too felt the call.

With his harried mother trying her best to cope with four children, little towheaded Billy McKay was allowed to run wild in the Pittsburgh streets. He was six when his father returned to the World from his second tour in Nam with a pocketful of medals and a hip full of shrapnel from an NVA 130 mm cannon. At this point Billy was already a member in good standing of a blue-collar Irish street gang. Despite a return of strict paternal discipline, he grew up big, powerful, and unruly. But that was also part of a time-honored tradition in the McKay clan.

When he was twelve, he was already almost six feet tall, and he never did go through a gangly adolescent period. He was always powerfully built, a natural athlete, a natural leader. He saw a Clint Eastwood movie, *Thunderbolt and Lightfoot*, about a bank robber who blew open vaults with a 20 mike-mike cannon, and it impressed the hell out of him. Then an adult told him that with his long, somewhat heavy features, curly blond hair, and thick muscular body, he looked like a stockier version of Steve McQueen. His feet didn't touch the pavement for weeks over that one; Steve McQueen was a heavy dude, as bad as you could get all the way around.

But eventually the USMC proved to be bigger, badder, and tougher even than Billy McKay. Rebellious as he was, he was also very bright, and it didn't take him long to figure out he couldn't win. At least, not by trying to slug it out head to head with ironbound regulations and drill instructors hard as drill bits.

So he learned to play the game, to shine his shoes and make his bunk and salute and march and drill like the ideal parade-ground soldier. When the sergeant told him to drop and do twenty push-ups, he did twenty-five. If the sarge thought he was being a smartass, he did another twenty-five and never batted a cool blue eye. Overnight he turned himself into something straight out of the manual.

But inside he was still the wild kid that had run the grubby Pittsburgh streets. Off base he was a hard-drinking hell raiser, busting heads and bars with fine abandon. He wasn't shy about using his pile-driver fists on his fellow Marines behind the barracks either.

Women flocked around him, drawn by his muscles and his tan and his spiffy dress blues, and by the ruthless rough charm in his ice-blue eyes. He used them and tossed them aside. Occasionally, just occasionally, he used his fists on them too. Afterwards he tended to stay drunk for a week at a stretch, hiding from himself in the bottle. Consequently, his otherwise perfect record got some smudges on it.

In 1982 Lance Corporal McKay, who had already made the trip up to sergeant and back once, found himself assigned to the peacekeeping force in Beirut. During that time he began to acquire his reputation for bravery bordering on sheer craziness. He had always had an affinity for violence. Now he proved to have an affinity for danger too, in a chaotic environment where supposed allies were damn near as dangerous as out-and-out enemies. He came home with his record bulging with recommendations and reprimands alike.

Despite his comparative youth, Staff Sergeant McKay was sent to Parris Island as a close-combat instructor. Drawing on his youthful street-fighting experience, his brawling in and out of the service, and what he'd learned in the rubbled-out streets of West Beirut, he proved to be an extremely, even brutally efficient instructor. What his students learned was reality, sometimes in rather stiff doses. When a fellow instructor, a gunnery sergeant with ten years and twenty pounds on him, remonstrated about the number of broken bones his pupils were cropping up with, he sent the gunny to join them in the hospital. Another busted jaw, and another bust back to the ranks for Wild Bill.

With a sigh of bureaucratic relief, the Corps's paper-shufflers approved his application for transfer to Force Recon. The level of United States military involvement overseas was skyrocketing. The pretense that the U.S. forces were "advisors" was wearing thin in half a dozen countries, from El Salvador to the Philippines, by way of Africa, the Mideast, and mainland Asia. More and more men were being committed as combat troops plain and simple. The name was "police action" now, but you got killed just as dead. "Send in the Marines" was the word being passed from on high with more and more frequency.

Before the Marines went in, they needed somebody to scout the way, secure possibly hostile landing zones. That was Force Recon's job. That became Billy McKay's job too, and he was good at it.

Enter the Studies and Observations Group, SWAC. During the Vietnam war, a wide array of covert operations against the North Vietnamese had been undertaken by the Green Berets, Rangers, Force Recon, the Navy's SEAL's, tribal mercenaries, the CIA, and various other special forces and commando-style outfits, under an umbrella program dubbed Studies and Observations Group, Military Assistance Command, Vietnam—SOG-MACV for short. The name was pure disinformation; since covert ops were politically sensitive, given the unpopularity of the war at home, a nonthreatening title was required for the program.

When the Rapid Deployment Force was replaced by the Southwest Asia Command in the mid-1980s, and operations both covert and overt began against Muslim and communist guerrillas from Morocco to Iran, SOG-SWAC was formed. It used the earlier name for the same reason the United Kingdom used the name Special Air Service when it revived David Stirling's dashing commando force in the fifties. The desert raiders of SAS had nothing to do with air services; the name was a cover, and was later readopted purely out of respect for tradition. Likewise, the Studies and Observations name. SOG-SWAC was looking for swashbucklers for deep-cover missions in Africa and the Mideast, fearless, smart, resourceful men.

Billy McKay was a natural.

For four years McKay found himself caught up in a world of intrigue, violence, and James Bond gadgetry, some of which occasionally worked. His battle-honed senses achieved a new razor edge, and not just on knife-in-teeth missions against enemy supply dumps and command posts. In the Mediterranean theater, your ally in the back streets of Tripoli might be your deadly enemy in the Desht-i-Kavir desert of Iran.

It was a complex, multisided conflict. The public was told that SWAC was fighting communist subversion, but that was only part of the story. Besides the Russians and Iranians, the U.S. had two other major foes in the Southern Med: the fundamentalist Islamic Front, and an array of Marxist groups loosely federated into the Muslim People's Liberation Front. Though most outsiders believed the two fronts were allied, in fact they were mortal enemies who had split militant Arab support between them after the PLO foundered in the mid-eighties. The IF fought for traditional Islamic values and against Western ones; despite its name, the Moscow-line MPLF was antireligious as well as socialist-revolutionary. The groups' mutual enmity was as close to a constant as existed in that strange struggle.

McKay's adventures among the bandicoots (the name that the Australians, the U.S.'s desert allies, gave the Muslims) would have been the stuff of newspaper headlines, if the papers had been allowed to print more than heavily censored (and beautified) pabulum about the secret war in the Mediterranean. It was a thrill to be indulging in exploits right out of the potboiling spy novels he'd loved as a kid. He might be in the North Yemen desert one week to snatch an enemy political officer, and the next emerging from the greasy waters of Abadan harbor in a black wet suit to deposit admonitory ace-of-spades "death cards" on the chests of the sleeping crewmen of a British freighter delivering Belgian-made FNC rifles to the Iranians. He shot up Iranian and Marxist-backed tax collectors on their appointed rounds in Egypt and Lebanon and Saudi Arabia, blew up Libyan refineries, and under the noses of the harbor police in Bari, Italy, replaced Soviet ammunition being shipped to Ethiopia with booby-trapped "bol bean" ammo that would explode when it was used.

McKay's exploits won him a commission to second lieutenant. But the strain took its toll. He was constantly living on the edge. The physical risks of the missions were daunting but not the whole story. Equally as bad was the constant possibility of betrayal, and having to listen to the ugly, persistent stories about covert-op teams being deliberately sacrificed in one or another gambit. He fought, bled, saw buddies die before his eyes. He had missions blow up in his face that had to have been compromised by his own side, and was once involved in sanctioning a Ranger captain who'd gotten caught passing mission data to the Marxist guerrillas. He saw, as few did, how futile the whole bloody, expensive effort was.

After fifty months, he threw in the towel, resigned from SOG, and took a furlough back to the States. It was a disappointment. The World wasn't real to him anymore. His family were strangers, his former friends were on welfare or going through monkey motions in some make-work Public Employment Agency job. People were wrapped up in trying to survive an inflation rate crowding the three-digit barrier. He had nothing to say to anybody, and idleness after years of nonstop action frayed his nerves as no danger ever had. In three weeks he was on a plane back to the Med and Force Recon.

Three weeks after that he was almost dead.

It was a typical mission. American and Israeli combined forces planned a raid from Egypt into southern Libya near the Sudanese-Egyptian border to wipe out an MPLF training camp from which guerrillas had been infiltrating teams into Egypt. Mike (the nickname for the MPLF) had acted with his usual arrogance. Moscow trained, the MPLF leadership had picked up the Russians' distaste for Arab ways, especially those of the ragged village and desert folk, and so word was out that the locals would be helpful to McKay's side.

McKay and his recon team would be inserted by helicopter well north of the camp, take a swing through the surrounding country to check the accuracy of their maps and the guerrillas' security, then get out by chopper or by humping it, depending on the situation. Simple. But McKay didn't like going in by chopper. Too hard to remain unobtrusive.

The higher-ups vetoed his suggestion that insertion be by HALO—high-altitude, low-opening parachutes. Libyan radar coverage was spotty at the best of times, even though many millions of petrodollars had gone to buy French- and British-made equipment to augment that which Qaddafi bought from the Soviets in the late seventies. A decade of ever more frequent hassles with American, Israeli, and Egyptian pilots had made the Libyans cautious about contesting overflights unless it looked as if a major strike was coming in. McKay figured a plane could drop the team, equipped with HALO gear, from altitude, and then swing back into Egyptian airspace before the Libyans had finished strapping themselves into the cockpits of their MiG-25bis Foxhound interceptors, assuming the intruders were even spotted and the Libyans felt pugnacious enough to deal with them.

But the brass said no. HALO insertion was risky, they said —as if choppers, slow and noisy and oh so vulnerable, weren't —and more to the point, they were expensive. Besides, the natives were friendly. It would be a piece of cake.

So it was—at first. The two Huey choppers hove in to a landing on a hilltop far from the nearest huddle of tumbledown mud dwellings. McKay stood in the doorway of the chopper, ready to jump the meter and a half to the arid, flinty ground. The heat of the sun beat off the rocks and washed against his face like surf. The air was thick with dust thrown up by the rotors.

From the corner of his eye, he saw a flash down the slope to his left. He shouted a warning, dove forward

—and the whole world vanished in a bright orange flare as the RPG-7v antitank rocket fired from cover blew the chopper, crew, and half his team to kingdom come. Somehow Sergeant Whitlock had been able to get the badly burned, battered, and unconscious Lt. McKay into the other chopper while its door gunner blazed manfully away at the ambushers with an M-60. The Huey lumbered off to safety, sieved by small-arms fire, and the next thing McKay knew he was in the Haifa hospital where Major Crenna found him.

The next thing after *that*, he was in another desert a world away.

CHAPTER
TEN

It was a small clearing, surrounded by tall pines, their tops black arrowheads against the overcast sky. High above, the uneasy rolling of the clouds made faint stars seem to race by in patches. McKay was only mildly surprised to hear crickets chirping brightly away as if the world hadn't just ended.

Closer by, cooling metal gave off soft creaks and pings along with the heat slowly radiating from the drab-painted hulls of the V-450's. A warm, moist breeze stroked McKay's face as he emerged from Mobile One. He nodded to President MacGregor, who was sitting on a mossy log between the two cars, eating rations heated in Mobile One's microwave. MacGregor nodded back and went on talking with George Mason, the gunner from Mobile Two, and a couple of the other Secret Service men from Parkinson's vehicle. The big chief agent was nowhere in sight.

The President had changed into an L. L. Bean shirt, jeans, and hiking boots, an outfit which was rather more practical for the fugitive life than the three-piece suit in which he'd fled the White House. The agents still wore their somber suits, and now had HK-91 assault rifles propped beside them on their logs. An air of gloom hung over the camp, a reaction to the cataclysmic events of the day. A camp fire would have lightened the scene in more ways than one, but it was out for obvious reasons.

From inside Mobile One came a crackle of static and a quick blur of voices. Sloan was monitoring radio traffic again, his face lit eerie red and green by the blow of his console. The rad meter was set on automatic; if radiation climbed significantly above background, a shrill beeping in the Guardians' earplugs would alert them. Meanwhile, Sloan tried to gather all the information he could about the general state of the world as well as the particular conditions of the country between this deceptively quiet haven and the Pennsylvania airfield where they were to rendezvous with the Company plane.

Even while it was keeping track of ambient radiation and wind direction, and helping Sloan scan the jumbled airwaves, Mobile One's computer was also riding herd on an impressive array of sensory equipment affixed to various points of the 450's titanium-alloy skin. Infrared scanners searched the woods for the telltale heat signatures of warm-blooded life forms and audio pickups. Instructed by the versatile computer to ignore the camp noises and the distinctive footfall patterns of the sentries, the scanners listened for the stealthy approach of a foe. Mobile One even sported miniature radars with both antipersonnel and sky-search modes, though with trees all around they were both shut down, useless for the moment. Additionally, the car carried all kinds of remote sensors that could be sown in the woods around the camp to detect intruders and relay word back to the car, but McKay had vetoed setting them out. Too much trouble and risk, he said, and they might have to de-ass the area in a hurry. Wouldn't want to leave all that expensive high-tech lying around the Blue Ridge Mountains. It wasn't real biodegradable.

All in all, it was very *Star Wars* and very splendid—and yet McKay was glad in his heart of hearts that Tom Rogers had lookout above the clearing. Mobile One's infrared eyes couldn't distinguish between the heat signature of a man and that of a white-tailed deer, and, computer-filtered or not, the "ears" could be effectively blanketed with white noise by a good stiff breeze blowing through the forest. The fancy-ass stuff actually did work well—if it didn't break and if its limitations were considered. Too many men put all their trust in electronic wonders, and woke up dead on that account.

McKay stretched, filling his big chest with air rich with greenery and summer and almost free of the petrochemical smells of the Eastern metroplex. The feathery touch of the night breeze, the fitful glimmer of stars, all reminded him of camping trips with his father as a boy, and of later, rare hunting expeditions to the Pennsylvania hills. For just a moment he wondered what had become of his family, his brothers and sisters who had married and moved away, his mother and father in their little house in Pittsburgh. He forced the thought from his mind. He had known, all the Guardians had known when they accepted this assignment, that they could spare no concern for their nearest and dearest, but only for the mission. Not that McKay was close to his family; it was one reason the Guardians had been chosen, lack of close ties. But still, for a brief, poignant moment, he wondered.

He shook his head and exhaled to clear his lungs of the smell of burned powder. That was an advantage of being a hero from all those books and movies and TV shows he'd loved as a kid. James Bond never had to spend an hour stripping and cleaning any of the nifty gimmicks he used. Maybe Her Majesty's Secret Service employed an army of flunkies to maintain the exalted double-oh operatives' weapons. That might have been one of the reasons the British Empire was in so much trouble these days. Or maybe all the goodies Q lashed up could fire forever without getting fouled with dirt and unburned powder. Unfortunately, McKay's Remington and the lightweight M-60 couldn't.

Reflexively, he took a turn around the little clearing. The two vehicles had been sprayed down with decontaminant aerosols and hosed down with water sucked from a mountain stream by a special pump rigged to work off Mobile One's engine. Now they were parked about five meters in from the closest trees and parallel to each other, with six or seven meters between them. In the margin between trees and cars, four Claymore mines had been set up next to rocks or with grass and leaves brushed over them to conceal them.

The Claymores consisted of hundreds of steel ball bearings imbedded in plastic explosive and rigged so they could be detonated on command. The Guardians had arranged them in a swastika pattern, following a lesson hard learned in Vietnam. Soldiers in that conflict used to emplace them facing straight out from their positions, which meant that they had to be put a good ways off to keep the backblast from cooking the good guys. It also meant that Charlie could creep up in the middle of the night, surreptitiously turn the damn things around, and then start hollering and busting caps. The GI's would touch off the Claymores and get faces full of steel marbles for their pains.

The way they were now positioned, if an enemy reversed the Claymores the charge would still fire outward. As it was, the deadly sprays of shot would barely clear the fronts and rears of the vehicles if the Claymores went. And things would look real grim for anyone who happened to be outside the little encampment.

McKay quickly satisfied himself that the Claymores and the wires that led to hand detonators stashed just inside Mobile One were well hidden. Hayes and Turpin were walking the small perimeter, the driver with a 7.62 HK-91, Hayes with his trusty Mini-Uzi. "McKay," young Hayes said softly.

"What's on your mind?"

The young agent stood facing him squarely. There was no moon; the intermittent starlight gave his skin a greenish cast. "I just wanted to tell you," Hayes said, his voice breaking like an adolescent's with barely contained emotion. Turpin stood a few meters away, holding the big black 7.62 assault rifle in patrol position, angled down across his lower body. "It was chickenshit the way you left our boys behind. Just chickenshit."

For a moment McKay just blinked at him. It took a moment for his mind to track. The events of the day were remote, disconnected, as though they'd taken place in a movie he'd seen some time ago.

Gotta give him credit for balls, McKay thought. The tousled top of Hayes's head came up to McKay's chin. McKay could have broken the Secret Service agent in two without half an effort.

"You have any combat experience, Hayes?" McKay asked.

Hayes shook his head. "I had a hitch in the Army. I served with LAPD for five years before joining the Service." He squared his shoulders. "But I learned you don't let your buddies down in a tight spot."

McKay's mouth tensed to a taut, sardonic grin. From what he'd heard, L.A.'s finest did a lot of shooting. Just not always at targets that could shoot back.

He could have explained to the youthful agent what anyone with battlefield experience would have known: that the men in Mobile Three had been beyond help by the time their comrades were in any position to get to them. But that would have smacked of making excuses. And that was one thing Billy McKay didn't do.

"Always glad to know what's on a man's mind, Hayes," he said, and stepped past him.

He pushed the incident out of his mind and made himself concentrate on business. The agents seemed sharp enough, well-disposed to him or not. But McKay stayed happy that Rogers was sitting on top of the hill keeping watch for strangers. Very little escaped the ex-Green Beret, whose keen senses had been honed to a fine edge during a decade of covert missions.

McKay walked back in between the cars and sat on a rock a little away from the others. Casey Wilson sat nearby, his eyes half-closed, his legs knotted into a lotus position. His rifle lay next to him in its case, ready for his turn on lookout. He was doing some sort of meditation. He was very into that sort of thing. McKay never could see the use in that Zen stuff, but it made Casey happy, and made him feel he could do his job better. And Casey was a good man, even though the others gave him a world of shit because he was young and looked younger.

And even though, in McKay's eyes, his background didn't exactly suit him for the task at hand.

Casey Wilson stirred as if awaking from sleep. He opened his eyes and got easily to his feet, picking up his rifle. "Time to relieve Tom," he said. "My turn in the barrel."

McKay roused himself from his reverie and looked around. The clouds had thinned some overhead, rushing by now in silvery wisps. Now that full dark had settled in the west, he could see patches of what seemed to be a false-dawn glow to the east, underlighting the restless clouds in orange and red and amber. His big jaw set. Nothing could be farther from the light of dawn than the glow of burning cities.

He stood and regarded Casey for a moment. The boy—the way he looked it was hard to think of him as anything else, even after all this time—was a good lookout, with an eagle's eyesight and, at need, an endless store of patience that was at variance with the nervousness he could sometimes display. And with that see-in-the-dark scope of his, and the flash and noise suppressor screwed onto the bull barrel of the M-40, an intruder trying to creep up on the camp would probably be dead before he knew it. There would be no sign to alert the victim's friends other than the supersonic crack of the bullet in flight, which could easily be taken for a branch breaking under a deer's hoof or some other normal forest sound.

But Casey still wasn't McKay or Rogers. *Dammit,* McKay thought, *he just isn't seasoned to this sort of thing.*

McKay made himself grin and say, "Go for it, Case," as if he trusted the young Guardian every bit as much as Casey thought he did. That was part of being a leader of these men, these Guardians.

Like the man said, no one told him it was going to be easy.

Casey grinned back, almost gratefully, it seemed. He moved off into the trees. He was good, McKay had to admit once again. He seemed to draw the darkness around him like a cloak as he disappeared, and McKay's skilled ears could catch only the faintest rustle of his passage upslope to where the hidden Rogers watched the surrounding nightscape. But still, but still . . .

"I'm coming in." The voice spoke quietly in McKay's ear. "Don't shoot at me." McKay glanced around, unaware of how much time had passed since Casey's departure. *Not good,* he thought. *Need to keep track of things like that.* Deep inside his skull a voice told him that this job was too big even for Big Bill McKay. *You've never grown up, Billy,* it whispered. *You're a boy in a man's body. You can't handle the responsibility. You never could.* He shook his head as if to drive the soft insinuating voice from it. He noticed that Turpin and Tim Hayes had frozen on their perimeter walk and stood peering into the circle of dark trees.

Suddenly Rogers was there, standing perfectly still, a third of the circle away from where the agents were watching. "Over here," Rogers said over the communicators. Hayes's and Turpin's heads snapped round. "Circled and came up from the south to make sure my back trail was clear."

He sauntered into camp, holding his Galil almost negligently before him in patrol position. "You shouldn't have snuck up on us like that!" Hayes sputtered.

"I didn't," Rogers said without rancor. "Everything's clear, Billy. There were sounds from the highway that runs north of us, commotions, shots sometimes, and there're people moving in from the east. We better shove off pretty early tomorrow or we might have company."

McKay nodded. "Don't want to keep the Company boys waiting either." Rogers gave him a quick perfunctory smile. Ignoring the glares of the two agents, he nodded to the President and clambered into Mobile One to get his ruck and bedroll.

McGregor picked himself up off his log. "I heard what you said, Lieutenant," he said with a wan smile. "I guess I'd better turn in." Though the underlids of his eyes sagged like worn-out leather purses from fatigue, McKay guessed the President of the United States wouldn't sleep much tonight. It was too bad MacGregor had never picked up the soldier's trick of sleeping anywhere and anywhen. He had been in the military—nobody much held high office in the U.S. these days who hadn't—but he'd gotten an ROTC commission and done his Army time in West Germany in the quiet days of the seventies and never had to learn the hard lessons that were second nature to men like Bill McKay and Tom Rogers.

Parkinson appeared in the side hatch of Mobile Two. His coat was off, his Mini-Uzi hanging from its shoulder holster. "Shall I have one of the men bring your bedding out, Mr. President?"

"I think the President'd better sleep in Mobile One tonight," McKay said.

Parkinson glared. "In a tin can full of high-octane gas, *Lieutenant*?"

McKay drew in a deep breath. "It's a risk. But there's more to risk sleeping in the open. Somebody tosses a grenade in here, or opens up from the trees—he's too vulnerable."

MacGregor offered a conciliatory smile. "I'll let you men work it out between you." He disappeared into Mobile One to get his toilet kit.

Anger flared inside McKay. *Typical goddamn politician* flashed through his mind. He frowned. It wouldn't do to start resenting the man whose life he was committed body and soul to protect. And besides, MacGregor was right. It was his responsibility, not the President's.

He looked at Parkinson. The chief agent had stepped from the vehicle and stood with his powerful legs spread, arms flexed, fists on hips, head lowered in a challenging position. "A Molotov or a rocket, McKay," he said. "That's all it'd take. And whoosh! No President."

"If somebody wants to start trouble, won't it likely be because they want to steal our vehicles, not blow 'em up? And who's gonna be lugging Coke bottles full of gas or antitank weapons around these woods? We've got a lot more to fear from deer rifles and Saturday night specials."

Parkinson stood looking as if he were a bull and McKay a skinny Spaniard in skintight pants and holding a cape. "Is that an order?"

"Yeah. If that's how you want it."

Parkinson shook his head. "You fucking glamor boys," he said. "This is our job. *Our* job." He turned and pulled himself heavily back into the V-450.

McKay felt the hostile eyes of the other agents. The worst of it was, Parkinson wasn't really an asshole. He was not just a wounded ego-tripper, all mouth and no brains. He was a damned good man, and there was stone-solid reason behind every last point he had locked horns with McKay over. It was a shame the two of them couldn't get together.

And yet it was absolutely vital for the success of this mission that they did get together. This mission was one to which McKay had devoted almost two years of his life—and maybe a whole lifetime before that, if you looked at it a certain way.

"Sweet dreams," he told the hostile faces of the agents, and went to get his bedroll and, with luck, some sleep before his turn to spell Casey Wilson.

CHAPTER
ELEVEN

"Eagle, this is Safe Haven," the voice rapped from the compartment speakers of Mobile One. The sound was clear and crisp and invigorating over the rush of wind from the open hatches as the car boomed along the dilapidated asphalt, heading northeast in the shadow of the rocky tree-clad ridges of the Alleghenies. "Eagle, do you read?"

A cheer rang off the insides of the V-450's curved hull. "Hear that?" Casey crowed. The boy was driving with his hatch popped, and his blond hair was blowing in the breeze. "We're almost home!" President MacGregor smiled a gaunt smile of relief. Agent Hayes laughed aloud and slapped McKay on the back. Only the burly ex-Marine remained silent and unmoved.

"Did you copy, Mobile One?" Even Clete Parkinson sounded excited as a schoolboy hearing the final bell of the last day of the term.

"We copied, Mobile Two," Sloan radioed back excitedly. "We're sending an acknowledgment now."

"Not so fast." McKay spoke without thinking.

Suddenly the Super Commando was full of eyes. "What do you mean, Billy?" Casey asked, ducking back inside and twisting around in his seat to gape at his CO.

"Go back to driving," McKay growled. Casey turned back, looking hurt, even though he'd slewed the car dangerously near the side of the Pennsylvania back-country road.

McKay felt Sloan's dark eyes trying to chip through the hard mask that had settled over his tanned face. *He thinks I'm nuts.* A corner of McKay's mouth curved up. *Maybe I am.*

"What the hell's the hang-up?" Parkinson demanded. "Acknowledge their damned transmission. We got a package to deliver."

McKay ran his hand over his short bristly hair. "Do it, Sloan," he said gruffly. The commo man gave him another heartbeat's penetrating look, then turned back to radio their response to the CIA base in the Alleghenies somewhere across the Pennsylvania line from Cumberland, Maryland.

"Good to hear from you, Eagle," the affected drawl of the CIA operator crackled back. "Come ahead on in."

"Let's go for it," Parkinson called.

"Casey," McKay rapped. "We've got a cache nearby, don't we? Bring it up on the map screen."

"Got it, Billy. What's up?" Wilson said.

"Head for it. We're going to top off the tanks. We're damned near out of gas."

Frowning, Casey started to turn again, thought better of it. Sloan gave McKay another look. "Tell Parkinson about our change in plans," McKay said.

"What is *wrong* with you, McKay?" the agent's gruff voice demanded in return. "We almost got the President home free. Why do you want to mess with gassing up?"

"We've been burning fuel pretty fast and free. And we may need to boogie in a hurry."

"Are you out of your mind?"

Nothing like discipline, McKay thought. "You were Special Forces, Parkinson. You should know as well as anybody something may go wrong with the pickup. Something always *does*."

"You're going too damn far, McKay. You're endangering the life of the President of the United States, all on account of your paranoia. . . ."

"We'll be at the base soon," McKay said. "When we get there you can file a protest, all official-like."

The rosy glow of the burning Eastern seaboard had begun

to diffuse into the gray murk of false dawn when McKay spotted them. Lying behind a moss-covered log with the smell of dew-wet grass and earth heavy and heady in his nostrils, he laid the light-amp electronic binocs down and picked up his old Zeiss night glasses, just to confirm what he thought he saw. A few small shapes dotted across the flank of a low ridge to the east. After them spilled more, dozens, then hundreds, like an army of driver ants on the march across the Blue Ridge.

Even as he watched, some faltered and fell by the way. The others came grimly on at the slow slog of utter exhaustion. Men, women, children: refugees fleeing the devastation of the megaplex who had been turned out by the smaller towns of the piedmont that knew too well how pressed they'd be to care for their own. They straggled onward, westward, with no goal save some illusion of a shelter that didn't exist anymore. Maybe some had rucks, but most were traveling light, too weary to tote any farther whatever provisions or private treasures they'd rescued from the holocaust. Many of them—hell, most—probably hadn't walked any farther than their garages in years. But desperation forced them to damp the fire in their lungs and drive aching, jelly-weak legs to take another step and yet another.

He shoved the Zeiss glasses back into their leather case and slung the electrobinocs around his neck. The pathetic doomed horde struggling across the mountains probably posed no threat to the President. But you couldn't tell, and anyway, they'd have enough trouble fighting through other mobs of refugees on the road to the CIA rendezvous. Might as well bug out before they got caught in this one.

He picked up his M-60, checked the hang of the half-moon-shaped Aussie ammo belt box clipped to the side of his light-weight machine gun, and started down the grassy slope.

The roads through the Alleghenies were blissfully clear. The roads from the coast had all been hopelessly clogged since the day before, and this permitted very little vehicular traffic to spill far from the main routes. And the people of the mountain towns and villages were tending to stay put and await events at home. Sloan's radio confirmed what McKay surmised: that the nation's relocation plan was breaking apart on the shoals of small-town America's not unreasonable determination to preserve what it had for itself, its loved ones, and neighbors. That determination had already led to innumerable firefights, according to broadcasts Sloan picked up. Some battles had broken out between refugees and townsfolk, others between the residents of small towns designated relocation centers and National Guard troops trying to force them to accept the fleeing masses. *Bad news,* McKay thought. *Guard's gonna be more trigger-happy than usual.* He didn't let himself think any deeper on it than that.

They made good time as the morning sun burned off the thick cottony mist. The hills were an aching green, growing rockier as they worked west. As much as they could, they avoided the small settlements dotted among the mountains. Here and there they passed through them, though, the quiet mountain places, wide spots in the road, a gas station with yellow Pennzoil signs flapping in the wind, a small store, a few houses set back from the highway among the trees that clung to the slopes. They were all lifeless, abandoned looking. But McKay had the sensation now and again of watching eyes, fearful faces hanging well back in shadow, frightened people peering over the tops of chintz drapes as the squat armored cars rumbled past in a stink of diesel fuel. The occupants had hunkered down to see what the new world brought by thermonuclear fire was like.

McKay's main worry was the black storm clouds piling up in the west. There was a chance they'd drop contaminated rain, which wouldn't make the pickup at the CIA field any easier. But throughout the morning, the clouds closed in only gradually across a sky gauzy with a high cirrus overcast.

Then they came to a major highway, and the story changed.

U.S. 48 was the sort of nightmare even MacGregor seemed to be getting accustomed to. After the comparatively easy run along the back roads, neither McKay nor Parkinson was in a mood to trifle with the logjam. While Mobile One's guns covered from the tree line, Two drove straight up to the highway. Parkinson popped out, and with his throat mike channeled through the 450's loudspeaker, explained to the weary refugees that a way through had to be made for a top secret government mission. He was good, McKay had to admit, his deep voice rich and modulated as an anchorman's, letting the crowd feel that they were in on something special, a mission to save what was left of America.

And why the fuck not? They are, in a way.

There was a bad moment when somebody broke from the crowd gathered alongside the unbroken line of stalled cars and rushed the agent. McKay's lips snapped into a snarl, and he longed to be outside the steel cocoon covering Parkinson with his Maremont. Parkinson may have been a prick, but he was also McKay's buddy.

He could actually *feel* Rogers' fingers taking up slack on the triggers of the .50 and the 40 mike-mike. Then he saw that it was three kids who were running forward, saw Parkinson hop from the front deck of the Super Commando and drop to one knee to greet them. He did something for a moment, the kids went running back to their worried-looking parents, who had come timidly forward, afraid to get too close to the ominous steel monster.

Rogers sighed and eased off on the trigger switches. Parkinson straightened and started giving orders, and damned if the crowd didn't hop to like good little troopers, jump-starting a couple of dead cars, literally picking up a little Japanese box and moving it onto the shoulder, and standing obediently back as Mobile Two bulled a stalled pickup and a van with an orange sunset scene on its side out of the way. Parkinson hopped up behind the turret of the 450 and, clinging to a handhold, rode to the far side of the highway.

Mobil Two drew up the opposite slope of the shallow valley and stopped. "Okay, Mobile One, come across," Parkinson said, and this time the loudspeaker didn't magnify his words for the ears of the refugees. "Unbutton and have everybody stick their heads out and wave."

"Are you f—" McKay had been about to say, *fucking crazy,* but something made him stop. Parkinson had P.R. training as a special agent of the Secret Service. Maybe he knew what he was doing.

"We have to give the people a show. They helped us heroes out. Now we have to pay off. Noblesse oblige, McKay."

"What say?"

"Look it up. Now haul ass. And have the President keep his head down—don't want to get carried away here."

"Okay, college boy," McKay said. Casey stuck his head out the driver's hatch, Sloan, out the radio operator's. McKay and Agent Hayes climbed half out of the rear hatch aft of the lozenge-shaped turret. Rogers had popped the top of his cupola. They all waved and grinned as if running for office as Mobile One cruised smoothly down the slope and across the path cleared by Two and the onlookers.

The crowd burst into applause. It tore McKay up inside, it really did. Here they were cheering him and the rest as if they were conquering heroes—and all they were doing was driving on, leaving the homeless and the helpless to whatever fate awaited them. But it made him feel good too. He shook his head; he didn't understand this. He slid back down the hatch. With him went the image of Rogers sitting with head and shoulders in the breeze, staring backward, a human killing machine looking for just this moment, maybe the only time in his whole life, like a lost little boy.

"Ain't that a lick," the turret gunner was saying as the rear hatch slammed to. "Ain't that just a fuckin' lick."

MacGregor was shaking his head. "Amazing." His voice shook.

"You did a hell of a job back there, Parkinson," McKay said. "But what was the deal with those kids?"

"The damnedest thing, McKay. They remembered my days in the NFL. *They wanted my goddamn autograph.*"

Thirty minutes later the call from Haven came.

The cache lay west of their line of travel to the CIA base. The two cars drove toward it in moody silence for twenty minutes. Haven had called back twice, asking for an estimated time of arrival. McKay had simply said there was a slight delay and left it at that.

Am *I being paranoid?* McKay wondered. He thought about the last time he'd been called that.

It had been on the eve of that last mission into Libya, when he'd wanted to HALO in rather than be inserted by chopper.

Drive on, he thought.

The holocaust could come at any minute, Major Crenna had told his Guardians, and consequently the Project had caches stashed all over the U.S.: concrete bunkers stuffed full of food, fuel, spare parts, and ammo, accessible only to those possessing a certain code, hidden so well that only an intensive search was liable to turn one up. If the shithammer fell while the President was whistle-stopping in the Midwest or addressing a newspaper convention in San Francisco, the Guardians would be assured of enough bullets, beans, and benzene to get the Man to Heartland.

Privately, McKay wondered at how comprehensive the whole scheme was. There were a lot of resources tied up for such a small unit as the Guardians, and a very chancy proposition it was that they'd ever be needed. But he wasn't sorry to have the caches to fall back on. Especially in the matter of fuel, which was liable to be held pretty closely, rationed wherever the authorities could get their hooks on it. And the caches would make it unnecessary for the team to drive up to a fuel dump and tell the guards, "Fill 'em up, boys, we got the President in the back." Very poor security, that.

The cache lay in a clearing similar to the one they'd spent the night in. A mountainside had been hollowed out beneath an outcrop of granite boulders. McKay used his I.D. plate and access code on a panel hidden in a rock and pulled open a camouflaged molded-concrete door. This cache wasn't large enough to drive into—the door was only big enough to admit one man at a time—so McKay dragged a hose out to Mobile One, which was parked next to the entrance. He and Rogers then took up stations on top of the outcrop; in their green-and-tan-mottled forest cammies, they blended effortlessly into the patches of scrub oak among the rocks. Sloan manned the turret, Hayes pumped the diesel fuel, and Casey kept Mobile One ready to move in case of trouble. Mobile Two kept watch from a nearby hilltop. When One was refueled, the cars switched places. McKay and Rogers stayed on watch. McKay would rather they both were back inside the 450, ready to roll and bear the President to safety if trouble broke, but Parkinson was pissed at McKay for this delay. Doing a little extra was good diplomacy, McKay reckoned.

"My men are competent to keep their own lookout, McKay," Parkinson said angrily when Two's tanks were full and McKay slid down to secure the cache again.

Fuck me, McKay thought. He stuck his card back in the slot cut into the rock, tapped the keypad and slid the door shut.

"Let's ride," he said.

"Almost there," Casey remarked. His words came through the Guardians' earplugs. His head was out of the hatch, and the words were whipped away on the wind as Mobile One bombed down a narrow road that wound through wooded green hills. Except for when they had been covering Mobile Two on its strange crossing of U.S. 48, they'd driven unbuttoned all day long. As long as they were away from traffic or towns, McKay figured the risk from snipers was nominal. Casey and Turpin could make better time this way, and the cool mountain air rushing through the cars cut down that locker room tang and gave the air conditioners a rest. The blowers ate gas pretty fast, and after their last stop McKay was especially conscious about their fuel supply. They couldn't *always* count on being in range of a cache when they went dry, no matter how grandiose Project Guardian's preparations were.

"Pull off here," McKay said as they approached a dirt track leading off into the pine woods to their left. "You too, Parkinson."

"But there's just a half-klick to go, Billy—" Casey began.

"Yeah. Now pull off."

McKay was too cagey to be relieved that Parkinson hadn't offered any protest to the new delay. He jumped out of Mobile One as soon as the vehicle came to stop at a curve in the dirt road, shielded from view of the paved road that led to the airfield by trees and thick undergrowth. Parkinson climbed from Mobile Two, also hidden from the road, with leaden, long-suffering deliberation. "What is it this time, McKay?" he asked.

"We're making a swap. You're coming with us, Sloan's going into your car."

"Why?"

"Because Mobile Two isn't going in with us. It's going to hang back in the woods and wait for my all-clear."

"What the fuck for?"

"Because I'm paranoid."

Sloan was staring at him from the right-hand forward hatch. "Why the change, McKay?" The handsome squarish face frowned in puzzlement. It was clear the former Navy man thought he was being separated from his teammates because of some deficiency McKay saw in him. The fact was, McKay needed a man he could rely on in Mobil Two. In case things broke wrong, he wanted someone who'd obey his orders without question. The resentful Secret Service agents might hesitate or jump the gun. Sloan was the Guardian he could most easily spare.

He didn't like to command by saying "Because I said so." Not that he tried to lead by consensus. But he always felt that if he explained his orders when he could, his men would take his word for it when the chips were down. Most especially he didn't want to stonewall a team such as the Guardians. You didn't do that with an elite, tightly knit outfit. *But I can't very well go into my reasoning while Parkinson and his men are on the line*, McKay thought. *So you're just gonna have to take my word for it this time, Sam.*

He walked along Mobile One's flank and clapped the other Guardian on the biceps. The irony didn't escape him—a raggedy-ass Marine lieutenant laying hands on the sacrosanct person of a Navy commander. It was like a parish priest slapping a cardinal on the ass. "I'm relying on you, Sloan," he said, hiding the grin he felt. "I want you to take Two through the woods till you can get in a good position overlooking the field. Then radio us and we'll roll on in."

Sloan frowned. "What do I—we—do?"

"Just wait for my word."

Sloan shrugged, hauled his rangy form out of the car, and dropped to the ground. "This seems to be going the long way around the barn, McKay. What's the problem?"

"No problem." He glanced at Parkinson, who stood on the rutted road between the two vehicles shaking his head. "Just look at it as a tactical exercise."

They drove out of the woods on the paved road. The CIA field lay to the north, an asphalt strip next to a huddle of wooden buildings and a tattered orange wind sock, all nestled in a broad meadow. It looked like just the sort of small private airfield the drug enforcement agencies had been trying to get outlawed over the last few years.

Agents in dark suits like Parkinson's emerged from the building as Mobile One rolled into view. They all wore sunglasses despite the darkening day and looked like the old Blues Brothers to McKay. They waved Casey to park the 450 next to the largest building.

Before they de-assed the vehicle, McKay took the full-flap Kevlar holster off his belt and replaced it with his Milt Sparks combat rig, including a six-pack and a double magazine holder. Going in to visit the company boys, he wanted to be able to get the Colt out in a hurry. Just in case.

He picked up the Maremont and slapped the receiver affectionately. "Ready to roll."

Parkinson looked at him and shook his head. "You're crazy, McKay."

"Didn't you deal with the Company when you were in Special Forces?" The agent shook his head. McKay rubbed his chin. He felt fatigue wash over him and realized just how much he hoped this *was* on the up-and-up. The pressure was already starting to grind him down. *Maybe I'm getting old*, he told himself. *I never used to burn out this quick, even on the shaggiest-ass missions*. But he knew he'd never had a mission like this before, never had so much riding on his shoulders.

"Well," he said, "let's just say I hope I *am* crazy." Rogers picked up his Galil, and Casey Wilson the sniper's rifle. McKay pushed open the side door and stepped out.

"In here," said a doughy, balding man of middle years and height, who held a Franchi SPAS riot gun casually in one pudgy hand as he looked askance at Casey's Rolling Stones cap and his yellow Zeiss shooting glasses. He escorted them through a lounge with a dead bar and gum wrappers and squashed cigarette packs scattered like leaves on the floor, and a few sofas upholstered in cracked Naugahyde along the walls. Several more suited, sunglassed agents watched them from the sofas as the newcomers entered a small office with a large occupant.

"Mr. President." The tall heavyset man in the blue-and-white polo shirt stood up from behind a green metal desk and came around in front of the picture window that looked out on the runway. Extending a sunfreckled hand, the man said, "It's a privilege to be able to serve you in this, the hour of our country's gravest need."

Reluctantly, McKay leaned his machine gun against the wall beneath the wide window. The other Guardians did likewise. Parkinson looked relieved.

MacGregor smiled back at the big man as heartily as he could. His eyes were sunken, giving him an intense, ascetic look. A shock of brown hair hung down his forehead. He looked like a bean-sprout visionary teenager, gone off into the mountains to seek revelation in his L. L. Beans and waffle stompers.

The man pumping his hand so enthusiastically had a sharp Anglo-Saxon nose, eyes a limpid blue behind tinted glasses, and a gorgeous head of wavy silver hair. He seemed as straightforwardly tacky as his office, with its warped and peeling pseudo-walnut paneling and its framed pictures of fifties aircraft. Except for the Peacemaker riding in its holster on his right hip, he might have been about to damn the drizzle that was blurring down outside the office windows and take off for a round of golf at the country club.

"I'm very grateful to you, Mr.—"

"Ott. Bill Ott. Langley sent me up here personally when the alert went out yesterday morning. They wanted me to be on hand to handle this rendezvous." He gestured around expansively. "My men are crawling all over this field. The pickup will go off without a hitch, Mr. President. You can rely on that."

MacGregor nodded gratefully. He was obviously taken a bit aback at the agent's ebullience. "Thank you, Mr. Ott. These men brought me here at great risk and effort to themselves."

He introduced his five companions: the three Guardians, Parkinson, and young Hayes from Mobile One. Ott gave McKay a lingering inspection. "McKay, huh? Didn't you serve a hitch with SOG-SWAC?"

McKay's blood temperature dropped a few degrees. *Don't be so damned nervous.* "I'm sorry, sir," he said in as businesslike a tone as he could muster. "I'm not at liberty to discuss my previous assignments."

Ott gave him a say-no-more nod and wink. "I understand, Lieutenant. All I can say is, I'm honored to meet three of the famous Guardians—" He left the obvious question unspoken.

McKay dropped his eyes. "We, uh, we had some casualties, sir." *If Parkinson or Hayes says anything, we're fucked.*

"I understand." Ott nodded gravely. McKay stole a glance at the Secret Service men. Parkinson stood there scowling like a black Zeus waiting for his thunderbolts to recharge. Hayes was just opening his mouth to speak when the big agent dug an elbow into his ribs. Parkinson may have thought McKay was nuts, but he was too much SF not to back his play.

"Mr. President," the tall Company man said, "I'd like to

introduce a few of my own men. Ed Holloway, Dave Morgan, and my personal aide, Jesus Martinez.'' He nodded to three of his men crowded in the little room; their dark, sober outfits contrasted with their boss's informality. Holloway was the Pillsbury Doughboy with the fancy shotgun who'd led them in here. Morgan was a fresh-faced type who looked like a thirty-year-old kid.

Martinez didn't look much like a Blues Brother, though, McKay had to admit. He looked like a lean, brown, Cuban shark in a suit. He wore a Smith & Wesson model 29 in a shoulder rig, a genuine Dirty Harry .44 Mag. A certain type of man—and McKay had met lots of them in his dealings with the Company in the Med—hauled the unwieldy mass of iron around because Clint Eastwood did, and ol' Clint was a real man.

Martinez also looked like the kind of man who carried one because he thought it was good for killing people with.

The other three agents standing around as if they were there to hold the scuffed linoleum in place obviously didn't rate introductions. It didn't make much difference, McKay reflected. None of the names they'd been told was likely to be real.

"Sit down, gentlemen," Ott said, indicating a collection of depressed-looking armchairs over beneath the yellowing Constellations and DC-6's. MacGregor, Hayes, and Wilson sat down. Rogers, Parkinson, and McKay remained standing. "Refreshments while we wait, anyone? We have beer, soft drinks, or the hard stuff. Whatever you'd like."

One of the unnamed agents went to a dented little refrigerator next to Ott's desk to act as bartender. MacGregor accepted a premixed martini. Ex-cop Parkinson refused anything alcoholic, as did Hayes, with a regretful glance at the Scotch being poured for Tom Rogers. Wilson was handed the Coke he'd asked for.

"Beer," McKay said.

"What kind? We got Stroh's, Tuborg, Heineken, Dos Equis—"

"You got Budweiser?" Raised eyebrows, then a nod. "I'll have a Bud."

Ott had himself a daiquiri in a glass filled with crushed ice the agent took from the fridge. "So tell me how it was, those last hours in the White House—if you don't mind talking about it?'' Ott asked.

MacGregor waved a weary hand. "Oh, it's okay, I don't mind." He was obviously beginning to let down now that he was on his way to safety. He could barely keep his eyes open, but he answered the smiling agent's inquiries as completely as he could. McKay leaned against the wall, sipped his Bud, and kept his eyes open.

He was starting his third beer as Ott said, "Yes, it's tragic, President Lowell's disappearance. He knew how to keep a firm hand on the reins—though I'm sure you'll prove a worthy successor, worthy indeed. What is it, Bullister?"

A fat man with an Uzi slung around his thick neck came in. "Just got word. The transport's on its way in."

Even as he spoke they heard the drone of the plane's engines. Ott nodded and smiled even more broadly. "Excellent. Mr. President, you're almost on your way!"

MacGregor just rubbed his pale, stubbled cheeks and tried to smile.

McKay and Parkinson moved over to the window. The pickup plane was coming out of the west, banking in to approach from the north. It was a big-bellied C-130 transport, a four-engined Hercules.

"Wrong again, McKay," Parkinson said from the corner of his mouth as the big plane touched down at the far end of the strip. "Okay, boys, let's get ready to pull out."

But McKay was staring hard at the taxiing plane, willing its outlines to become distinct through the haze of falling rain. There was something wrong, he sensed. Its topside looked okay, standard mottled camo colors. But the sides looked dark. Not like a transport. Like—

"That's a gunship!" he exclaimed and heard Hayes gasp. McKay spun around with his hand going for his .45.

"Not so fast, Lieutenant." The Company men were all pointing guns at them, except for Ott, who sat behind his desk looking very on top of the situation. "You won't be accompanying the President on this trip, I'm afraid."

CHAPTER
TWELVE

"You'll never get away with this, Ott," McKay said, speaking with exaggerated deliberation as Bullister sidled over to him and fished the .45 out of its holster, his fat lips set in a moist, triumphant smile. "Kidnapping the President's the worst mistake you could make."

Ott shook his head sadly. "You disappoint me, Lieutenant. I didn't expect such a trite response out of you."

Covered by Holloway and by Martinez's big-bored Magnum, the other Guardians and the Secret Service men had been disarmed. Bullister oozed around the wall, deposited the confiscated side arms on his chief's desk, and moved back around behind Holloway to place himself between the door and McKay and Parkinson. *Sam, don't let me down.* . . . McKay muttered to himself, subvocalizing.

"Mobile Two acknowledging, Billy," Sam's voice whispered in his earphone. "We're on our way."

Ott frowned at him. The mike and the tape that held it against his larynx were flesh-toned, very inconspicuous, like a round Band-Aid over a shaving cut. And to the best of Ott's knowledge the five men who'd driven in with the President were all that remained of the team that had broken out of the embattled White House the day before. Even if the agent noticed the throat mikes, he'd have no reason to believe the Guardians had help within the half-kilometer range of their communicators.

The roar of the gunship's engines filled the office, vibrating off the window, then diminished as the craft pulled to a halt two hundred meters away. Its port side faced the buildings; the whole awesome array of its weaponry gazed impassively at the watching men. McKay felt a crawling in the pit of his stomach. A hiccup of fire and nothing would remain of buildings or occupants but smoking fragments.

President Jeffrey MacGregor sat in a straight-backed chair, staring in stunned bewilderment into the muzzle of an Uzi. "Take the President on out, boys," Ott said. "It's not much to serve as Air Force One, Your Honor, but—" He smiled and gestured graciously as two burly agents hustled MacGregor to his feet and out the door.

Quickly McKay sized up the tactical situation. MacGregor was out of the way; already his two escorts had marched him a quarter of the way to the gunship. One of the nameless agents remained, over by the wall that faced the window. He held an Uzi by his hip, covering Rogers, Casey Wilson, and Tim Hayes, who stood in a loose triangle in front of him. To his left Dave Morgan held a Colt Python on the trio in a two-handed police-academy stance. Bullister and Holloway stood by the window to McKay's left, keeping themselves in front of the hardware stacked against the wall. Martinez had stationed himself in front of Ott's desk.

McKay's half-full can of Bud chilled his hard palm. He turned deliberately to face the window, away from the yawning muzzle of Holloway's Hollywood shotgun and fat-faced Bullister's Uzi. "We'll get the President safely on his way," Ott said. "Then we'll let you gentlemen go on yours. You've done a good job, a splendid one; but high policy decisions have been made that necessitate taking matters out of your hands. . . ."

From the corner of his eye, McKay could see Parkinson swelling with fury. He had gotten himself mousetrapped and lost the President—the ultimate failure for the chief of the Secret Service's presidential detail. The insincerities flowing from Ott's mouth like chemical waste from a fertilizer factory were helping pump Parkinson's rage to the bursting point. In a moment Parkinson's Service training would assert itself explosively. And if that moment came too soon . . .

The Guardians' mission doesn't involve throwing yourself in front of the President to stop a bullet meant for him, Crenna had told them in that sweltering classroom in Arizona. *You have to have a certified death wish for the Secret Service to put you on presidential detail. That's their job. Yours is to stay alive and defend the President to the last breath of your body.*

Parkinson's chest expanded mightily as he drew breath. *Keep it cool, for Christ's sake!* McKay mentally begged. Reflected in the glass he saw Martinez turn his head toward the Secret Service man, like a tiger shark sensing the thrashing of an injured fish.

From the south, distinct even above the deep-throated drone of the idling engines, came the deliberate, crisp pounding of a .50-caliber machine gun. Martinez' head turned forward, brow creasing above his glasses in consternation.

McKay pivoted on his right heel and threw the beer can into the Cuban's face. The shades exploded in green shards and Martinez went down, his .44 spurting infinite noise and an orange flame-ball at the dropped-tile ceiling.

McKay was already spinning the other way. He saw Parkinson hacking Bullister's forearm with a knife-edged hand. The unnamed agent by the far wall yelped and started to squeeze the trigger of his Uzi, but Casey Wilson moved with the reflexes of a fighter ace. His hand closed around the stub of the barrel, burning his fingers but protecting McKay in the process.

The Uzi stuttered as McKay batted the muzzle of Holloway's riot gun away with his left hand and drove the stiffened fingers of his right into the pudgy man's solar plexus. McKay then grabbed the gagging CIA man by the collar and belt and pitched him through the window.

The room was a whirlwind of violent action. Even as towheaded Dave Morgan had triggered off his .357, Rogers had dropped out from in front of its muzzle. From the floor he fired a smashing side kick into the man's groin. As Morgan collapsed he rolled past, going for the stacked guns. Still holding on to the hot barrel of the Uzi with his seared fingers, Casey was taking his man down with a foot sweep as Agent

Tim Hayes vaulted out through the broken window. He hit the ground running after the men bundling MacGregor toward the waiting gunship.

Showing more fortitude than McKay would've credited him with, Bullister was grappling with Parkinson toe-to-toe, clinging to his submachine gun with the strength of the deranged. McKay tried to get past, to his M-60. The battling pair reeled in front of him. He gave Bullister a six-inch punch in the kidneys. Rolls of flesh shielded the Company man from the full force of his blow, but for just an instant he was distracted from his wrestling match with Parkinson. In that heartbeat, Parkinson pushed the Uzi barrel forward with his right hand, jabbed his left thumb into the trigger guard, and squeezed.

Five bullets burped from the Israeli-made weapon, clawing away Bullister's flabby face, blasting his cerebrum all over the ceiling, and setting his Blues Brothers suit on fire. His limbs spasmed, hurling him and Parkinson to the floor in a blood-soaked Apache dance.

McKay dropped to one knee, grabbed the chopped 60 by the barrel and straightened, turning, reaching for the pistol grip

—and found himself facing Ott. The CIA chief stood behind his desk, leveling his weapon at the center of McKay's chest. McKay struggled to bring the machine gun to bear.

Ott pursed his lips and shot him.

"Jesus," Ben Turpin remarked in Mobile Two as the C-130 taxied up in front of the sorry-looking structures. "That's funny."

Sitting in the commo seat with his head out of the hatch, Sam Sloan felt alarm stab through him. "What do you mean?" he asked the driver, whose narrow sandy-haired head was poked out the port hatch.

"The paint job on that Herkie-bird," Mason remarked from the cupola. "Its sides black like that—night camo. That thing's a gunship—a truck killer. AC-130H, probably. If it's anything like the ones I saw down in Chile, it's carrying four twenty-mike-mike Gatling guns, a one-ought-five howitzer, and a new-model quick-firing Bofors forty millimeter." He rubbed at his round face. "The forty mike-mike can shoot a depleted uranium slug that'd rip open a T-87's top armor like a tin can, though the Pentagon's never gonna admit that. And the Gatlings spit out a hundred rounds a second each."

The screen of underbrush and the half-fallen tree from which hung a curtain of Spanish moss suddenly seemed vulnerable as cellophane to Sloan. "Why would they send a plane like that to pick us up?"

Turpin champed lean jaws on his chewing gum. "Dunno, glamor boy. Not much elbow room in one of those babies, all the ammunition they carry." From inside the hull Sloan heard a worried buzz of conversation between Popejoy, the radio operator he'd displaced, and Garcia and Goldberg, the other two Secret Service men of the Super Commando's crew.

"Maybe that sonofabitch McKay's not so crazy after all," Popejoy's voice came over the intercom. "I—"

"Belay that chatter!" Sloan snapped, suddenly pressing the headset of Mobile Two's radio against his ear as if to squeeze more sound from it. "—never get away with this, Ott," Bill McKay's voice was saying, tiny and wavering with the weak signal it rode, but distinct as a death sentence. "Kidnapping the President's the worst mistake you could make."

"Oh, holy shit," Goldberg said from inside the car. The message had come over the compartment monitor too. Sloan sat as if stunned. *Oh, Lord, it's all come down on me.*

"Mobile Two acknowledging, Billy," he heard his voice saying. "We're on our way."

"Roger, Two. Give it thirty seconds."

Sloan checked is watch. *God, I don't know what I'm going to do. I'm way out of my depth. I'm a blue-water man, I don't belong here, I, I—*

He felt the eyes of Turpin and Mason on him. Time flowed, stretched. *You've got a piece of paper that says you're a commander, Sam,* he told himself. *So command.*

He brushed his hair out of his eyes. *Pretend you're back in the Gulf of Sidra.* "Mason, line up that fifty-cal. on the cockpit of that bird. When I give the word, you blast them. Turpin, get ready to roll."

Not too bad, he reassured himself. Electric motors whined as Mason adjusted his aim. *Even if you sound a bit too much like Billy McKay for comfort.*

Turpin turned pale, worried eyes toward him. "You want us just to cruise on out onto that field?"

Even the hard-bitten Secret Service driver was shaken at the prospect of driving out into the face of that hideous firepower. Oddly, the thought calmed Sloan down, brought him into full command of himself. It was the crunch, with lives on the line. He'd been here before.

A plan was forming in his mind. "That thing's guns fire to portside only?"

"Affirmative," Mason said.

"Then, Turpin, you drive like hell for the starboard—the right side. If we can stay off its bow or left beam, we should be fine."

Two men, insects in dark suits, had emerged from the main building. They held a man between them by the arms. "Christ on a skateboard!" yelped Mason, holding a pair of binocs to his eyes. "That's MacGregor!"

"Time to go, boys," Turpin said. He gunned the big diesel with a blat.

"Belay that." Turpin gaped at Sloan. "We wait for our mark. Eight seconds . . . six . . . five, four, three, two, one—*fire*."

The world exploded in thunder as Mason loosed a long burst from his M-2. The muzzle blast tossed leaves and shattered branches in a whirlwind. "Now, Turpin!" Sloan shouted, but his voice was lost in the roar of the .50. He punched the driver on the arm. "Go like a sonofabitch!"

He dropped into his seat as the 450 leaped ahead. His fingers fumbled the hatch shut. Mason was firing short bursts as Turpin boomed onto the tarmac. Whether the gunner was making any strikes or not Sloan couldn't tell. Powerful as the .50 was, it was hard to imagine it making much impression on the huge gunship.

Almost a kilometer away, MacGregor struggled briefly. One of the agents hit him behind the ear with the butt of a pistol. He sagged and the CIA men began to run forward, impeded by their limp burden.

"Goose it, Turpin, push it hard!" Sloan was shouting, but his voice was lost in the babble from the compartment behind. The lives of the six men crammed into the thin steel shell of Mobile Two lay in the palms of Turpin's sweaty hands. The diesel howled like a banshee as the skinny driver pushed it for all it was worth.

Slowly, inexorably, the C-130 began to turn.

McKay fell heavily to the floor. Smiling, Ott swung his .45

to cover Casey, now hatless, who sat straddling the unnamed agent. "Hold it there, gentlemen," Ott told them.

Rogers and Parkinson froze, the Guardian in the act of reaching for his Galil, the Secret Service man trying to struggle out from under Bullister's corpse. His face a network of scarlet, Martinez was struggling to his feet at the foot of Ott's desk.

"It's unfortunate Lieutenant McKay acted so rashly," Ott said. "But if you behave in a rational manner, there's no reason—"

He broke off in midsentence. His eyes bulged behind yellow lenses.

Billy McKay had rolled onto his back, Maremont held submachine-gun fashion in both hands. No dark stain smeared the front of his tan-and-green fatigues.

The first copper-jacketed slug struck a shocked William Ott in the joint of his right hip. Long before the pain message had reached his brain, another punched through his belly to the right of the navel. He began to buckle, and the third round caught him in the center of the chest, holing his heart clean through. The fourth bullet hit the outside of his left eye socket and tore off his glasses and the silver-haired side of his head.

Snarling like a rabid dog, Martinez whipped his .44 up to blow McKay away with a round that McKay's vest couldn't stop. Tom Rogers was quicker, though. He had his Galil now and fired a snap shot from the hip. It took Martinez in the gut. The hydrostatic shock of a sixty-three-grain bullet traveling at three times the speed of sound pulped a section of his intestine and the bullet itself nicked the tip of his left kidney. His tan turned to ashes and he collapsed.

Parkinson had eeled out from under Bullister when McKay fired. Now he rolled out the broken window and lit out after Hayes and the pair dragging the President toward the Hercules. A man appeared in the door. Casey had his side arm out, a Smith & Wesson 29 just like Martinez. He snapped two quick shots double-action and the man disappeared.

Wincing at the pain of his cracked ribs, McKay sat up, braced his back against the wall, and fired the machine gun dry in waist-high bursts, left to right, through the wall into the adjoining room. Screams rang out above the yammer of the M-60, then silence. Pausing to kick Dave Morgan in the head as the blond CIA man tried to recover his Python, Rogers went out the door. Casey was a heartbeat behind, scooping up his rifle and his fallen cap.

McKay heard shooting outside the building. He got to his feet, leaving the empty 60 for Bullister's Uzi. Three agents stood in front, blazing away at Parkinson, who in his single-minded drive to rescue his President was making no attempt to dodge. McKay knocked two of them spinning with an eight-round burst, and the third man turned in time to catch a short burst in the chest. McKay dropped the empty Uzi, recovered his M-60, and raced off after his buddies.

Rogers and Wilson ran through the blood-spattered lounge, past two shattered corpses, and burst out the side door. An agent with an Uzi stood on Mobile One's front deck. Rogers knocked him off with a short burst before the man knew what was happening. The ex-Green Beret scaled the side of the V-450 like a cat and disappeared down the open hatch.

Casey paused to take stock of the situation. Runners were strung out in a frantic bead between building and plane. Parkinson was moving fast, gaining on Hayes, who seemed to have twisted his ankle and was limping badly. Well in front of them, the Company men were within twenty meters of the open crew-entry door just aft of the AC-130H's twin nose wheels. They were clearly going to win the desperate race.

Casey didn't hesitate. He flowed to one knee, assuming a kneeling firing position—not the most stable, but stable enough, and more important, fast. He thumbed the electroscope to straight optical three-power magnification. His targets were inside two hundred meters, the range for which the seven hundred was zeroed. He blanked his mind against the pain of his seared left hand.

The cross hairs centered on the back of a short-haired head. Without conscious thought Casey squeezed the trigger. The rifle bucked, carrying his field of vision off the target.

The rifle came down, and Casey saw that the Company man had bought it. MacGregor slumped, obviously semiconscious, as the man on his right was frantically trying to drag him to his feet. Casey worked the bolt and lined the sights up on his ear.

The man turned his head. Casey looked him in the eye and fired. The CIA man's mouth opened in a scream as he saw the firefly wink of the shot that blew his head away.

Casey lowered the heavy rifle for a second. A strange feeling came over him, replacing the steel calm with which he'd fired. *I've never killed a man like that before. Not face to face.* His aerial kills had been against *machines*. This was different. Nothing separated him from the men he'd shot but a few meters. . . .

"Casey," Rogers' voice said calmly in his ear. "That gunship's rolling—trying to get Mobile Two under its guns."

Casey stood. The eerie feeling passed as the imperative of immediate action asserted itself. He could hear a mosquitolike whine, even over the clamor of the gunship's four Allison turboprops: the electric motors that spun the multiple barrels of the Gatling guns.

"On the way, man." He went in a side door of Mobile One, clipped his rifle in its brackets in the hull, and slid into his seat. The engine had been left running. He hit the gas, felt the power swell.

Unimaginable thunder deafened him.

Mobile Two plunged arrow-straight down the runway. "Go, Turpin, go!" someone was shouting behind Sloan. Sloan himself had nothing to say. His mouth was set in a thin line, quirked up slightly at the corner in a fatalistic half-smile. Deep down he knew they weren't going to make it. The AC-130H was coming about, pivoting to bring its guns to bear. He could see the squat black muzzles jutting from its bulging flank, swinging relentlessly away from profile, giving them a full frontal view of Death.

"Here she comes," somebody breathed. Mason's machine guns screamed their futile protest overhead. Packed full of ammo as the 130 was, there was a good chance a few good fuselage hits would send it skyward in a bright orange flash. But the fireball would swallow MacGregor as well; Mason had to aim high and hope for the best.

Then the Hercules was broadside to the V-450.

"For what we are about to receive," Sloan murmured in the traditional blasphemous battle prayer of the saltwater sailor, "dear Lord, make us thankful."

Fire blossomed form the gunship's side.

As McKay emerged from the side of the building, a wall

of sound hit him and staggered him like the shock wave of a nearby shellburst. He looked out at the airplane. Its tail was turned toward him, hanging like a vast crucifix against the gray, weeping sky. Twenty-meter tongues of flame licked from the beast, slavering toward Mobile Two, which was heeled over on two wheels as Turpin slewed hard left to avoid the more than four hundred rounds a second the gunship was spitting at him.

The earthquake noise stopped, leaving a deafening stillness. Mobile Two came out of the turn, dropping all four wheels to the pavement, and then broke hard right and past the bulbous black snout of the behemoth.

Tim Hayes had reached the President. MacGregor was on his knees, shaking his head groggily. The redheaded agent knelt by his side, pulling the President's arm around his neck. Clete Parkinson put on a final burst of speed, fifty meters away from MacGregor—

—and pitched face-first onto the rain-slick asphalt.

The man who went by the name Jesus Martinez let the heavy barrel of the .44 Magnum fall back to horizontal. So much for Parkinson, the big nigger—though the satisfaction he normally felt when he made a kill dissolved in the liquid fire the other gringo's bullet had made of his guts.

McKay dove in the open side hatch of Mobile One as Casey let in the clutch and rolled ahead. He heard the laboring engines of the AC-130H change timbre, but had no time to wonder what was going on. "Tom! Somebody shot Parkinson. Check the building," he called, hurriedly dropping the empty ammo box and snapping a fresh one into place.

Tom Rogers traversed the turret right as the 450 nosed out in front of the main building. He was mildly startled to see the Cuban standing there with that hand cannon of his, his face a bloody death mask and the front of his trousers shiny-sodden with his blood. He was hard-core, Rogers had to give him that.

"Hold it, Case." Mobile One bucked to a stop. Rogers depressed the muzzle of the M-19 as the Cuban took in the slack of his trigger.

The grenade launcher burped once. The arming range of one of its 40 mm projectiles was roughly ten meters. Jesus Martinez stood fifteen meters away.

The high-explosive dual-purpose armor-piercing round

caught him under the left arm and blew away his torso. For a moment the legs stood alone, blood burbling from the severed trunk. Then they fell.

Holding his M-60 in one hand, McKay looked out the door in time to see the Cuban fall. Then he looked to his left. "Jesus, Casey, that fucker's turning this way!"

It was true. Cheated of its prey by Turpin's evasive maneuvering, the gunship had reversed direction and was turning counterclockwise, hoping to catch the scuttling steel beetle when the gunship swung back by to pick up the President. The muzzles of its armament were tracking back toward Mobile One.

For Casey Wilson, a lightning decision was called for, requiring flawless judgment and titanium nerves. He made it.

He hit the gas.

McKay was flung backward against the engine compartment. Rogers managed to hang on as the 450 turned southwest and jackrabbited forward, straight through the field of fire of the multibarreled Gatlings, the howitzer, and the Bofors automatic 40. He watched with fatalistic fascination as the yawning gunports slid by. Casey had guessed the gunners wouldn't be expecting the car parked innocuously beside the building to get up to anything; they were concentrating on lashing back at Mobile Two, which had been stinging them with a steady stream of fire from its two machine guns. He was hoping to get clear of their guns before they woke up.

It worked. But the Company gunners were quick. The full broadside burst loose at Mobile One in a savage firestorm. The shell stream from the gunship's foremost 20 mm howled past so near astern Mobile One that the suction of the projectiles' passage rocked it back on its suspension.

Unfortunately, the Hercules was still wheeling as its gunners opened fire. A 105 mm shell went in the broken window of Ott's office as the 40 and the Gatling guns blasted the clustered buildings to matchwood.

Casey's whoop of triumph was overridden by Sloan's anguished cry: "Oh my God, *the President!*" McKay looked back to see the six foot tires of the gunship's left main landing gear looming over MacGregor and Hayes.

The lumbering leviathan had moved forward and right in its first attempt to get the impertinent armored car into its sights. Now it reversed, backing its port engines and throttling up the starboard ones, coming backward and left to catch Mobile Two as it streaked in from behind.

Clete Parkinson had struggled back to his feet. Like McKay and the other Guardians, he was wearing a Kevlar vest. It wouldn't have sufficed to stop the hot hand-loaded round from Martinez' pistol, even at this range, but the Cuban's aim had been off. The heavy jacketed slug had hit a rib on the left side of Parkinson's chest and been deflected, following the rib around his body and plowing an agonizing furrow just beneath the skin.

The AC-130H was backing straight onto Hayes and MacGregor. The President was scarcely able to stand after the blow on his head, and Hayes's ankle had turned to Silly Putty. They lurched along in a pathetic three-legged race they could not hope to win. Parkinson pulled out his mini-Uzi and ripped a high-speed burst of 9 mm into the rear cargo door. The Parabellum slugs didn't even penetrate the monster's skin.

"Here!" Hayes shouted. He heaved the President upright and threw him forward. MacGregor reeled on rubbery legs. Parkinson hooked strong black fingers in the front of the President's plaid shirt and pulled him backward onto the asphalt.

The main gear fairing caught Tim Hayes at the backs of his knees. He pitched forward, caught himself on his palms. Then he shrieked like a wounded horse as the gunship's eighty tons rolled over his legs and up the length of his body. Parkinson felt the rubber of the tires kiss the soles of his shoes. He held the President flat against the wet asphalt as the whalelike bulk of the Hercules blotted out the gray sky overhead.

Turpin swerved Mobile Two to a skidding halt. Goldberg, Popejoy, Garcia, and Sloan came spilling out the side hatch like kids off a school bus and ran ducked over toward Hayes and MacGregor. Mason had the two turret guns cranked up to their full 55-degree elevation and was blasting the tail section, trying to cripple the elevators. It was the first time he'd been able to fire for effect since the first, apparently ineffectual, blast at the cockpit. He hadn't even been able to shoot at the engines for fear of setting them ablaze and chancing blowing the President to Nebraska.

Sloan saw MacGregor stumble into Parkinson's arms, winced as Hayes disappeared under the twin tires. Goldberg stopped, threw a G-3 to his shoulder, and began cranking single shots at the gunship's firing ports. Sloan had left his Galil behind; the thought of spitting feeble .223 rounds at a monster that hadn't been visibly affected by .50-caliber slugs was too pathetic, and Sloan wasn't suicidal enough to shoot rifle grenades into fifteen tons of high-explosive ammo hanging over his head.

As Parkinson and the President vanished between the main gear and the nose wheels, Sloan saw a 105 gunner, alien-looking in flight suit and helmet, fling up his hands and fall away from his piece. Then Sloan took a running dive forward onto his face. Popejoy and Garcia flung themselves down beside him, and then the airplane swung harmlessly over them. They got up and ran to where Parkinson was trying to haul MacGregor to his feet as Turpin burned rubber around the tail of the gunship and came for them.

On the far side of the gunship, Goldberg stood his ground, firing deliberately. He killed another man at the howitzer, then turned his attention on the gunship's Bofors gun. A loader was trying to stuff a heavy ten-round clip into the quick firer's receiver. Goldberg put two rounds into him through the port.

Then he came into the firing arc of the rear Gatling. The helmeted CIA man behind it hit the firing switch for a one-second burst. More than fifty rounds of 20 mm high explosive struck Goldberg simultaneously, literally disintegrating him in a cloud of flame and flesh. But even as Goldberg died, his comrades were bundling the President into Mobile Two.

Turpin accelerated away from the gunship, hightailing for the tall timber. At the same instant, Mobile One came to a halt three hundred meters from the airplane, facing its slowly swinging tail. "We're clear, Billy," Sloan's voice said. "Run, for God's sake."

Casey tapped two fingers on the wheel. "No way, Billy. If we let that beast get airborne, we're fucked. Those things eat armored cars for *breakfast*."

Strapped into the commo man's seat, McKay nodded. He'd seen Spectres at work before. It wasn't the sort of thing you forgot. Once the monster, so clumsy on the ground, lifted its elephantine bulk into the air, it would become an inescapable killing machine. The cars couldn't outrun it, and computerized television cameras using inferential mapping could pick the alien shapes of the V-450's out from under cover of the pine forest. The gunship's whole arsenal was slaved to those goddamn cameras. All the Company crewmen had to do was get you on their screen and hit a button, and *zango!* you were gone. Just like the world's biggest video game.

In another few seconds the plane's guns would be aiming their way.

"Tom? Casey?" McKay asked.

"Go for it," Rogers said, calmly as ever.

"You know it, Billy." Casey was practically vibrating in his chair with the desire to come to grips with the monster. The pain of his burned fingers was totally forgotten. He'd never killed a plane the size of a Herkie before. Even if he was only going to be the driver for this fight and Rogers the shooter, he was so hungry he could taste it.

McKay popped the hatch over his head. "Do it."

He pushed himself into the rush of wind as Casey accelerated. He braced his legs against the floorplates of the V-450 and held the M-60 in both hands. He wasn't sure how much he'd contribute to this showdown, but he hungered to strike at the black iron beast, so huge and impervious and arrogant.

But the monster was hurting now. Having fired his quicker-cycled 7.62 dry, Mason was firing short bursts from the .50 over Mobile Two's rear deck as Turpin raced for the tree line, aiming for the aircraft's engines. The left outboard of the beast was beginning to spark and drool black smoke. With his own head out the right forward hatch, Sloan craned his neck to try to see around the turret.

Casey floorboarded Mobile One in a straight-in firing pass. The Hercules' engines were shrieking now. Its pilots had realized what was happening and were trying to swing the guns around faster. Fast as the Super Commando was moving, the hurricane of explosive shells began to catch up with it.

His face twisted in a fighting grimace, McKay held down the trigger of his M-60. He might as well have been pissing against the prop wash of those mighty engines. *This is it,* he thought. *But at least the President's clear.*

Then Tom Rogers began to play rock 'n' roll on his M-19. Billy McKay had never heard a sweeter sound.

A white phosphorus grenade burst ten meters ahead of the gunship's nose, sending out a starfish of smoke and incandescent metal. The next round was also white phosphorus. It popped through the window next to the system engineer's seat and filled the cockpit with screaming death. With a virtuoso's touch, Rogers walked the 40 mm rounds along the fat fuselage of the monster.

The Hercules blew up like the Death Star.

Billy McKay popped down the hatch like a prairie dog. White-hot debris whistled over his head and rattled off Mobile One's hull.

Howling like a coyote, Casey lined Mobile One out for the trees as fifty thousand rounds of ammo started going off behind.

CHAPTER
THIRTEEN

"I'll meet your five million," Ben Turpin said, thoughtfully chewing the stub of his cigar, "and raise you five million."

"Shit," Popejoy said, throwing a scrap of paper into the pot. "This is getting too rich for my blood." Turpin picked up the deck to deal the draw cards.

"What the hell is this?" McKay demanded, emerging from Mobile One. Casey Wilson and three of Parkinson's men were sitting on the grass between the vehicles, playing dealer's choice in the dark. Their throat mikes were turned off, as they always were in camp, lest casual conversation clog the comm channel. "Did they pass a big hazardous-duty pay raise for the Secret Service, or has inflation finally gone bugfuck?"

"One card," Casey Wilson said. He was sitting in a lotus position on the grass, with his hair in his eyes and a serious expression on his young face. The fingers and palm of his left hand had been coated with a white Vitamin E ointment and bandaged.

"He's drawin' to an inside straight," Turpin said, and grinned. "I can always tell."

The wiry agent looked up at McKay. "We're playing for markers," he said, holding up a sheaf of IOU's as Garcia drew a single card. "I figure this whole pot's worth about a tenth of an ounce of gold in the world as we're about to get to know it. Two cards, Popejoy? And two for the dealer." He dropped his winnings, picked up a penlight to illuminate his catch, nodded, and flicked off the light.

Casey picked up his one card, read it by the light of the stars, slipped it into his hand.

"I'll open for a million," Garcia said. He was a darkly handsome man of medium height with a trim black mustache on his upper lip and sideburns that came near to flouting Service regs. Like his fellows, he was in his shirt-sleeves with his tie loosened against the muggy nighttime heat of eastern Ohio.

"Raise five," Casey said.

Turpin cocked an eyebrow at him. "Could it be?" He looked up at McKay. "You play the game, big fella?"

"Used to," McKay said. "Lost too much."

Dollar signs glinted in Turpin's eyes. "What'd you lose?"

"My temper, mostly."

Turpin blinked. Garcia grinned. " 'Let the Wookiee win.' "

"We gonna play or we gonna talk?" Popejoy demanded. "I'll see you clowns."

"Not so fast," Turpin said. "Put in another five million if you want the privilege of seeing the cards these hands have touched." The other players called. "All right, Frito Bandito," Turpin said.

Garcia's grin widened. "Skip straight." He laid down the three of hearts, five and seven of spades, nine of clubs, and jack of hearts.

Popejoy goggled. "What in the fuck is a skip straight?"

"That," Garcia said.

"How did that shit get in the game?" Popejoy demanded. He was a short, stocky man with crew-cut blond hair. "Nobody's counted fucking skip straights since Chester Alan goddam Arthur."

"*I* announced it when I dealt," Turpin said glumly. "Skips, blazes, dogs, and tigers count. Shit. I should know better than to try to hustle you, Garcia." He shook his head. "I always said they shoulda shipped you wetbacks back across the border."

"I'm not surprised," Garcia said. "You Jews've been trying to shut the door on everybody else since the days of

Samuel Gompers. What you got, Popejoy?''

Popejoy grimaced and threw his cards facedown on the grass. "Drawing to a pair with a kicker again, Jerry?" Turpin asked sweetly. Popejoy glowered. "Okay, fly-boy, show 'em."

Impassively, Casey laid down a jack-high straight.

Turpin stared at them, working his cigar in a circle with his teeth. "Don't you know you can't go on bucking the law of averages forever, sweetie?" He tossed in his hand. "My three kings don't look so world-beating now, somehow."

Casey raked in the pot with an expression of Buddhalike smugness.

After they busted the ambush at the CIA airfield, the two cars had rendezvoused a few klicks to the west to exchange personnel and get Parkinson's and McKay's wounds tended to by the curiously gentle hands of Tom Rogers. Using the back roads, moving cross-country when those began to choke up near Pittsburgh, they had made surprisingly good time since leaving behind the pillar of black smoke that was the gunship's pyre. They'd skirted well south of Pittsburgh, into West Virginia and thence into eastern Ohio. Though the overcast had started to break up when they hit the Ohio River between Wheeling and Wellsburg, the Allegheny Plateau at their backs was being lashed by lightning and heavy rains. The broad river itself had only begun to rise, though; the current was sluggish enough to ford, and they swam the amphibious Super Commandos as necessary. Shortly thereafter they'd laagered in for the night in this little hollow, beneath a bluff furred with buckeye chestnuts, while Clete Parkinson kept watch.

"McKay," Sloan's voice said in the Guardian leader's ear. "I'm picking up a newscast on the radio."

"I'll be damned," McKay said. "Pipe it over the communicators."

"—Pereira today declared himself Emperor Pedro the Third of Brazil, including Paraguay, Uruguay, and Argentina. Fighting continued in Patagonia, but government sources expect all of Argentina to be pacified in the next few weeks."

"Where's it coming from?" McKay asked.

"Radio Akron, they call themselves," Sloan said. "They're not using call letters."

"In Europe," the announcer said, in a radio newsman's professionally crisp tones, "the provisional government of

West Germany in Düsseldorf today accepted the sovereignty of the Internationalist Council. The Council, an organization of business and political leaders from throughout the Free World based in Zürich, announced a Federated States of Europe yesterday in the wake of the destruction sown by the thermonuclear exchange between the U.S. and the Union of Soviet Socialist Republics. American General Mark Shaw, commander of NATO forces locked in battle with the Soviet Army, could not be reached for comment on this development—"

"Where are they *getting* this stuff?" Turpin asked.

"Apparently some communications satellites survived," Sloan said. "What I'm not sure of is how the station's broadcast equipment managed to make it through all the electromagnetic garbage. Wright-Patterson and Rickenbacker got hit pretty hard, and so did Cleveland. And Pittsburgh—sorry, Billy."

McKay sucked in a deep breath. "That's okay. How about a cigar, Turpin?"

The agent shrugged skinny shoulders. "Sure. They won't let me smoke 'em in the car anyway. That's why I chew gum." He picked up his suit coat and fished in an inside pocket. "Here you go."

"—Mayor van Zandt announced distribution of food supplies will begin in the next few days," the announcer was saying. "Ration cards are being printed and will be available at supermarkets and shopping centers. In the meantime, Police Chief Owens is requesting all able-bodied males between the ages of fifteen and fifty-five to register for participation in voluntary emergency services—"

"Voluntary." Turpin snorted through his prominent nose. "Let 'em try *not* volunteerin'. Welcome to the Brave New World, boys and girls."

"That's enough, Sloan. Thanks." The newscast shut off.

From a pocket of his vest, Turpin produced a disposable lighter and rolled blue and pink hundred-dollar bill. "Light, McKay?" He stuck a fresh cigar in his mouth, flicked the lighter to life, and set the c-note afire. "Pretty, ain't it? Makes me feel like Daddy Warbucks. But shit, these things aren't good for much but tooting coke these days, and the doctor made me give that up on accounta my sinuses." He lit his cigar and held the burning bill up for McKay. "Doesn't much matter. They'd have been worthless in a few years anyway. Feds were turning 'em out so fast . . . why, I quit Treasury detail; couldn't hack hassling penny-ante counterfeiters in order to save the number one counterfeiter from competition, and anyway I wanted to act out my death wish. Oh, Jesus, excuse me, sir!''

He dropped the flaming note and jumped to his feet, brushing burning fragments of paper off the front of his trousers. Jeffrey MacGregor shook his head and gave him an amused, weary smile. "It's okay, Agent Turpin. May I talk to you, Lieutenant?''

McKay nodded and the two men moved off to stand next to Mobile Two. MacGregor had been napping in the darkened vehicle since dinner. The sedative Ott had dosed his drink with to render him compliant hadn't entirely worn off yet.

The President glanced back at the men, clumped in a circle in the dark while Garcia dealt a hand of high-low seven-card stud. "They . . . I don't mean to criticize them, I owe them far too much. But they don't act like men who've just lost friends.''

"Beg pardon, sir, but yes, they do. They've all lost buddies before. You learn not to act too broke up about it. You'd be Section Eight in no time if you let it get to you.''

"You mean they don't *care*?" A look of pain washed over his handsome features.

"They care, Mr. President. They care a lot.'' He hesitated. He was not accustomed to putting his feelings into words, especially ones that ran this deep. "There—there may be some marriages as close as what you get between men who've gone into combat together. But not many I've seen.'' He shook his head. "But this is wartime. Men die. You just got to carry on.''

"Wartime.'' MacGregor moistened his lips and looked off to where Tom Rogers sat on lookout half out of Mobile One's turret. He was silhouetted against the unquiet eastern sky, where purple lightning flared. A few farmhouses could be seen dotted among the dark hills, but they showed no lights. The power grid was down, and the farm folk realized that fuel for generators was going to be in mighty short supply for a time.

Or maybe they realized it was best not to call attention to themselves in the world after Armageddon.

"Yes, sir.''

"It's hard to accept . . . but then, it's hard to accept that the Central Intelligence Agency would try to kidnap the President of the United States."

"Maybe not, sir. The Agency has a tradition of being a law unto itself. And besides, maybe Ott was playing a game of his own. Cowboying's an old tradition with the Company too."

"Do you think so?"

A pause. "No, sir."

"Do you think the whole Agency's in on this? They're trying to stage a coup d'etat?"

"I don't know, sir. Don't have enough to go on. But there's something big going on . . . bigger even than Ott realized, I'd guess."

"How do you mean?"

McKay leaned back against the hull of Mobile Two. "That plane was a Hercules AC-130H gunship with updated weapons and avionics. Not a luxury jetliner."

"Well, we knew that."

"Yeah, but think of the implications, sir. They didn't need all that firepower just to collect you. But it would've come in awful handy if somebody wanted to be sure nobody stayed alive on the ground who knew what had gone down."

"A double cross?"

McKay grinned lopsidedly. "Maybe."

"What does that mean for us?"

A burst of raucous laughter came from the circle of card-players. "It means we're going to have to be awfully alert from here on in."

And lucky too, he thought. But he didn't say it.

Sloan emerged from Mobile One carrying his Galil with the M-203. He wore a vest sewed with little pockets to carry two dozen 40 mm rounds for the launcher. They were smaller than the grenades fired by the M-19 but still packed quite a punch.

Sloan nodded to McKay and the President. "I'm going up to spell Parkinson," he said. "I left the fallout monitor on. We shouldn't take any rads unless the wind changes, but we can't be too careful."

"I think I'll turn in," MacGregor said, yawning. "Good night, gentlemen."

McKay said good night. MacGregor climbed back into Mobile Two and Sloan started trudging up the bluff.

McKay watched him go with mixed feelings. Today for the first time the Guardians had seen combat as a team, and to his mind they'd performed beautifully. They fit together like pieces of a well-designed machine, played off one another like members of a jazz band. He was pleased and proud.

But each man still had his limitations. Sloan had a way to go as an infantryman and would have a tough time against a potential foe with the cunning and skill of Rogers or Parkinson or McKay himself. Yet those three could not bear the whole burden of guarding the camp themselves and still keep alert enough to be effective. And it would damage Sloan's morale if he were left out of the watch rotation. Every member of the Guardians was theoretically able to do anyone else's job.

McKay shook his head and drew thoughtfully on the cigar, shielding the coal with his hand without even thinking about it. Command. You'd think it'd be pretty straightforward, but somehow it never was.

Parkinson called in to say he was approaching camp and please not to fire him up. Rogers slid down out of the cupola and came out One's side hatch as the big agent walked into camp carrying a G-3. "Clete," he said, "I need to see you and Billy a minute."

Parkinson nodded. McKay grinned. Rogers was the only man in the group who called the Secret Service boss "Clete." Even MacGregor called him "Mr. Parkinson." His men mostly called him "sir."

"Wanted to check your regenerators," Rogers explained to the two. He was carrying the pouch that held Mobile One's medical kit. "Pull up your shirts."

The two obeyed. "Yours is unplugged, Clete," Rogers observed reproachfully, inspecting Parkinson's bandaged chest.

"Damned thing kept hanging up on branches," the agent said. "I had to take it off."

"You didn't *have* to. What you have to do is wear it until that broken rib heals. We need you operating at full capacity." He turned to his own superior. "How about you, Billy? Behaving yourself?"

Silently, McKay turned so that Rogers could see the tiny unwinking red eye of the pilot light on the calculator-sized electronic stimulator taped to the small of his back. "Good boy," Rogers said. "Here, Clete, roll up your sleeve. It's time for an injection of Reficin." He produced a hypospray, held it against Parkinson's bulging biceps, and fired a measured dose of the healing-stimulating enzyme into his bloodstream. Then he waited while Parkinson, looking sheepish, reattached the electrical unit to the probes that reached down to the bone on either side of the fracture of his rib. Pulses of electric current would help the bone knit in a remarkably short time, even as the unit taped to McKay's back would help mend the crack in his rib.

"Keep it on, Clete." Rogers slapped the big agent on the shoulder. "Good night, Billy. I'm going to turn in. You are too, in a few minutes."

McKay grinned. "Yes, Mother." The stocky Guardian went back into Mobile One.

Parkinson uttered a low, disbelieving laugh. "Not many men try to talk to me like that."

"Rogers is a real Jekyll and Hyde. Most of the time you'd think he's got all the emotion of a shark. But let him play medic and he turns into a head nurse in drag. Also, he talks more than he normally would in six months."

He was suddenly aware that Parkinson and he were talking without snarling at each other. Parkinson didn't miss it either. "I see your boys are playing cards with mine," the agent said. "Is Turpin cheating them too badly?"

"I think he's running aground on Casey's Zen mystic rap," McKay said, trying not to show his surprise at Parkinson's friendly attitude.

It was inevitable that the barrier between the Guardians and the Secret Service men would begin to break up. They had fought and bled together, and some of them had died. And they had worked well as a team. You didn't go through hell together without forging a mutual bond.

"I misjudged you and your men, McKay," Parkinson said, his deep voice rough. "You aren't just glamor boys. But no matter how good you are, McKay, this is our job. Our men have been laying their lives on the line for the President since before you were born. Remember that."

A heavy weight seemed to settle on McKay's shoulders. "I will," he said in a flat tone. "You can bet on it." Shaking his head, he turned away for a tour of the perimeter.

A footfall behind him made him turn. "Lieutenant McKay," Turpin said.

He looked back at the darkened cars. "The game break up?"

The skinny agent grinned around the unlit stub of his cigar.

"Naw. Got tired of losing to that Zen-freak kid of yours, and I thought I'd stretch my legs awhile." He shook his head. "I can't believe the way he filled that damn inside straight."

"Careful you don't wander out where the Claymores are."

"Actually, I wanted to talk to you, McKay. You and the Chief still aren't getting along too well, are you?"

McKay said nothing. "Never mind," Turpin said. "I know the answer to that. And I thought I should explain a few things."

"Nobody needs to explain anything to me," McKay said gruffly. He started to turn away.

"Wait a minute, will you? At least I want you to understand that Parkinson's not just another uptight bureaucrat with a hair up his ass."

"Agent Parkinson's a good man," McKay said in a level voice.

"Fuckin'-A straight. And you have to understand just how hard he worked to get where he is. He was a ghetto kid from Detroit, ten brothers and sisters, welfare, the whole nine yards. Mom had a whole string of live-in boyfriends." He spit out a fragment of tobacco. "His old man got shot in a holdup when he was fourteen. That was it for Parkinson. He ran away, living with friends, staying alive by working odd jobs. He got into football, and that got him into college. All the time he wanted to prove to himself that he was really somebody, not just a worthless nigger. That's why he quit the Rams to join the Army. He wanted to prove he could do something more than chase a little ball around a field.

"Now he's done it. He's a black in a white power structure. He's got the most coveted job in the Service: bossing the presidential detail." He took the cigar from his mouth and studied it. "And along come the lily-white Guardians, horning in on his territory."

McKay bridled. "That's not fair! We're—"

"All pretty WASP. You're the closest thing to an ethnic on the team, and I don't think Parkinson sees a Mick-Polack as exactly a soul brother."

"Just why the hell should that make any difference? You think the Irish and the Poles got treated with kid gloves when they came over here? The blacks and the Spanish aren't the only ones who had a hard time."

Turpin grinned. "Don't I know it. But that's how it looks to

Parkinson. He maybe can't help wondering if the Guardians would ever have been formed if the chief of the White House detail had been white."

It was dark outside the great picture window that gave out on the southern mountains of the Swiss province of Bern. The light inside the room made the window a huge mirror, reflecting the image of a burly man sitting behind a huge desk of blond wood. A square hand held a gilded telephone handset to one ear.

"We failed," a voice said across what may well have been the most secure phone link in the world. "Few personnel survived at the base, but from interrogating them, we can only surmise the President escaped."

The man frowned. "I thought the gunship dispatched was supposed to insure that the President would not escape if anything went wrong with the pickup, as well as guaranteeing the . . . silence of the base personnel. This is just rank incompetence." His voice was deep, broad, and stark, his accent evoking the Russian steppes of his past.

"Those responsible have paid, Excellency. There's nothing left of that Hercules but a burned spot on the runway."

"But what about *your* responsibility for this, Trajan?" Tiny random crackles illuminated the long silence that stretched between Langley and the Swiss uplands. "Consider *your* responsibility, my good friend. Then assure me that your errors will be rectified at once."

"A-At once, Excellency." Very little could so much as dent the composure of the man code-named Trajan, but the thought of the big man's displeasure came very near shattering it. "All our domestic assets will be diverted to this project immediately."

"*All* of them, Trajan."

"As you say, Excellency." A pause. "We've got word most of Europe has submitted to you. Congratulations."

The attempt at flattery was fruitless. "It was inevitable, Trajan. My Council promises to restore order where now there is only chaos. But Europe is nothing. I must have America. I must have the blueprint. It is the keystone of my master plan. And that means I must have the President. Or have him neutralized."

"You will, Excellency. Our hunter-killer teams are on the

trail at this very second. MacGregor hasn't got a prayer."

"Splendid. For you especially, my very good friend. Your future is in MacGregor's hands, one might say."

A powerful hand laid the gold receiver down in its gold cradle.

"We have company, McKay," Sloan said. "Coming up fast from the rear."

McKay was riding on the rear deck with his legs in the open hatch, getting some fresh air and trying to ignore the long lines of refugees trudging along the hopelessly clogged highway. He twisted around and peered into the east, shading his eyes against the morning sun. A moment and he saw it, a small black dot silhouetted against the fluffy clouds piled on the flat Ohio horizon. The aircraft was skimming just above the road.

The back-road strategy had played out that morning in central Ohio. Midwesterners seemed more hip to the existence of the little-traveled country roads than Eastern seaboard residents—or maybe they'd just had longer to filter onto them. In any event, by midmorning McKay and Parkinson had decided to take their chances with Interstate 70.

It was working fairly well. The road was clogged with lines of immobilized vehicles, but county crews were already out trying to clear the highway. To the sides fugitives streamed away from Columbus, which had been badly hit by near misses aimed for the stratotanker base at Rickenbacker. The cars rolled along the shoulders of the highway, only occasionally having to turn off into the fields.

They had just clambered back onto the right-of-way. A semi, its driver possibly blinded by a flash from one of the Rickenbacker strikes, had slewed across the westbound lane and busted the barrier onto the eastbound, wiping out at least a dozen cars in the process. With no medical services immediately available, the wounded had died where they lay. Now they were stacked by the side of the road with a tarp spread over them while a bulldozer tried to shove the semi into the ditch. Sheriff's deputies with shotguns in hand stood by, eyeing the 450's warily as they rolled over the even furrows of soybean plants.

"They guarding the dozers or keeping the looters off?" Turpin wondered aloud over the intercom.

The back of the trailer had popped open, spilling cartons of toilet paper onto the road. "You wouldn't think looters'd be too keen to get their hands on that," Sloan commented.

"Like, it might not be such a bad idea, Sam," Casey had replied. "Be awhile before they see another roll of Charmin." It was about that moment the little radar spinning on top of Mobile One's turret had picked up the bogey closing rapidly from the east.

"It's a chopper," McKay said, and even as he spoke he could feel the beat of its rotors vibrating the hot, still air.

"Trouble, McKay?" came Parkinson's voice. Mobile Two was fifty meters ahead of the other car.

"I don't know," McKay said, studying the fields rolling by on both sides. A stand of trees eight hundred meters to the northwest was the only cover anywhere nearby that came any higher than the hubs of their tires. "I sure as hell hope not."

The chopper flashed by low overhead, a lean sharklike shape with stub wings. "Cobra," Casey said. "Old crate."

"Still has a bite," Turpin said. McKay recognized the helicopter as an AH-1T TOWCobra, originally built for the USMC. It carried a three-barreled 20 mm gun in a chin turret, and eight missiles in tubes under the stub wings. It may have been an old crate, but gunships just like it had been knocking the snot out of the tanks of the Eighth Guards Army in Europe just days before. It flew on about five hundred meters, curving right away from the road, then pivoted to face the armored cars.

"I have a bad feeling about this," McKay said.

White smoke blossomed under the left wing as a rocket was fired from a port outboard launcher.

CHAPTER
FOURTEEN

"Turpin, break left!" Casey shouted. Wailing like a banshee, the missile hurtled past the coffin stern of Mobile One and struck the jackknifed semitrailer. Blazing rolls of toilet paper puffed out streamers of smoke from a sudden orange fireball as the shaped-charge warhead exploded.

Whether he had spotted the missile launch or not, Parkinson's driver reacted instantly to Wilson's warning. The ten tons of Mobile Two swung hard into the unmoving line of traffic, sideswiping a little Chevy electrocompact so that it rolled right over the top of a lowslung Thunderbird in the left lane, and blocking itself from the Cobra's line of fire with the bulk of a hardware company's panel truck.

Even as he screamed the warning, the young pilot's battle-trained reflexes blasted into action. He braked Mobile One hard and threw the wheel right as if going into a bootlegger reverse. Refugees scattered like frightened chickens as the big V-450 swung broadside to the killer missile's line of flight with a keening of tortured rubber. As soon as the vehicle's angular snout was aimed for the soybean fields north of the road, Casey hit the accelerator.

Clinging to handholds on the rear deck for all he was worth, McKay was almost flung out of the hatch as the Super Commando darted forward. It slammed through a chainlink fence as if it were tissue paper. Jagged wire ends raked McKay's arms as he flung them up to protect his face.

Sitting in the forward cockpit of the attack helicopter, the gunner wore a helmet interfaced with the guidance mechanism of the missile. When the chopper's weapons system was in Launch mode a cross hair was projected onto his faceplate; as long as he kept it centered on his target, impulses transmitted down a hair-thin wire steered the twenty-kilogram missile toward its objective.

However, even the chopper's computer-enhanced aiming system wasn't infallible. Turpin had effectively hidden Mobile Two from view. Casey's violent evasive maneuver, shooting off at right angles to the Cobra's line of sight, had spoiled what fighter jockeys called the gunner's "tracking solution."

As Mobile One bounced over the furrows of soybeans, Tom Rogers traversed his turret left. *"Don't shoot!"* the President shouted, horrified at the thought of what the high-explosive— and worse, white phosphorus—rounds would do to the hapless refugees on the highway below the chopper. But Roger was already triggering off a long burst. He wasn't aiming for the tiny target that the Cobra, narrow as a racing shell, presented as it swung to track the fleeing V-450. Even at five hundred yards, he didn't think he had a chance of hitting it from the wildly jouncing armored car. Instead, he dropped a pattern of grenades between the aircraft and Mobile One. A wall of dense white phosphorus smoke erupted, cutting the chopper off from view.

McKay was inside the compartment, tearing at clamps securing a molded compartment lid to the hull. "Turn us back to the highway, Casey," McKay shouted. Casey turned right as hard as the uneven, yielding earth would permit, and sent the car racing back for the highway.

Its twin Pratt & Whitney engines howling, the Cobra burst through Rogers' smoke screen like an angry hornet. Its chin turret swiveled, seeking prey. The gunner fired a burst toward Mobile Two as Casey busted the fence again. President MacGregor let out a moan of anguish as the armor-piercing shells ripped through the line of men, women, and children. Hits danced in firefly sparkles on the side of the V-450. Sloan hit the override, cutting off reception from the personal communicators of Mobile Two as shouts of pain and confusion rang in One's earplugs.

Mobile One boomed into the space cleared to the west of the now-burning semi and bucked to a halt as the Cobra streaked by. The bulldozer operator had stayed in his seat, as if uncertain of what to do with the blazing truck. Through a view port, McKay saw the man's florid face go slack with surprise, and then a 20 mike-mike round hit him and knocked him off his yellow steel steed.

McKay threw open the left-side hatch and dove free, clutching a Stinger missile launcher to his chest. Casey gunned the engine and Mobile One leaped ahead, crossing the space the dozer had cleared and wheeling right to run along the shoulder of the eastbound lane. McKay hunkered down to arm the shoulder-fired surface-to-air missile, hoping he was out of sight of the helicopter. The heat of the blazing truck seared his face. From somewhere came the agonized, heaving moans of the injured dozer driver.

The V-450's both carried Stinger launchers with one round prepped and ready to go, attached to the reusable gripstock and guidance system. The Stinger was designed with a built-in IFF, identification-friend-or-foe interrogator, to prevent its being fired at friendly aircraft. Given the Guardians' mission, Crenna had seen to it that theirs had the IFF device disabled. Which was a good thing, since an automatic transponder in the Cobra constantly broadcast a signal identifying it as friendly.

McKay heard the pitch of the rotors change as the Cobra swung around for another firing pass. The slow thud of .50-caliber machine guns drummed in his ears, and the quicker firing of a 7.62. Mobile Two wasn't out of the fight yet, he noted with satisfaction. As the roar of the Cobra's engines increased, McKay knelt and peered through the launcher's sights.

The chopper was right on top of him, flame flashing from the rotating muzzles of its M-197 cannon. He hoped Casey was managing to keep clear of the lethal stream of 20 mm rounds. As the Cobra zoomed past, he pivoted to follow.

The infrared and ultraviolet sensors in the guidance unit picked up the heat of the Cobra's twin exhausts. McKay heard the shrill beeping of the annunciator telling him the weapon was locked on target. He drew a breath, let out half, and squeezed the trigger. The missile leaped from the launcher with a whoosh as its ejector motor boosted it to a safe distance from McKay, then streaked suddenly ahead as its main rocket drive ignited.

The Cobra was rapidly overtaking Mobile One. The CIA gunner grinned beneath his insectile faceplate and Air Force mustache. The car's driver was good, weaving all over the beanfields and up onto the road in his efforts to elude the chopper's cannon, but he wasn't good enough. Another couple of seconds—

He felt a sudden hammerblow transmitted through his seat as the Stinger struck the starboard exhaust port of the chopper at almost twice the speed of sound. The pilot shrieked as blazing fuel enveloped him. The gunner just had time to throw futile hands up before his face, and then the Cobra dove full-speed into the plowed earth of Ohio.

The attack helicopter disappeared in an orange-and-black blossom of flame that rolled over a dozen luckless refugees. Some ran screaming from its midst, sexless and without identity, wrapped in cocoons of fire. McKay grimaced and lowered the launcher. Nothing to do for them.

"Report—Casey, Parkinson?"

"We're fine, Billy," Casey's voice came back at once. "Couple of rounds glanced off the rear deck, but they didn't penetrate."

For a heart-stopping moment, Mobile Two didn't reply. Even as McKay remembered he was cut off from hearing their communicators, Garcia's voice came through his earplug on the frequency of the car's main radio. "Popejoy bought it, and Mason's leg got laid open. We had a fire in the turret, but we got that put out. Everything—uh, everything's under control." He sounded shaken.

"All right. Pull on out. We'll bury Popejoy when we get clear of this mess." McKay straightened. He could hear the cries of the wounded to the front and rear as Casey drove back to pick him up. The chopper had hosed the crowded highway with shots without concern for the refugees packed onto it. McKay had no idea how many were hurt. Nor did he want to know.

A hatch opened and MacGregor's white face appeared as

Mobile One pulled up. "The people, my God, the *people*," he said. "We've got to help them!"

McKay hefted the launcher into the car. "I'm sorry, Mr. President."

MacGregor's face registered momentary incomprehension. "You—you can't mean you're just going to drive off and leave the wounded?"

"I'm sorry, but that's exactly what I mean, Mr. President." He climbed into the 450 and slammed the hatch shut. "Fire her up, Casey."

Casey glanced back and bit his lip. His eyes were wide behind the yellow lenses of his glasses. "Roger, Billy," he said after a split second's pause. The car started rolling.

MacGregor grabbed McKay's arm. "Lieutenant, I *order* you to help those people. Do you hear me?"

It was a moment McKay had been dreading since the beginning of Project Guardian. He grabbed a strap and lowered himself into a fold-down seat. "I'm sorry, sir. I can't do that."

"What do you mean?" MacGregor's voice trembled with near hysteria. "I gave you a direct order!"

McKay took a deep breath. "My orders are to do everything I can to get you to Heartland Complex in safety, Mr. President. And to allow nothing to interfere with that assignment."

"I'm overriding your orders! I'm the Supreme Commander of the Armed Forces—"

"Mr. President," McKay said softly, "that doesn't matter. In our charter, it plainly states that the Guardians are outside the chain of command of the armed forces."

"But I'm not just some National Guard general trying to commandeer your vehicles!"

McKay shook his head. "That doesn't matter, Mr. President. I—we—have a mission to perform. Until we carry out that mission, *no one* is able to change our orders."

MacGregor stared wildly around the compartment. Sloan was half turned in his seat, listening to the dispute. His eyes met MacGregor's for a moment. He turned away.

"Parkinson! Agent Parkinson, do you hear me?"

"Yes, Mr. President."

"I'm ordering a halt to help those poor refugees! I can't get Lieutenant McKay to obey me."

A pause. "He's right, Mr. President." The words rolled out ponderously, as if each were of boulder weight. "Your safety is the overriding factor. And please, sir—don't ask me to overrule Lieutenant McKay again. I—I can't do that."

MacGregor slumped into a seat. McKay regarded him calmly.

"Do you realize the *power* this gives you?" MacGregor whispered.

"Yes, sir." McKay's eyes were the blue of an Arctic sky. "And I don't give a shit.

"That's why I'm a Guardian."

CHAPTER
FIFTEEN

"Be seated, General." The big man waved expansively from behind his desk.

The tall man in military green let his eyes wander around the room, from the wide blond oak desk across the lush maroon carpet, to walls of prestressed concrete dressed to resemble stone and finally to the wide window looking out on the Bernese Alps. He looked, in fact, everywhere except at the big man himself. "Thank you," said General Mark Shaw, Commanding Officer, USAREUR. His voice was subdued, perhaps by the thick carpet. "I prefer to stand, uh, Chancellor Maximov." The General seemed taken aback by the unruffled, imperturbable quality of the office, so totally at variance with the chaos of the world outside.

The man behind the desk nodded his massive head. "Very well, General. You asked to see me." *After a paid minion on your staff put the idea in your head, and then convinced you it was your own*, the big man thought with a touch of smugness. It pleased him when he got value for his money. He spread his big muscular hands. "I am at your disposal, General."

General Shaw blinked. He was tall and lean, flat-bellied despite his fifty-three years, and narrow-faced, with a firm-looking squared-off chin that contrasted oddly with his rather fussy mouth, long straight nose, eyes that seemed to be perpetually squinting, and high broad forehead. His hair was gray at the sides, though still brown on top, and cut short, emphasizing his large ears. His uniform was rumpled from the helicopter trip across Germany.

Shaw had good media presence—it had been an important factor in his rise in today's Army; you couldn't get prestigious assignments if you looked like a fool on camera. And he carried the fatigue of the last ten days well, so that it showed only in hints of dark half-moons beneath his eyes and the slightest stoop to his shoulders. He commanded a force that, in the tense months before confrontation spilled over into open war, had swelled to over half a million men. He had led them well, if not overly imaginatively.

Yet he was ill at ease before this heavyset civilian in the plain black suit.

"I won't mince words, Chancellor—"

"Please!" The man held up a hand. "No need to be so formal, General. You may simply call me Mr. Maximov. It makes me feel much more at ease."

Shaw looked at him a moment, then nodded briskly. "Very well. I have just over a hundred thousand troops on active status, plus almost a hundred thousand wounded." His face grayed perceptibly as he spoke. His command had suffered horribly, more from the thermonuclear exchange that devastated Europe than the bloody week of war preceding it. "The casualties need medical attention badly. My troops need food and clothing. I'm out of communication with the States. What intelligence I have indicates that it'll be one hell of a long time before we get any more support from back home." He looked grim. "If ever."

Maximov nodded. The intelligence General Shaw received had originated with the CIA, which was to say with Maximov himself. Not that it was false, exactly. Merely shaded to emphasize the untenability of General Shaw's position. And that of his two hundred thousand surviving soldiers. "I'm sure you will be equal to these exigencies, General," Maximov said.

For an instant Shaw looked the man full in the face, and Maximov read despair in the pale gray eyes. Then the General looked away. "I don't know if I am," he whispered.

Maximov leaned forward attentively. "Perhaps I can be of assistance?"

Shaw stared at the rug. "Mr. Chancellor, you have become the de facto ruler of western Europe."

"Say, rather, the survivors of this tortured continent have chosen to entrust stewardship over their destinies to the Internationalist Council, which I have the honor of chairing."

Shaw nodded. "Whatever. What I've come to say is . . . my army—what's left of it—can't exist in a vacuum. We need support, supplies. Already there've been desertions, bands ravaging the countryside. If we could be assured of a source of supply—and if, if maybe my men felt they had a *purpose* . . ."

Maximov waited indulgently. Typical of Americans to lapse into tongue-tied adolescent confusion when matters of real import came under discussion. As a culture they were used to dealing with surface things, appearances. *In the old days*, he thought, *this man would simply kneel before me and offer his sword. Or perhaps the banner of his regiment.* Stubby fingers tapped ruminatively on the green blotter. *Maybe there's something in restoring those old ways. My New Order could use a few old traditions for window dressing.*

Wearied by strain and fatigue, Shaw's mind was wandering in and out of focus. He had honestly not expected his men to do well against the Russians. For so long he, his peers, and the Pentagon had all been convinced of the innate superiority of the Soviet system. The well-ordered society, where everyone knew his place and kept to it, where dissenters weren't mollycoddled, where the military occupied the pinnacle of the social order . . . *Funny that such a strong-looking man would have such a sissified telephone*, he thought vaguely. He forced himself to the words: "Chan—Mr. Maximov, I would like to conditionally offer the services of myself and the United States Army in Europe to your new Federated States of Europe."

Maximov raised a brow. *"Conditionally,* General?" He gave the words the slightest touch of steel.

"Pending the restoration of order in the United States of America," Shaw said hastily. "Our first duty is to our country, of course."

Maximov nodded. "Of course." He pretended to ponder the offer for a moment. "I accept your concern, General. May I point out that by tendering your . . . assistance . . . to the FSE, you are serving the interests of the United States in an immediate way?"

Shaw looked puzzled.

"Your men were dispatched to this continent to help keep order," Maximov continued. "Unfortunately, that proved impossible. Yet it is now your opportunity—dare I say your *destiny*?—to play a vital role in the restoration of order to Europe. And once that is achieved, who knows? You may well be called upon to help bring order to your own unfortunate land once a strong and united Europe stands at your back."

Shaw was standing straighter and his eyes showed traces of a fervent gleam. This was something he could understand. Order, keeping the peace. That was the U.S. Army's global mission, after all. And if he and his men could be sent back stateside once things were straightened out here, wouldn't they show the civilians how a strong, proud country should be run!

Maximov restrained a smile. The bird had not only taken the bait, he was helping pull taut the snare. "In a way, this war, tragic as it was, has been beneficial," he said, sensing the time had come for the tough talk of *realpolitik*. "The unification of Europe has been a dream whose realization was long overdue. And if the whole world can be likewise unified—in the proper hands, of course—" He saw there was no need to complete the sentence.

"Mr. Chancellor," General Mark Shaw said, "I'm your man."

"I thank you, the suffering millions of Europe thank you—" *Almost said "masses,"* Maximov chided himself. *I mustn't let the headiness of success lead me into unfortunate lapses of terminology*. "And ultimately, the people of your own great nation will thank you for your services. To them and to all of free humanity."

He stood and offered his hand. Though the General was six-foot-one, Maximov loomed above him. Shaw took the hand, shook it crisply. "One thing, General," Maximov said. "The Soviets—"

"Marshal Beriev and I have had an unofficial cease-fire going since the bombs started falling," Shaw said briskly. "They've shown no signs of breaking it." His continuing bewilderment was apparent; Western military dogma had held that the Soviets were prepared to fight a protracted nuclear war as an adjunct to a campaign of conventional-style conquest. Even now he had difficulty accepting that this concept was as false as the image of an invincible Red armored thrust through the weak heart of western Europe.

"But if they do," he went on, chest swelling with an unexpected pride in his men gained over the seven hard days of land warfare preceding the One-Day War, "then we'll finish the job we started before they pressed the button in Moscow!"

"Very well, General. I have every faith in you. I suggest you return to your troops now." He pressed a button on the blond desk and his aide held open the office door. "And may God bless you for what you've done today."

Shaw saluted, turned, and walked out the door, somehow looking as if the creases on his uniform had been restored.

Maximov's aide escorted the General out. Maximov's hand moved to a box on the desk and flipped open a lid painted with an icon of the Holy Mother of Kazan. Inside were Russian cigarettes, harsh black Ukrainian *makhorka* rolled in paper and glued to cardboard tubes. The Russian's traditional first sign of upwardly mobile westernization had been to switch to milder Western cigarettes. It was axiomatic that no one enjoyed smoking *makhorka* cigarettes. Maximov did. Or chose to pretend so. Perhaps it clashed somewhat with his image as a modern industrialist, cosmopolitan and urbane. But it fit the self-image of a man born on the bleak steppes of the Ukraine, of untamed Don River cossack stock, whose father had died fighting the hated Russians while he was still being carried in his mother's womb, whose mother had escaped with him into Turkey while he was still a small boy. He lit one, swiveled his chair to face the window, and drew rank blue smoke into his lungs.

A light on the console on his desk flashed green, signifying that his aide had returned from seeing the General off and wished admittance. Maximov stabbed the button to unlock the door. Apparently carved oak, it in fact consisted of oak veneer over a heavy steel-and-foamed-concrete core, cunningly counterweighted to make it manageable. Even a shaped-charge antitank weapon would have trouble penetrating it.

The aide slipped inside and shut the door. "You've seen the General off?" Maximov asked in Russian.

The aide nodded. "Poisoning your lungs with that vile black Ukrainian trash again?" He spoke the flawless pseudo-Muscovite Russian that was as sure a sign of rising status in the Soviet *apparat* as a public school accent used to be in the service of the British Empire.

Maximov raised a bushy eyebrow. "I take vitamin and

amino-acid supplements to minimize the ill effects.''

The aide's finely sculpted right eyebrow arched in derision. ''Those chemicals. You'll kill yourself.'' A boyish grin. ''Now that you've achieved what you've worked so hard for.''

''Bah. Next you'll have me give up vodka.''

The aide leaned against the doorjamb. ''It would be beneficial.''

Maximov scowled. ''A man needs his vices, Ivan Vissarionovich.''

''That's why I keep myself healthy for mine.'' The grin widened.

''You Georgians have always been sodomites.''

''And you Ukrainians boorish swine.''

Maximov hoisted his cigarette in sardonic salute. Had another man spoken thus to him he would have killed him with his own hands. He'd done so, in fact, back in his younger, more boisterous days. But if anyone had earned the right to speak to him thus, it was Colonel Ivan Vissarionovich Vesensky, formerly of the *Komitet Gosudarstvennoi Bezopasnosti*—the KGB.

A tall man, almost as tall as Maximov himself, with a skier's lithe build, classic profile, swept-back blond hair, Vesensky was a secret agent who actually resembled the popular image of a master spy. And a master he had been before the holocaust, jet-setting around the world as the star troubleshooter for the State Security Committee. He had been a well-known and cordially hated thorn in the side of the CIA, the British Foreign Office, the French Deuxième Bureau, the Mossad, and the West German DNB. At forty-three he had been the youngest man ever to wield so much influence within the stodgy gerontocracy of the KGB.

He was also a traitor.

And he had a vice. It went beyond his taste for the good life, as evinced by the impeccably cut double-breasted blue Savile Row blazer he wore over white linen trousers, an outfit completed by the two rows of brass buttons down the breast and a scarlet scarf knotted rakishly around his lean throat. Those tastes could be written off as augmenting his cover as a European playboy-athlete, though the Committee's comptrollers despaired noisily whenever he submitted his accounts. Nor did it have to do with his origins as a member of a despised— meaning non-Russian—ethnic group. His being a Georgian wasn't exactly a secret, though he didn't generally advertise it. As long as he performed, the old men who headed the Committee were willing to overlook his origins. He had a real secret, which could have resulted in his fall from grace with the KGB. Maximov knew his secret well enough to joke with him about it.

And yet, in the shadowy demimonde of intrigue and power politics, Vesensky was the closest thing Maximov had to a friend.

"Besides, I wouldn't want to end this life before achieving my aims," Maximov added.

"You've got Europe—" Vesensky held out a tanned palm. "Right *here*. And more on the way."

"America! I want America! That's where power lies."

"I take it that fool Trajan hasn't found MacGregor yet." Vesensky sneered. "I'm glad he rebuffed my attempts to recruit him for the KGB. I have *some* national feeling left, after all."

Maximov drew on his cigarette. "He claims MacGregor's capture is imminent."

"But the President is heading for the Midwest," Vesensky pointed out. "The CIA's assets aren't as numerous there as on the Coast. And that region was hit hard. It'll be tricky to track him through the fallout." He rubbed his hands together. "Still, you have Shaw's submission."

Maximov was staring out the window. "Yes," he said, rubbing his jowls. "His men will prove quite useful shortly, I've a feeling. And beyond that, once Europe is truly pacified, the Americans will offer much less resistance to an invading army, especially if it is an American one."

"You think that will be necessary?"

"Only if Trajan fails there." A blue light on the console winked on. Maximov smiled. "Splendid. Our other guest has arrived. Will you be so good as to show Marshal Beriev in, Ivan Vissarionovich?"

CHAPTER
SIXTEEN

"What'll you do when we get to Heartland, Ben?"
Casey asked over the comm as they cruised through rolling
farmland in the middle of Indiana. They had had to detour to
the north of Indianapolis, which had been hit twice with air-
bursts. Now they were passing through the clear zone between
the wind-borne contamination from the groundbursts that had
inexplicably been dropped on Chicago and the fallout from
the near-misses that had blasted Grissom Air Force Base and
the countryside around it. They could have veered south
rather than north, but that would have entailed passing
through the fallout from the Minuteman complexes in west-
central Missouri, which was widespread and heavy. The crews
of the two 450's were enjoying a chance to breathe fresh air
while they could. The atmosphere inside the vehicles was
beginning to go pretty stale despite state-of-the-art climate
conditioning.

"Well, now," Turpin drawled from Mobile Two, in a bad
imitation of a broad Western accent, "I reckon I'll settle down
with one of them Earth Mamas—you're too young to remember them; they're from the late sixties, back when God and I
were young. I'll find me an Earth Mama with long frizzy hair

and tits down to *here*, and get a nice little farm, and settle down to raise granola.''

Casey laughed. ''You don't *raise* granola, Turpin,'' Sam Sloan said in mock outrage.

In Mobile One they could almost see Turpin shrug, though Two was a hundred meters ahead, starting around a curve that passed a low, hummocky hill. The sky was gray and sullen, the air heavy, wet, and hot. ''You're a farm boy, Sam. You know that sort of thing. Me, I've always been altogether urban, but I do feel a sea change coming on—''

His voice broke off as something struck Mobile Two from the front.

The warhead of the Viper light anti-tank weapon—LAW —was too feeble to penetrate the sandwiched-alloy frontal armor of a modern tank, but it was more than adequate for the thinner skin of the V-450. The nose of the vehicle was angled to the right of the projectile's line of flight. The rocket struck the turret base on the left.

Gunner Mason had time for a brief agonized scream as gaseous copper, accelerated to almost 45,000 miles an hour by the explosion of a shaped charge of plastic explosive, lanced through the Super Commando's armor and vaporized his body from short ribs to knees in a near-incandescent jet. The blast detonated a dozen rounds of .50-caliber ammunition stored in belts around the turret, setting off a chain reaction of lesser explosions.

Though the lower part of the turret shielded him from the brunt of the blast, Clete Parkinson was flashburned and hurled back against the starboard side of the car. He slumped, senseless, as more secondary blasts from various munitions stashed in the vehicle began to flash off, filling the compartment with smoke and whizzing fragments of shattered metal.

His back clawed open by steel splinters, suit coat smoldering, Turpin fought to control the vehicle as it lurched into the ditch on the north side of the highway. Behind, Casey Wilson, having slowed for the curve, whipped the massive Mobile One into a screaming bootlegger turn and bolted back for the protection of the hill to the left of the road as Tom Rogers scattered 40 mm grenades and .50 cal. rounds down the highway past the stricken car.

''Shit,'' McKay grunted, clinging to the rear of Sloan's seat. ''Looks like the Company's finally caught up with us. With the heavy-duty shit they're slinging around, that ain't no bunch of road gypsies.''

As Mobile One bounced over the hill's shoulder, skinny Ben Turpin climbed out of Two's driver's hatch. From a stand of white oak and the ditch beyond another curve two hundred meters farther down the road, the ambushers opened fire on the car with M-16's. Ignoring them, Turpin heaved the massive inert bulk of Clete Parkinson, manhandled up to him by a sweating, bloody-faced Garcia, out of the V-450. Puffing, his hatchet face red from exertion, Turpin rolled his unconscious chief onto the forward deck.

Garcia grunted as a tumbling 7.62 round, cooked off by the fire raging in the rear of the compartment, hit him in the neck. He fell to the floorplates, spurting blood. An instant later the auxiliary fuel tank blew, swamping him in a wave of flame. ''Phil!'' the driver screamed.

By then the hidden riflemen had found their range. Bullets hit Ben Turpin in the thigh, stomach, and chest. He uttered a strangled coughing cry and rolled Parkinson off the blazing car onto the loose rich loam of Indiana. Two more shots caught him and he pitched forward into the ditch.

Once behind the hill, Casey whipped Mobile One around again. He carefully drew forward along the flank of the rise until the 450 was hull-down from the attackers, with only the low one-man turret exposed.

The ambush team poured fire at Turpin, who was struggling to pull his still-unconscious chief clear of the burning armored car. The Viper man had another round prepared and ready to go in case the second car showed itself again. He was cursing himself under his breath for not letting the first car come closer and then nailing the second car with his first shot. That would have given them a better chance to bag both. Langley was breathing hot and heavy down their necks on this; it was giving them all a bad case of buck fever.

He saw the turret of the second Super Commando appear beyond the grassy shoulder of the hill as if disembodied. ''Shit,'' he muttered. It was a lousy shot. He shouldered the launcher and peered through the sights.

Tom Rogers had spotted the muzzle flashes of the attackers' M-16's. He let go a long burst toward the clump of oak trees. A half-dozen high-explosive grenades spattered down on the ambushers' position. The AT missileman's flesh fused with the plastic of his launcher in the heat of blazing phosphorus.

The Guardians went into action like the well-tuned machine they had become. Casey stayed at the wheel, ready to bolt if anything threatened Mobile One and the President. Sloan took over for Rogers in the turret while the ex-Army man collected his medical kit and Galil. McKay was already out of the car with an Aussie ammo box on his 60, snooping and pooping overland toward the ambush site.

Sloan covered him, firing judicious bursts of .50 caliber at anything that looked as if it might be moving in the area where the attackers had fired from. Rain had fallen heavily over the last few days, and the grenade rounds had only set a few trees and patches of grass alight. Nonetheless, the fire was enough to keep the handful of survivors of the killer team out of the little wood.

For an old patrolling hand like McKay it was a walkover. Stunned by the ferocity of Mobile One's riposte, eyes stinging from poisonous phosphorus smoke, the ambushers could only cling to the side of the ditch and try to keep out of the way of the car's heavy machine gun. They were so preoccupied with Sloan and the 450 that they never noticed McKay working his way around on their right flank until he cut loose on them from fifty meters with his lightweight machine gun. One managed to scrabble up onto the ditchbank next to the road. Sloan blew him back down in a spray of blood.

Rogers was working on Parkinson when McKay came back. Turpin lay to one side. The Guardians' medic had done what he could for him, pressing the plastic wrappers from bandage packs over the sucking entrance wounds in his chest to stop air from entering his chest cavity and collapsing the lung. Then he had staunched the bleeding of the other wounds and given him a spray of painkiller. But it was painfully obvious Turpin wasn't going to make it.

Turpin managed a feeble smile as McKay walked up. "Good news . . . Doc," the wounded man wheezed. "I finally got that death wish of mine under control."

McKay knelt by his side. The air was thick with the scent of wet earth and greenery and the jarring stink of burning flesh and diesel fuel. "Don't talk. Uses up your strength."

"That doesn't make any difference now, glamor boy. Know that . . . as well as you." He coughed up bloody foam. "You listening, fly-boy?" he asked.

"Yeah," Casey said over the comm link. "Yeah, Ben, I'm here."

"Got to know something. That straight you drew to the other night back in Ohio—was that really open inside?"

A few heartbeats' blood trickled into the black dirt before Casey responded. "Uh, no. It was, like, open at both ends. Drew a ten."

"Shit." Turpin spat blood. "An old hustler like me out-hustled by the Kung-Fu Kid! It's got to be time for me to—" A paroxysm seized him, arched his back off the ground and shook him hard. When it let him go his eyes were glassy-blind like the eyes of a stuffed red fox.

"Mother fuck," McKay said.

They found the CIA vehicles hidden from the road behind a fold of ground. A Blazer and a battered white station wagon, loaded with munitions of various sorts—guns, LAWs, grenades—and ultra-advanced radios with silicon lattice electronics and computerized filters and scramblers, much like the ones the Guardians themselves used. Sam Sloan appropriated the communications equipment. It was vital to know how the Company had known to ambush them on this deserted Indiana back road. With this gear it was quite possible the Company itself would tell them.

They picked up some of the grenades and a number of loaded Uzi magazines—standard thirty-two round size, but they would fit into Parkinson's Mini. Then they laid Ben Turpin's body in the back seat of the Blazer, folded his hands over his favorite deck of cards, and tossed in a Willy Peter grenade. Leaving his funeral pyre trailing black smoke into a gray sky, they drove hard for the west.

Putting Sloan in the turret and McKay in the comm seat to fret over one of the captured CIA radios, Rogers settled Parkinson on an air mattress in the back of Mobile One to finish patching him up. His left hand and the left side of his face were blistered; his right clavicle was cracked. Though concussion had put him out, Parkinson was coming around even as they loaded him into Mobile One. He was groggy and confused, but responded well to external stimuli and his pupils dilated properly when Rogers shone a light in them. Otherwise, aside from massive bruising, scattered scorch marks, and some metal fragments buried in his hide, he was not badly damaged. Rogers immobilized his right arm and applied appropriate medication, including a new electrostim unit for his cracked ribs. In short order, he left the agent resting under MacGregor's watchful eye and took over the turret again, leaving instructions with the President on how to spot signs of cerebral compression or hemorrhaging.

McKay had managed to raise traffic on the captured CIA communicator. Confident in the security of their high-tech scramblers, the Company boys were broadcasting in the clear, but McKay wasn't getting anything very useful beyond a general impression that for whatever reason Langley wanted their asses *bad*.

"Here's where I earn my pay," Sloan remarked as he took over from the ex-Marine. He keyed into the car's primary computer, a bubble-memory Televideo with a thousand megabytes of RAM and a bewildering assortment of software. He accessed the voice-recognition mode, gave the computer a set of key words to search for, and set the beast to scanning CIA freaks.

They were approaching a crossing with U.S. 421 when he came up for air. Casey had slowed the big car apprehensively. "It's okay, Case," Sloan said. "They're not waiting for us right here. Our friends in the Company have sure been busy, though. They're interviewing refugees along our projected line of travel. They've got a fair idea the route we're following, but only fair. They're getting pretty desperate to nail us. They've sown twenty or thirty hit teams in what they hope are our probable paths. One got lucky."

"I don't know about *that*," Casey remarked with a tight grin. "They didn't look too lucky when Tom and Billy got through with 'em." He goosed the 450 and it shot across a 421 dotted with abandoned vehicles.

McKay said, "They must have a pretty damn good idea where we are now." His face was grim. The Company would be vectoring every killer squad in the Midwest onto them. So far they'd been lucky. And he knew all too well how quickly luck could dry up.

But Sloan shook his head. "Apparently the team we hit didn't have time to report contact with us." His handsome down-home face rumpled in a puzzled frown. "They've already lost contact with several teams. There's a big flap on in Illinois because they think we wiped one out north of

Peoria.'' He shook his head. ''Something's going on out there I don't altogether understand.''

MacGregor was shaking his head. ''Why is the CIA trying to kill us?''

''Maybe they figure they oughta run things, and you're in the way,'' McKay said. ''All that matters right now is making sure they don't get to you, sir.''

''How do we do that?'' Casey asked.

McKay settled back in his fold-down seat with his arms across his chest. His eyes met MacGregor's. ''That's a good question.''

''If they're tracking us by talking to the locals,'' Rogers said, ''why don't we go where there aren't any people?''

Sloan asked, ''Where'd that be, Tom? This is still a pretty populous part of the country.''

''It *was*,'' Casey said.

McKay was rubbing his heavy jaw. ''You mean right through the fallout, Tom?''

''Yeah. Enough heavy stuff blew into southern Illinois from the Minuteman complex around Whiteman base that there shouldn't be many people left to talk to the Company. Even Indiana probably ain't too healthy, down by the Kentucky line.''

MacGregor's face had paled. He mouthed the words, *my God*. Parkinson started up from his air mattress. ''No!'' he croaked. ''You can't take the President through the thick of the fallout!''

''You been hit on the head, Clete,'' Rogers said softly. ''Better take it easy.''

''This four-fifty'll keep fallout out a lot better than it will LAW's,'' McKay said. ''And if they get another Cobra on our asses, we're gonna find out what trouble's all about.'' He chewed the inside of his mouth a moment.

''All right, Casey,'' McKay ordered. ''And from now on, we're not stopping for nothin'.''

So began a desperate race across the poisioned flesh of Middle America. The Guardians began to take shifts, one driving and keeping tabs on the radio and another in the turret, while the others slept as best they could on air mattresses dogged down in back. MacGregor offered to do his part, and McKay let him take a shift as commo man. It wasn't all that hard to

scan the frequencies, trying to glean information on the state
of the stricken nation, and the radar and radiation monitors
had alarms that would bring Sloan in a hurry if they turned up
anything out of the ordinary. Parkinson, on the other hand,
was able to man the turret, if not drive, but Rogers wouldn't
permit him to take full part in the rotation despite his protests.

Early in their odyssey, they discovered the poison was more
than just radioactive dust. Within three hours after turning
south toward the fallout zone, with radiation only slightly
above background, they began to see pillars of smoke climbing into the sky. "Farmhouses burning," Rogers said.

So it proved to be. They passed one blazing merrily a
quarter-mile off the road. "That hasn't been burning any four
days," McKay said. "More like since this morning."

"Something pretty weird going down," Casey said.

They found out what it was after traveling another few
miles south. In the greenish late afternoon light, they saw
another black column stretched up to the putty-colored clouds
from the undulating green land to their left. They came up
over a swell of ground to see a pickup truck bouncing along a
dirt road from the burning farm. As the truck approached the
paved highway, they could see cans and crates piled in the bed
and three armed men riding with them.

"Stop this thing, Casey," McKay said.

MacGregor came forward as Casey braked the 450. "What
on earth?" he asked, peering through the driver's view slit.

"Looters," Rogers said.

"I don't believe it," the President and Casey said simultaneously, though with different inflections.

"Believe it," Sloan said tiredly.

"We're not the damn police," McKay said, "but this is too
fuckin' much. Tom."

"Roger." The car vibrated to the thumping of the M-19,
then, briefly, to the tooth-jarring rattle of the heavy-barreled
M-2. They drove onward past a newly sprouted tree of black
smoke.

When the bombs came down, all was confusion. That was
to be expected. But by the day after the One-Day War, the survivors had begun to come out of their shock, overwhelmed
rescue services were operating, and local authorities were mak-

ing every effort to keep order. For a time it seemed the damage could be controlled.

Then things began to run out. Fuel supplies for power-generation plants diminished. Stations pumping water to urban areas shut down. Food stocks disappeared. Medicines —even sterile bandages—became unavailable.

Slowly, inexorably, the realization spread: *there wasn't going to be any more*. Not in any future the stunned and increasingly desperate population could foresee. No food, no fuel, no international relief organizations such as had existed to aid the victims of the century's previous wars. *Nothing*.

In fury and in fear, like an organism gone mad, what remained of America began to tear itself apart.

"You know what this reminds me of?" Casey asked as they drove through southern Illinois. The weather was hot outside —a hundred rads an hour and falling. It was an extraordinary radiation count for the early afternoon of the fifth day since the war, but the Soviets had spewed a lot of megatonnage in groundbursts all over Kansas and Missouri in their attempts to neutralize the deadly missile silos scattered in a triangle whose points were roughly Kansas City, Jefferson City, and Joplin. Even here, a hundred miles east of the nearest known ground-burst—a wide miss that hit on the western outskirts of St. Louis—Sloan's computations gave a peak figure of over 1,000 rads/hour a few hours after the barrage stopped.

"What's that?" McKay asked, sipping a cup of coffee and peering out the vision blocks of the turret. There wasn't much point in scanning the landscape for attackers, but you couldn't be too careful.

"Ever read the Amber books by Roger Zelazny?" Casey asked.

"Uh-uh."

"I have." Sam Sloan came forward to the commo seat, carrying a plastic tray of prepackaged dinner. He and young Wilson were both science fiction and fantasy buffs. McKay never saw much point to all that far-out stuff, though he kind of liked the *Star Wars* pictures.

Casey gestured with his chin. "It's like one of the hellrides through Shadow he talks about. Everything changes as you move along."

"And every scene is worse than the last," Sloan agreed, chewing, "and none of it seems quite real."

Little moved in the terrain rolling past the vision ports of the V-450. To their left was the usual line of stalled cars caught in a terminal jam while fleeing a stricken city—in this case, East St. Louis. Few had made it from the Missouri side; an airburst had dropped the highway bridges into the Mississippi. To their right was flat farming land dotted with clumps of trees.

But there was something subtly wrong with the picture. The grass was going yellow. Leaves were beginning to drop from the trees. No birds turned in the cloud-filled sky above. Nothing moved, in fact, except the wind and that which it stirred.

The scene wasn't altogether lifeless, of course. Turtles and cockroaches were not overly troubled by this level of radiation. Nor were some plants, and a wide range of microbes. And perhaps, just perhaps, hidden away beneath the once-green landscape were pockets of human survivors huddled in concrete wombs, hoping that their food and water and whatever means they used to cleanse the air all held out until the rad count outside dropped to survivability.

Sam Sloan let his tray rest in his lap and played the fingers of one hand across his console. "I don't like it," he murmured. "The hull has a very low transmission factor, but we're still taking rads."

Billy McKay traversed the turret left, telling himself it was to scope out the countryside south of the dead traffic, and had nothing to do with the body of the beefy woman, her skirt up around pale sausage-thick thighs, who lay facedown in a pool of long-congealed vomit with the body of a child sprawled next to her. "What does the Company have to say, Sloan?" he asked.

The fingers moved. "Not much," Sloan said. "Right now they seem to be trying to keep track of their assets. Rioting's cropping up all over the place, and a lot of their teams are getting caught in it. I don't think they're worrying about us too much just now."

Servos whirred as the turret tracked right again. McKay was a city boy, but still the sight of this lovely rural land slowly dying sickened him. "Swing us north, Casey. Get us out of this shit."

Thunderheads flailed the land with lightning. None of the men riding in Mobile One could remember having seen such a variety of color to the vast discharges before: purple, blue-white, red, orange, greenish-yellow. The rain came down in solid sheets from above, beating off the V-450's hull with a noise like a stampede.

Crossing the Mississippi was a problem that had been eating at McKay since the ambush in Indiana. Fallout wasn't the issue; Casey had cut hard north at McKay's order, and when they reached the river late that rainy night, they were near Keokuk and the Iowa border, north of the heavily irradiated zone. The problem was the river itself. Under the best of conditions, the Mississippi was too broad and had too strong a current for the car to try swimming, and the incredible rainstorms that had whipped the East and Midwest since the War had lashed the river to a raging, frothing flood. Besides this, the road bridges were certain to be jammed with derelict cars. According to the few radio reports they were still able to pick up, attempts had been begun to clear bridges in a number of places, but those had broken down in the eerie spasm of violence that now possessed the country. McKay had an extremely unsatisfactory vision of their finding some craft that would bear Mobile One's ten tons—by the 1990s, ferries weren't too common anymore—and then trusting to Sam Sloan's nautical skills to get them to the other side without their becoming part of the flotsam of cars, bodies, and houses rolling endlessly downstream.

In the event, it turned out to be no problem at all. "Highway bridges are clogged, Billy," Rogers observed. "But what about railroad ones?"

Casey's maps revealed a newly constructed line, built as part of an attempt by the federal government to revitalize the railroads that crossed the Mississippi north of Keokuk. It lay across open country on both sides of the engorged river, so that they wouldn't have to fight through any urban areas coming or going. It was all so damned simple that it had to be an omen.

At midnight of the fifth day of their journey they rolled across the utterly deserted bridge through pounding rain. The Mississippi raged beneath them, impotent to halt their ghostly passage. Polychromatic lightning stabbed at the land, the bridge, the turbulent water. Once onto the sodden soil of Iowa they cheered and pounded each other on the backs like high school jocks after a big victory. It was a clear shot to Heartland, just over two hundred miles away. They were home free.

But somehow things never quite work out so easily.

CHAPTER
SEVENTEEN

"Shit," Billy McKay said, staring at Mobile One. The Super Commando had skidded crosswise, almost blocking the two-lane country road. One wheel lay splayed out to the side like a foot with a twisted ankle. "Fifty miles. *Fifty fucking miles!*"

A dawn wind blew around them, cool after the hard rains of the preceding days. Today was coming up murky, the sky to the east the sullen red of an open wound. The land lay shining, fresh, and green around them. In appearance, this part of Iowa was similar to Illinois. Also Indiana. But not, thank God, in having a radioactive dead zone of the kind through which they had driven to escape their pursuers. The rain that intensified until driving became impossible—they had to lie up for several hours after crossing the Mississippi—had failed to dampen the exhilarated relief they felt at being so near their goal.

And here, so close to the safety of Heartland they could practically stretch out their hands and *touch* it, they had gotten stuck.

It was the rain that did them in. Water running in the ditch next to the road undermined the verge of the blacktop on an inside curve. The pavement itself looked normal. It wasn't until Casey felt the surface start to give beneath them that he had any notion anything was wrong. A five-meter-long crescent of asphalt had broken off under the car's weight, and all his skill and feline reflexes hadn't managed to stop Mobile One from snapping the axle of its right rear wheel.

As they stood out on the road looking grimly at the disabled vehicle, Casey pushed his cap up on his lanky blond hair and scratched his head. "We walk from here, looks like."

Parkinson growled a protest. McKay shook his head firmly. "No way the President is going to hump it fifty miles overland."

"I can make it," MacGregor said. "I'm used to hiking." His fondness for nature and camping was part of the youth appeal that had gotten him on the ticket with Lowell, whose campaign managers perceived he himself had little appeal for the young.

"No, sir," McKay said, trying to keep his impatience from crisping the words. "It's too risky."

"We've seen some traffic since we left the fallout belt," Rogers said from the open hatch of the turret. "We could appropriate transport."

"That's a good idea," Parkinson agreed. "There's a farmhouse just up the lane. They may have something that still rolls."

McKay gestured at the stricken vehicle. "We got transport right here, complete with armor, air conditioning, fancy electronics, and enough firepower for a goddamn infantry company. I do not see us riding the rest of the way to Heartland in a Chevy pickup with no shocks, and brakes that haven't been checked since 1972."

"But Wilson's as much as said he can't fix it," Parkinson said. With one arm strapped down and wired up to healing stimulators, he was in a particularly grumpy mood.

"There's a cache within a few klicks of here," McKay said. "Could you get Mobile One rolling again with stuff from it?"

Casey shrugged. "Take awhile, man. But, yeah. I think the parts are there."

"Our luck isn't as bad as it might have been." McKay looked around. "Case, can you drive this wounded water buffalo a little ways? I think we should try to get it out of sight."

"I can move her a little way. She's got four independent axles. Fortunately."

"Let's shift her over to that farmhouse, get off the highway and out of the open."

"Do you think that's a good idea?" Parkinson demanded. "Might be people there."

McKay sighed. After all they'd been through, Parkinson still wasn't easy to get along with. "Now, Clete," Sloan said, "we don't want to come back and find her propped up on blocks with the engine gone."

Parkinson's scowl deepened. "This isn't a joking matter."

"It's not a joke, Parkinson," said McKay. "Somebody could get awful itchy-fingered looking at this thing. And you know how easy it is to defend an immobilized AFV." It wasn't, and ex-SF man Parkinson knew it. "Now, let's saddle up and move."

Settled in at one side of a dirt track bisecting fields of shoulder-high corn, the farmhouse was sixties ranch-style brick and stucco, faded red and tan with low-pitched roof and shaded by a windbreak of trees that obviously predated it. Chickens scratched on the lawn around a yellow plastic trike and a quiescent Rainbird sprinkler, and pecked at the dirt next to a driveway in which were parked a battered white Ford station wagon and a dark green Bronco with white stripes. Outbuildings of purpose unintelligible to McKay stood out back. An immense lime-green John Deere tractor was parked next to one of them. It had the blurred and faded look of a piece of machinery no longer in repair. A golden-Retriever-colored mongrel trotted, barking, out to meet them as Mobile One chugged up the road, dragging its wheel like a clubfoot.

Casey stopped on the dirt road in front of the house. Rogers aimed the turret away from the house. "Anybody home?" Sloan asked, his voice amplified by the car's loudspeaker. The curtains remained drawn over the picture window. "Place looks pretty dead," Sloan said over his shoulder.

"This isn't the most reassuring approach," Parkinson said. "I think the car intimidates them."

"It's what it was designed for," McKay said. "Any suggestions?"

"Cover me," Parkinson said, and popped the starboard hatch.

McKay's jaw and cheek muscles tautened. He wasn't thrilled about Parkinson acting on his own like that. On the other hand, it didn't seem the time to force the issue, and besides, Parkinson seemed to know what he was doing.

What he was doing was walking up the walk and knocking on the door. "I'm not exactly sure how reassuring a sight *he* is,'' Sloan remarked. A six-three black ex-football player with his left hand bandaged and his right strapped across his huge chest, burn blisters spattered across the left side of his rugged face, wearing a charred and tattered white shirt, with a black tie, black shoes, and dark blue suit pants, and a Mini-Uzi in a shoulder holster, was not the kind of thing you'd expect to turn up on your front porch in the middle of Iowa.

He waited, knocked again. The dog stood off to one side and barked, wagging his tail. "Don't worry, Billy,'' Rogers said from the turret, as if reading McKay's mind. "We can cover him all right. These fifty-cal. rounds'll go through both walls of that place like it was modeling clay.''

"My God,'' MacGregor said. "A farmhouse in Iowa and we're talking about it as if it were an enemy stronghold!''

"Let's hope it's not,'' McKay said.

A few moments more and the door opened. A woman stepped out, quickly shutting the door behind her. She was cutting middle age close, with a plain pioneer woman's face and indeterminate brown hair done up in a bun. She was wearing a plaid shirt and jeans, and had a good figure. McKay eyed her through a view slit, rubbing his jaw appraisingly.

"We got nothin' here,'' she said. Mobile One was buttoned up in case the reception was hostile, but the words came clearly over Parkinson's throat mike. "Just some seed corn, few days' food. Refrigerated stuff's already started to spoil.'' She cast a defiant look at the armored car, bulking squat and massive in front of her home. "How we're going to eat if you don't let my Carl and the others go's a mystery to me. Haven't you people thought of what's goin' to happen when the food runs short in Luxor?''

Startled at her vehemence, Parkinson stepped back. "Ma'am, I'm sorry, but I don't have any idea what you're talking about.''

"Don't give me that, comin' around in your tank like that! Just take everything then, if you have to. You'll be gettin' awful thin when the snow lies thick on the fields and the corn's rottin' beneath.''

"Let me talk to her—'' MacGregor began, starting for the hatch. McKay grabbed his arm.

"No, sir,'' McKay said. The President tried to pull away. McKay's face stayed impassive, but his grip was unbreakable.

Parkinson glanced back at the car, not quite sure how to proceed. *Wing it*, he told himself. "We're from the government, ma'am, on a special mission—"

She sneered. "And I'm Merith Tobias," she said, naming a voluptuous television star.

"—and I assure you, whatever's going on in Luxor, we have no knowledge of whatsoever. In fact, maybe we can look into it ourselves."

"No fucking way," McKay muttered. Parkinson jerked slightly at the comment coming through his comm earplug but kept his composure.

"If you'd just let us come inside, you could tell us what's happening around here," the Secret Service agent said.

"All we want right now's to park this thing out of sight of the road, Parkinson," McKay said.

The woman agreed to let them pull around next to the tractor. "Then you can come into the house. No way I can stop you anyhow."

Casey parked the 450 in the indicated spot, and McKay joined Parkinson inside the farmhouse. He took Sloan with him. Sloan was a farm boy himself, and had an easy, reassuring way with women. He might help put her at ease. That left Casey and, more importantly, Rogers with the car in case trouble broke—or in case MacGregor became insistent about coming inside to talk to the woman himself.

To McKay, a rural living room looked a lot like a suburban one—two couches in an L, fireplace with an old-timey brass clock on the mantle, magazine-strewn coffee table and a couple of end tables, a sort of bar setting off the kitchen-dining room, the whole thing roomier than what he'd grown up with. There were a few toys in front of the sofa, which stood beneath the picture window, an Atari computer with joysticks tucked into a stand under the TV, a well-made silvery model of a World War Two Mustang on a plastic stand atop a bookcase stuffed with almanacs, loose-leaf ledgers, and some Time/Life series books with fake cordovan bindings. By the looks of the place—and the woman—she had several children, ranging from elementary school to teenage, but none was in evidence.

Sloan had come to the same conclusion. "Like the frontier days. She's got the kids hidden away and told them to keep quiet," he murmured as the woman went into the kitchen.

"I thought she was supposed to stand off the Indians with her trusty shotgun."

"May've figured it wouldn't do any good. Not too many Indians rode armored personnel carriers."

"You might as well sit down," she said when she returned. She was carrying a plate of vanilla wafers and some paper cups filled with water from a bucket in the sink. She set them on the coffee table as McKay and Sloan sat down on the sofa by the window. "Not much I can offer you gentlemen. We don't run the generator unless we have to, to save fuel, so I have to pump water by hand. If you want hot coffee, you'll have to wait. Carl rigged up a kind of wood stove out back. He was going to get one going in the kitchen before—"

She bit her lip and sat on the raised hearth. Parkinson came into the living room sipping water from a Dixie cup and sat on the other sofa. "Mr. Parkinson here was telling me you didn't know nothin' about those National Guard types over to Luxor."

"He's right," Sloan said. "We're just passing through, Mrs.—"

"Oh. I'm sorry." She brushed a vagrant strand of hair away from her eyes. "Forgot my manners. I'm Sally Ledoux. My husband's Carl. We—we have several children." Her eyes were fixed on the well-worn grayish carpet.

What, does the National Guard eat kids? McKay wondered. "I'm Lieutenant William McKay, U.S. Marine Corps. This is Lieutenant Commander Samuel Sloan, U.S. Navy."

"You seem kind of a mixed bag." Sally Ledoux tried a smile. It was a good effort.

"We're a special team," Sloan said smoothly. "Now, what seems to be going on here?"

"It's that General Westerfield and his city trash. National Guard, they call themselves. They're just common criminals, even if they do have uniforms!" McKay and Sloan traded glances. In their green-and-tan cammies, haggard after almost a week on the road, they didn't look too respectable themselves. "They were based in Des Moines, but that got bombed, and then there was fallout from Omaha. Just by the grace of God we don't have that here. Except maybe that would be a quicker way to go than being starved by those hoodlums in Luxor!"

"But what have they done, Mrs. Ledoux?" Parkinson prodded gently.

"Came in here and took over. Declared martial law, said they were establishing a new order." Her face was a mask of bitterness. "A new order, all right—them on top and us on the bottom."

"Ma'am," Parkinson said, massaging the knuckles of his right hand with his left, "you may be judging them rather harshly. It's necessary for someone to take command, assert authority before anarchy sets in. Perhaps some of their measures seem unduly harsh, but—"

"But nothing! They're bandits! They're roundin' up able-bodied men into work gangs, makin' em fortify the school-house for 'em while they go around to all the houses and take all the food people've stored."

"They have to prevent hoarding," Sloan said.

She looked at him scornfully. "You sound like a country boy yourself, Commander. You ought to know better. Folks around here look out for each other. Nobody'd starve if they'd just let us get on with things. You talk about hoarding—what do you think General Rodey high-and-mighty Westerfield and his goons are doing? He's got the State Patrol helping him too. They take what they want, and they just shoot anybody gets in their way. My sister's man, Earl, he tried to make 'em leave the medicine for little Jerry, that's Ann's little boy, he's a diabetic. But they said they were im-pounding all medical supplies, and Earl and Ann could apply to the military government to ration them out some. Earl said, over his dead body, and they said fine, and they shot him right there in his living room with Ann and Jerry and little Lisa watching! And after he served his country in El Salvador—not like those draft-dodging National Guard bastards!"

Sloan let out a long breath between pursed lips. "Crenna said it would happen," he said softly. *"Sauve qui peut."*

McKay frowned. He'd picked up enough French in North Africa to understand what Sloan said, but all this talk was making him impatient. It was too goddamned bad General Westerfield and the boys had decided to make the people of Luxor, Iowa, into their personal serfs, but it was none of their concern. They had a mission to complete. Luxor would have to look out for itself.

To be polite, he took a vanilla wafer. It was stale. He chased it with water and stood. "Sorry to be rushing out on you, Mrs. Ledoux. Commander Sloan and I have an errand to run." He looked meaningfully at Sloan. The lanky brown-haired man gulped the rest of his water and stood up. "Thanks for the refreshments, ma'am. We'll be back in a while."

She didn't look up.

"Gosh, it's good to be stretching my legs again," Sloan said for the twenty-third time since they'd left the farmhouse. "I'm losing all my muscle tone. Maybe I should jog back to the Ledoux place."

"You'll look funny carrying a fifty-kilo tire and a new wheel for the four-fifty," McKay said sourly. Actually, he was pleased to be stretching his legs again too, but he wasn't going to admit it to Sloan.

"Me?" Sloan crinkled up his forehead in mock surprise. "You're the foot-slogger type. I was going to let you carry the stuff, and I'd keep a lookout."

McKay hefted the Maremont one-handed. Even after all his years as a soldier he loved doing that. It made him feel very John Wayne. "Not me. I'm your heavy-weapons section. Besides, this pig's enough to tote all by itself."

It felt strange to be shooting the shit like this with Sloan. They had never exactly been at ease with one another. They were Guardians now, no more and no less, but neither could quite forget where they both had stood in the military caste system. Nothing like getting shot at together to break the ice, unless you were Clete Parkinson and had a hair up your butt about proving you weren't a worthless welfare nigger.

The clouds had dissipated. The day was hot but lovely, the sun bearing down on their camouflaged boonie hats and stinging their shoulders. The fields and softly swelling hills were green and placid. They had made their way cross-country from the farmhouse, avoiding other farmhouses they passed, using the cover of trees and cornfields. This was such a milk run, it was a good opportunity for Sloan to get some practice snoopin' and poopin'. McKay didn't feel bad at all about leaving Rogers back at the Ledoux place eating tough cookies with the others. Casey and Tom could take turns watching the car and the President, whom McKay had gotten to promise not to reveal himself. Sally Ledoux seemed an all right kind of lady, kind of sharp looking even, if you put a bag over her head. But as always, McKay was unwilling to take unnecessary chances.

The cache lay next to a small stream beneath a bluff in a couple of acres of woods a half-klick from the nearest paved state road. Pushing their way between green cornstalks, the two Guardians came out on a dirt road running past the woods.

McKay froze.

"What?" Sloan asked. Instinctively he brought up his Galil. His left hand slipped from the perforated metal sleeve that held the M-203 on the rifle's barrel to the trigger of the grenade launcher.

"Voices." McKay subvocalized, letting his personal communicator carry the words to Sloan. "Casey, Tom? Do you read me? Shit. Must be too far even for the car unit to pick us up."

"Atmospheric interference's probably still pretty bad from the War," Sloan said. He glanced up the tree-clad slope. "Better check it out."

"Yeah."

McKay kept watch while Sloan dashed across the graded road, scrambled up the steep grassy cut, and then up ten meters of clear slope to the trees. He went belly down and covered for McKay with the grenade launcher while McKay followed. Not for the first time he admired the fluid grace and speed with which the big man moved, weighty machine gun and all. Hunched over, the two of them ran to the crest and went flat. The voices were louder, all masculine, bored and bantering. McKay's nose twitched. "Cigarette smoke," he whispered. He crawled forward to peer over the lip of the bluff. "Fuck me," he said.

Sloan slithered up beside him. He pantomimed a whistle. "This just isn't our day."

There was a deuce-and-a-half truck pulled up alongside the stream, olive drab with camo stripes of tan and earth brown. A man in an old-fashioned steel helmet and Army fatigues with corporal's stripes on the sleeves sat on the hood, watching a dozen or so men hauling the Guardians' supplies out of their cache while another six kept perfunctory watch up and down the stream. The hiding place had obviously been blasted open, none too expertly if McKay was any judge. Which he was.

They oozed back down out of sight. "Can we take them?" Sloan asked.

McKay studied him a moment with fresh appraisal. This Navy dude was pretty hard-core, he had to admit. It was good to know that he didn't leave his balls behind when he left the high-tech confines of a cruiser. Not that it was cowardly to charge an AC-130H in an armored car the way he had in Pennsylvania. But even that was a different proposition from suggesting two take on twenty right out on the ground, with no armor but their Kevlar vests.

"They're not alert," Sloan went on. "Nobody on the high ground—everyone's watching that damn stream as if they expect the *Merrimac* to come steaming up and shell them."

To McKay this was elementary, but he was pleased Sloan remembered his lessons when the stress was on. A lot of troops didn't. Even very promising ones. But McKay shook his head. "They may have buddies. Let's go back for some help and wait till nightfall. As shitty a job as they did blowing the cache, it'll take 'em awhile to get everything dug out."

They walked back down the slope. Why they didn't hear the truck approaching, McKay would never know. But just before they reached the lower limits of the trees, there it was: another National Guard two-and-a-half tonner, a canvas-back with a helmeted driver, slowing down at the foot of the slope.

"Hey, you!" the driver shouted, braking all the way to a halt. "Stop right there and put those guns down, or we'll—"

He never finished. Sam Sloan threw his Galil 203 to his shoulder and popped the dual-purpose grenade right in the window. A bright flash filled the cab.

He let the Galil's whole thirty-five-round clip go in one long yammering burst as soldiers bailed out the rear of the truck. McKay bellyflopped onto the damp black dirt at the wood's edge and opened up with his M-60, the muzzle blast kicking a commotion of composting leaf flakes into the air.

The National Guard squaddies just freaked when the 60 let go. Half of them had come out without their M-16's. One who had his dropped it and threw his hands over the top of his helmet as if trying to cover his ears. McKay blew him and two others away and then walked his fire in short vicious bursts along the side of the truck.

Sloan had dropped at his side and was fumbling to stuff another magazine into the Galil. Well, he'd got things off to a hell of a start before he began suddenly acting like a troop in his first firefight.

"Grenade!" McKay shouted. At once Sloan let go the mag and slid forward the barrel assembly of the M-203, opening the breech while he reached into his twenty-four-pocket vest for a fresh round of 40 mike-mike.

One young hero started firing upslope across the truck's

hood. The 5.56 rounds cracked overhead into the trees. McKay blazed off the last seven rounds in the box right straight through the hood, and the helmeted head went away. McKay broke the empty box away from the receiver and swapped it for another in the modified Rhodesian ammo pouch he wore on his chest. He was having a lot of success not thinking how his cracked rib cage felt after he'd thrown it on top of the three Aussie boxes the pouch carried.

Sloan fired the next grenade right through the shredded canvas into the truck bed, and it blew with a familiar starfish of dense white smoke. Screams rang from the road. McKay turned to check upslope. Still clear that way.

"Reload, then go for it," he told Sloan. "I'll cover." He turned around and started firing very short sporadic bursts. If the Guardsmen thought the firefight was still going on this side of the bluff, they might not be too eager to stick their little heads out. From behind he heard the truck's gas tank blow and hoped Sloan had had sense to cross well clear of it.

"I'm across, Billy," Sloan's voice said in his ear. "Your turn." He got up and ran, skidding on his butt down the cut—the temptation was to say fuck it and leap, but he didn't need a busted ankle just now—and raced across the road. As he made the corn he heard the thump of Sloan's 203 and the boom of a Willy Peter round going off in the woods.

"That should slow 'em down," Sloan said.

They split up, moving fast across the furrowed ground. McKay saw no point in doing anything more to slow pursuit. He doubted any of the Guardsmen could track a Brahma bull through a K Mart, much less Billy McKay, who in his time had had to elude Somali trackers who could practically trail a lizard across bare rock. And one thing McKay never doubted about Sloan was that he was more than able to run any weekend warrior into the ground. A marathon runner, he had the stamina of a camel. They moved fast overland, keeping tabs on each other by their communicators.

They heard shouts from the road, and the sound of more engines. From the sound of it, none of the Guardsmen was leaping ahead to follow them through the corn. No more sounds of pursuit reached their ears, but they didn't slow down.

In a little over an hour they were back at the farmhouse. Both men were soaked in sweat but privately pleased not to be especially winded. The sedentary months in Washington hadn't taken off too much of the edge Crenna had put on them at his holiday camp in Arizona.

They leaned their weapons by the front door and sat on Sally Ledoux's sofa. They'd been back in touch with the others for half an hour, but other than alerting them to the fact that the shit had hit the fan, they'd saved their breath and the story for when they arrived. Rogers, Parkinson, and MacGregor were all sitting in the living room, eating leftover fried chicken. "It was going to spoil anyway," Mrs. Ledoux explained. "You men go on and have some too."

McKay realized he was starving and picked up a leg off the platter and sat down, tearing a chunk off with his teeth. "We better get the car hidden better," he said. "Your General Westerfield isn't gonna be very happy with you if he finds out you've been sheltering us."

Sloan smiled. It wasn't an expression McKay had seen from him before, and it wasn't as pleasant as Sloan's usual run of facial gestures. "We damaged a few of them back at the cache," the radioman admitted, then he turned pale. "Uh, I think I'd better sit down too."

McKay looked at him. Like Casey Wilson, he had no doubt caused men's deaths before, but never like this, never face to face. The run back from the firefight had left him no luxury for reaction. Now it set in with a vengeance.

Sally Ledoux was staring at him. "You mean you fought with the National Guard?" She looked almost horrified.

McKay nodded. From somewhere back in the house he heard a door open. *Going to meet one of the Ledoux kids at last*, he thought.

"What are our chances for getting anything out of the cache?" Parkinson asked.

"If we'd been able to go in there tonight and take out the guards, they'd've been real good. Now—" He shrugged. "They're gonna cordon the cache off real good. And probably start combing the countryside for us. If—"

He stopped. The slim-built young man who'd just stepped out of the hallway was unmistakably his mother's son, with the brown hair, blunt features and long nose, all more becoming on a masculine face. But that wasn't what arrested McKay in midsentence.

It was the wide, wide bore of the Mossberg pump 12-gauge he found himself staring down.

CHAPTER
EIGHTEEN

"You make a move," the boy said, "I'll blow you away." His voice quavered, but the muzzle of the shotgun didn't move a millimeter.

The back door was kicked in. McKay's eyes flicked over to see a second youth, this one blond and stocky, come in holding a scoped bolt-action rifle at the hip. "Casey," he said low in his throat, "have you gone to sleep out there?"

"I hear movement, but nothing's showing," McKay heard Casey say. The man outside sounded stricken that he'd let his buddies down.

McKay didn't think so. It was his own fault. He'd been too hung up on keeping the car in a secure position where, unfortunately, Casey couldn't keep an effective lookout. Whoever had crept up on the house had stayed out of Casey's line of sight—which wasn't that hard, given the cornfields, the trees, and the outbuildings.

The door between garage and kitchen opened and more people came in, husky young men with guns. "We should have searched the house, Billy," Tom Rogers said sadly.

"Wouldn'ta done no good," said the boy with the rifle who'd come in the back. "Carl Junior here came for us when you drove up."

"Don't tell 'em anything, Mike," Carl Jr. snapped.

187

"Carl," Sally Ledoux said urgently. "These men are okay. They been fighting with the Guard people."

Carl frowned. "Is that true?"

"You see a black column of smoke a few klicks to the northwest of here?" Sloan asked.

"That's just those Guard mother—uh, turkeys, burning bodies at the dump," Mike said.

"Naw," said one of the newcomers. "I saw the one he means. Started up while I was on the way from Fergusons'."

"That was a National Guard truck. We shot it up. Along with the occupants." He swallowed a little at the memory. He couldn't get the screams out of his ears. McKay could have told him he'd hear them all his life. It was the sort of thing you got used to, or went Section Eight.

"Your mom's right," McKay said evenly. "Put the guns down."

Carl, Jr.'s jaw jutted. The barrel of the gun had begun to droop. He whipped it back up to the level of McKay's nose. "It might be a trick. We'll wait for Tanya."

"McKay—" Parkinson said insistently.

"I'm here," a new voice said.

They looked into the kitchen. A woman stood behind Mike. She was tall, with long red hair tied back in a bandana, and looked to be in her middle to late twenties. She wore a denim shirt, jeans, and a Browning 9mm auto in a holster on her right hip—Bianchi, serious leather, well-made. Her eyes were very blue.

If Billy McKay had ever seen a more beautiful woman, he couldn't recall.

The blue eyes met McKay's. "You don't look like the National Guard," she told him.

Sloan smiled disarmingly. "That's what we were just trying to explain to your young friends here—"

"Don't patronize them," the woman snapped. "They got the drop on you, didn't they?"

Sloan blinked. The response was usually different when he turned on the charm. "They did," McKay said. "But there isn't any point in all this. If you'll listen a minute—"

But the woman named Tanya obviously wasn't. She was looking intently at Jeffrey MacGregor. "Just a minute. I've seen you. You're the Vice President!"

"Aw, Tanya," Carl said. "Who the heck recognizes the Vice President."

"*I* do. I saw him on television too damn much during the last election. That reactionary Lowell was trying to add some youth and glamor to his ticket, so he signed on Jeff Mac-Gregor."

MacGregor winced. Parkinson scowled ferociously. "Now, hold on, miss," Sam Sloan said. "He isn't the Vice President."

"But I tell you, I've seen—"

"He's the President, miss," Rogers said.

"We're a special government team," Sloan went on over the sudden silence, "formed to safeguard the life of the President of the United States. We're trying to escort President MacGregor to safety."

Tanya stared. She was utterly nonplussed, and McKay sensed it wasn't a familiar sensation to her. "Put up the guns, boys," she said at last. "Mrs. Ledoux, if you don't mind, I think I need a drink. And then I think we have some things to talk about."

Her name was Tanya Jenkins. She was an attorney who had given up a junior partnership in a prestigious Des Moines firm to set up a practice in her hometown. In the days since Westerfield's men had arrived, she had become the nucleus of resistance against him.

Billy McKay had never met anyone like her.

She sat next to Mrs. Ledoux on the hearth while a half-dozen youths gathered in the living room to tell their story. Apparently, even as Mobile One was first dragging itself up the road to the Ledoux place, sixteen-year-old Carl, Jr., and his thirteen-year-old sister, Mona, had been slipping out the back door and into the corn. Mona stayed behind to watch events at the house while Carl went for help from the neighbors. Word went out through the grapevine that a small group of soldiers had turned up at the Ledoux place in an armored vehicle of some sort.

Hiding out at a farm outside town, Tanya had heard the news with curiosity. Already the Guard had learned to go about in force, especially when they ranged as far out of town as the Ledouxes'. She had gone to join the group collecting near the farm.

It was a curious crew. All kids in their teens, many of whose fathers were interned in town in work gangs or "protective custody." They had grown up as wise to the fields and woods around Luxor as McKay was to the Pittsburgh streets. It had been no great challenge for them to approach the farmhouse unseen.

"Mona said it looked like you guys could talk to each other from inside the house and stuff," Carl Ledoux said. "We figured you had radios of some sort, even if we couldn't see them. That's why we kept hidden when the two of you left, and didn't try to take out the ones who stayed. We knew they'd warn you."

The Guardians looked at one another. Ott and his CIA cowboys hadn't realized the importance of the personal communicators. This bunch of Iowa farm kids had. "Somebody is selling the rising generation short, it seems to me," Sam Sloan remarked.

"It's easier than thinking," Tanya said shortly.

Tanya had arrived in midafternoon. Once McKay and Sloan had returned, she gave the word to move. It had been easy enough for the youths to keep out of Casey Wilson's restricted line of sight. Carl had gone in the window of the room Elaine and Bobby, the youngest of the four Ledoux children, shared. The rest had stolen up to the back of the house and waited.

McKay was angry at himself for getting caught like this. He hadn't been expecting this sort of response. Even when he knew the area was a trouble zone, he only thought of opposition in terms of the National Guard. Nevertheless, he and his elite team had been caught out by a bunch of young punks and a redheaded piece of ass with a law degree.

"So you're taking the President off to a secret command post so that the government that brought this whole mess on can continue running things without much interruption. No, no, I know you weren't in on much policymaking, Mac-Gregor. You don't have to protest."

MacGregor gave her a lopsided smile.

She grinned back at him. "You're not what I expected," she said. "Take that as a compliment."

"I shall."

"But be that as it may, it really doesn't make much difference to me whether you get where you're going or not."

"Now, Ms. Jenkins, it's vital that the President assume command in this emergency situation—" Parkinson began.

"You make a crummy press secretary, Mr. Parkinson. You were a better running back." The agent blinked, and McKay wished he was able to shut him up so deftly. This Tanya was a pushy broad, but she had style. "What I was leading up to is that we have certain interests in common. And no lectures about getting the captain to the helm so he can steer the ship of state through troubled waters."

"Perhaps you're better cut out to be a press secretary than Mr. Parkinson," MacGregor said smoothly. "Permit me to offer you a job in my administration."

Tanya stared at him, then laughed, a hearty full-throated laugh. McKay liked the laugh, but he didn't like the way MacGregor and the woman were looking at each other. *None of my concern*, he told himself. *Besides, I can't hack these liberated types.*

"Ten points, Mr. President. But let me give you a counteroffer. You need to get General Westerfield's boys out of your cache; we need to get them out of our lives." She leaned forward. "Maybe we should work together."

"No!" McKay and Parkinson roared as one. "Out of the question!" the Secret Service man shouted, while McKay said, "No fu—uh—freakin' way!"

"Doesn't it make sense?" she challenged.

"The President's life—" Parkinson said.

"Bunch of amateurs—" McKay sputtered.

"They're sure better than the National Guard," Sloan interrupted. "And do you have any other ideas for keeping the President safe, with General Westerfield's troops beating the bushes for the men who shot up his truck?"

"Billy," Rogers said in that soft almost-Southern voice of his. "Sam's right."

That calmed McKay down. He trusted Rogers' judgment damn near as much as he trusted his own. *You are absolutely, repeat, absolutely forbidden to involve yourselves in the affairs of the areas you pass through when escorting the President to safety*, Major Crenna had told them at least three hundred times. But once McKay backed off and looked at it, they didn't seem to have a hell of a lot of choice.

Oh, well. Crenna knew Billy McKay had a long record of insubordination.

Parkinson of course thought it was a lousy idea. He roared a lot about exposing the President to danger but eventually gave in. The alternative was to take out overland with the Guard after them.

"All right, McKay," he grumbled at last. "But have you given any thought to just what you're going to do? You can't take on an army."

"What kind of morale do you figure the Guard's got?" McKay asked back. "We take Westerfield out, they'll fold."

"I sure as hell hope you're right," Parkinson said.

"One thing I'll say for this General Westerfield," McKay said, working the focus dial of his binoculars. "He's a fast worker. He's got that school pretty well fortified. Sandbags on all the windows, armor plating on the front door, roof emplacements, the whole nine yards."

Lying in the bushes at his side, Tanya Jenkins nodded grimly. "He's had lots of slave labor to fill sandbags for him."

Luxor, Iowa, was a quiet town of about five thousand, a place of easy, uncrowded streets, whitewashed houses with cozy porches pushing pitched roofs up among myriad trees, the whole thing seemingly untouched by urbanization. The area was dominated by a large hump of earth, forested on top, looming thirty meters above the western side of town. The locals called it Indian Knob and said it was an old Indian mound. Archeologists said it was a natural formation. Whoever was right, it was providing an excellent vantage point for McKay and Tom Rogers to scope out the town under cover of night.

With a clatter of steel treads on cement an M-113 armored personnel carrier rumbled down a side street toward Sherman, the main drag. A soldier rode half out of the hatch, holding the spade grips of a Browning .50 cal. in a bored-looking way. McKay felt Tanya's body clench with fury at his side. "Those bastards," she whispered. "Those filthy, fucking *bastards*."

"They hit us like a blitzkrieg just hours after we saw the mushroom cloud over Des Moines. We never had a chance," Tanya said, earlier that day. Dusty amber light filled the living room of the Ledoux house. They were waiting for full dark to make their reconnaissance and she was filling them in on what had happened at Luxor.

Major General Rodey Westerfield had enjoyed a reputation as a go-getter from the days he commanded a line battalion in Nam. Through the grapevine, he'd picked up an early rumor that the balloon was about to go up. He had hours before the onset of the War to mobilize as much of his current command in the capital as he could.

It was his initial intent to set up a military government in Des Moines, but fate decreed otherwise. By accident or intent, a one-megaton warhead went off over the Center of Science and Industry, a cosmic blink of an eye in which a hundred thousand lives evaporated. At the same time, Omaha and environs were hammered by groundbursts—upwind of Des Moines. As a consequence, his understrength battalion of just under four hundred men had been reduced to a company of two hundred, and Westerfield ran north to beat the fallout. On the way, he worked a deal with a captain from the Department of Public Safety and added fifty State Patrol troopers to his contingent.

Why his group wound up in Luxor no one knew. McKay guessed he wanted to try establishing himself in an out-of-the-way location where he wouldn't be seriously challenged until he could consolidate his power. "They roared into town at three in the afternoon," Tanya told them. "They had six of those armored personnel carriers, a few jeeps, and fifteen or twenty trucks. There were a bunch of State Patrol cars with them. They had loudspeakers. They ordered everyone to come down to the courthouse, but most people were afraid to leave their homes."

Tanya had been among those to go. Westerfield, a stocky man of medium height with a grizzled mustache, prominent ears, and two stars on his helmet, had stood on the back of an M-113 and declared martial law. "He claimed the Russians had invaded," she said. "His men were there to protect us. I never heard such a crock of shit in my life. If the Soviets couldn't conquer Western Europe, how could they invade us?"

He announced the terms on which order had come to Luxor. All able-bodied males between fourteen and fifty-five were to be registered. All stored foodstuffs, fuel, and medicine were to be surrendered. Possession of firearms was forbidden. A curfew was imposed; groups of more than two persons on the street would be fired on. Meetings were proscribed. The listening townspeople looked at each other in disbelief. "What would the Russians do to us that he's not?" they asked each other.

The General sent parties out immediately to begin carrying out his orders. He had a lot of men to feed. They met resistance from the start. Chief Hiram Talbot of the Luxor police had tried to stop the foragers. They'd blown his brains out in the street, then blasted the police station with machine gun fire and grenades, quickly overcoming the poorly armed town lawmen. The same peremptory treatment was meted out to anyone who failed to cooperate.

"After that it was like some sort of movie. Rape, looting, killing. They just ran wild."

Now Tanya pointed to the elementary school Westerfield had taken over for a command post, about four hundred meters southeast of them on Sherman. Vehicles, deuce-and-a-halfs, jeeps, and two M-113's were parked in the paved teachers' parking lot and on the playground on the north side of the school. In the middle of the nearby park a sandbagged emplacement had been set up. McKay turned the binoculars. "Jesus," he said. "A four-deuce mortar. That's pretty serious artillery."

"The morning after they arrived, they said that they'd been getting too much resistance and needed to make an example," she said in a low tone. "They set that thing up and bombarded a farmhouse a mile away on the outskirts of town." Her voice trembled. "There were two families in it, *two families*, and they hadn't even been to that house yet. They picked it at random, blew it open with high explosive, and then shot some incendiaries into it."

"Christ," McKay said.

"Then they started rounding up all the men they could. They've got them in a vacant lot next to the Methodist Church on Grand, around the corner from Ames Elementary there."

"I see it." Barbed wire had been strung around the enclosure into which were crowded about two hundred men. A couple of M-113's stood guard.

"They've got arms and things stored in the church. Some of their soldiers are there, some are billeted in the prefab classrooms behind the school. There's talk they're going to quarter the officers in people's homes."

"Where's the State Patrol?" Rogers asked. Like McKay, he was carrying an MP-5 with integral silencer instead of his usual long arm. If they ran into trouble, they wanted to keep its resolution as quiet as possible.

"They've taken over the Luxor Inn. It's a motel on the north side of town, near the cemetery."

He studied Ames Elementary again. There were spotlights emplaced on the roof, but none lit. He counted five machine gun nests on the flat roof of the school, one at each corner and one right over the entrance. The weapons themselves looked like Minimis, Belgian-made squad automatic weapons that fired 5.56 ammunition. Each was manned by two Guardsmen. They looked tense, alert. Across the street was a supermarket with a car wash next to it. A sentry walked the perimeter of the market's roof. Apparently the attack on their truck that afternoon had them worried. That wasn't going to make things easier for McKay's side.

He gave the glasses to Rogers. Silently, the former Green Beret scanned the town, particularly the prisoner compound and the fortified school. McKay was intensely aware of Tanya Jenkins lying beside him, her hip nearly touching his. She was breathing heavily, from anger rather than exertion. The smell of her sweat was strong in his nostrils. *Never thought I'd pull a recon patrol with a woman*, he thought. But she was the best guide available. And she'd done well, keeping quiet, moving from cover to cover as if she'd done it all her life, and she hadn't slowed the two old campaigners down at all.

Rogers handed back the glasses. As always, his thoughts were hidden behind his shark-gray eyes. "Let's go."

"Well, Tom?" McKay asked. It was the next afternoon. The two men were taking a break, squatting on the back porch of Sally Ledoux's house. Locusts buzzed in the trees. The yellow dog dozed a few feet away on a little patch of lawn. A rooster perched on Mobile One's rear deck, watching with pride as his harem strutted its stuff below. The sun shone bright and hot through sparse white puffs of cloud. "What kind of chance do we have?"

Rogers took a deep drag and gazed out past the yard and the barn to the fields beyond. A few magpies chased each other across the green rows, and sparrows fluttered around the trees. Otherwise nothing much moved except the smoke trailing up from the tip of his cigarette.

"Those kids are pretty good for locals," he said. "Give me a few weeks, I'd make 'em guerrillas."

McKay drew in smoke. "So what happens when we go in tonight?"

A shrug. "Maybe half of 'em lose their nerve somewhere along the way, either fade or freak out. Half of what's left will, you know, forget to work the bolts on their rifles or shut their eyes when they shoot, that kind of thing. At least most of them know *how* to shoot.''

"One thing," McKay said from behind a thin smile. "Westerfield's probably not gonna have much better results from his heroes."

Rogers laughed. "Fuckin'-A."

Tanya had gathered about thirty volunteers for the night's raid. They ranged in age from fifteen to twenty—not all of them boys, but McKay figured beggars couldn't choose. One thing Westerfield seemed to have succeeded in was rounding up any adult males who might have had military experience and an inclination to raise trouble. Rogers and McKay had already been to a farm a couple of klicks away to meet with the youngsters.

Security on this was giving McKay fits; too many people already knew where the President was, and there wasn't anything McKay could do about it. He could make sure that no one came to the farm who hadn't been with Tanya and Carl Ledoux yesterday. Other than that he had to trust to luck and the hatred the Guard had incurred in their week's occupation of Luxor to keep someone from informing on them.

McKay didn't trust either very far. In the Muslim countries of North Africa and the Mideast no one was hated worse than a traitor, and the penalty for informing tended to be a very picturesque—and prolonged—form of execution. Yet there were always informers ready to talk to you for the proper price. It didn't have to be money; the price was sometimes revenge or the chance to remove a rival. McKay had no illusions that the good farm folk of Luxor were made of sterner stuff than the Bedouin or Berber.

One bit of luck helped them out with communications. Westerfield's men didn't seem to have any radio direction-finding equipment. Though use of two-way radios had naturally been among the things Westerfield proscribed right off the bat, Tanya's fledgling resistance had found they could use CB's, ham sets, and walkie-talkies with impunity. It made the Guard boys mad as hell, but they hadn't managed to catch anyone yet. Hence they lacked RDF capability.

Also, they hadn't figured out how to tap into the town's computerized phone switching station yet. The would-be rebels were actually able to pick up the telephone and *call* each other. McKay had forbidden—and Tanya had seconded him, an unfortunate necessity—anyone to use either radio or telephone from the Ledoux farm. Messages moved by courier to neighboring farms before going out over the air. The only exception applied to the Guardians themselves. Sloan had hooked on to the TV antenna on the Ledoux house roof so that the team could communicate with each other over a greater distance.

Rogers put the cigarette to his lips, puffed it down to a roach, ground it out against the side of the cement stoop, and tucked it in a pocket of his camo blouse. He stood and stretched. "Tom," McKay said, then hesitated. "These kids could have taken us out yesterday."

The hens chuckled in the weeds. The silence seemed to grow. McKay wasn't sure what he was asking Rogers for, an excuse, absolution, or what. He wished he hadn't spoken, but he'd had to.

"Yesterday we weren't headed into enemy territory, Billy."

McKay spat out a vagrant bit of tobacco. "Hell we weren't. There's no friendly territory. Not anywhere."

"We know that now. Yesterday we didn't. Not . . . not inside." Rogers looked away. He wasn't comfortable discussing the things that went on inside a man. "This place—looked like safety. We wanted to believe it."

"We could have blown the mission."

Rogers shrugged. *Fuck it*, he seemed to say. *The past is gone*. McKay accepted the lesson.

He stood. "Tom."

"Yo?"

"Most of those kids are going to die, aren't they?"

"If they don't have the sense to bug out."

He nodded, slowly, heavily. Rogers opened the screen door and went into the house.

It wouldn't be the first time McKay had led green kids to their deaths. But it bothered him somehow. These weren't kids in uniform, with the buffer of a few weeks' boot camp between civilian life and battlefield reality. They were just . . . *kids*.

"Lieutenant McKay?" He turned. Tanya stood in the screen door behind him. "May I talk to you for a few minutes?"

"Yeah."

She stepped out. She wore a yellow shirt with the ends tied up under her full breasts. Her hair was tied in a blue bandana, and she had sandals on. She looked like a schoolteacher out for a picnic in the country, not a would-be guerrilla leader. "Walk with me?"

He nodded. "Better—uh, better not go too far."

She laughed and tapped the ear that held the flesh-colored plug. "You have those nifty little communicators in case anything goes wrong. But don't worry. We won't wander out of sight of the house, I promise."

They walked out past the windbreak line of trees, out into the furrows of corn, McKay tense, alert to the approach of danger, Tanya seemingly relaxed. Huge green grasshoppers flipped themselves off cornstalks and buzzed past their faces on wide wings.

"A lot of my kids are going to die tonight," Tanya said. Just like that, no preamble, no softening the blow with cushiony words.

McKay chewed the inside of his underlip. He felt tongue-tied with this woman, an experience he hadn't known with a woman since he lost his cherry at fourteen. He tried to tell himself it was because he was having trouble keeping his mind on business, trying to work with this gorgeous piece of ass, but that wasn't the whole story. Tanya put him off balance, and that was something he couldn't altogether admit to himself.

"Yeah," he said in the same tone Rogers had used with him. Suddenly the dam broke and the words came rushing out. "They haven't got any experience for this. They know how to shoot, but that's, that's only part of it. They grew up watching the rebels shoot the shit out of the Empire in the *Star Wars* movies. But in real life the storm troopers don't always miss. And death hurts, lady. It's painful and it stinks and it's ugly—"

He broke off suddenly and looked away. His cheeks burned with embarrassment, as if he were a schoolboy who'd pissed his pants in front of the whole class. He felt her take his hand in his. It was a strong hand, firm and solid, yet not unfeminine.

"Billy." She stopped. He stopped and turned to face her. "You don't understand," she continued. "The world's changed. There's no safety anymore. No one, parent or guardian or government, to shield them from the consequences of their own acts. Not for them any more than for us. They have to accept that. It's not an academic question. It's a matter of *survival*. It may sound harsh, but they might as well learn how things are tonight, on this raid, as later. And would the ones who die be better off starving to death this winter, or living as virtual slaves at the pleasure of Westerfield and his bully-boys?''

Her face softened, as did her voice. ''Tonight is going to be their best chance to learn the lesson they have to learn,'' she said, ''with you and your men to teach them.''

He was going to protest, say that that wasn't what he and the Guardians were in this for at all, but she did something that amazed him as much as anything he had seen or heard on this last week's run through Hell.

She slid her hands behind his bull neck, drew his face down, and kissed him. Hard, her tongue probing between his lips and urgently seeking his.

He responded hungrily, folding her to him. Then as suddenly as she had embraced him, he broke away. It was all he could do not to throw her down on the black dirt and take her there, willing or not, but for the first time in his life he had met a woman he could not treat so casually.

''What's going on?'' he asked hoarsely. He tried to turn his confusion into a joke. ''I've always been a ladies' man, but damn, I never kidded myself I was irresistible.''

''I'm acting,'' she said, ''like the heroine of a bad movie. And I don't care. You don't care for independent women and I don't like big overbearing jocks in uniform.'' Offended, he tried to break away. She gripped his shoulders. ''But you are a beautiful man, Billy McKay, and I know from the way you've been looking at me you like what you see. And you don't stop at those clichéd steel-blue eyes. There's more inside you than you're willing to show.''

She stepped away from him, reached up, and undid her hair. It fell down over her shoulder in a glistening fall of fire. ''Isn't this what they always do in the movies? When the heroine takes her hair down, it's time for the love scene.'' Her fingers worked at the front of her shirt. She wore no bra beneath, and her breasts were tanned, with broad burgundy areolae and stiffened nipples. ''Well, the world has become a bad movie. So I'm ready for the love scene. I may not get another chance.''

She kicked off her sandals. Her jeans slid down her hips, over trim thighs. Her pubic hair was deep red. With a growl, McKay came for her. She welcomed him with her arms and mouth and hunger, and for a time they forgot the world.

CHAPTER
NINETEEN

"I'm in position, Billy," Casey said from Indian Knob overlooking the darkened town. It was as if Wilson had whispered the confirmation in McKay's ear. *Wish we'd had these gimmicks in the Mid*, McKay thought.

McKay huddled with Tanya and the six members of their commando against the side of a dark, deserted house. The supermarket loomed dark behind the house, separated from them by a wall. Another of General Westerfield's many popular decrees had been that every house within a block of his headquarters should be evacuated. "Roger, Casey," McKay whispered. "Have you got the M-113's in sight?"

"Affirmative. We got one about six, seven blocks from you, heading east away from Sherman. The other's up to the north, by the bowling alley."

McKay grimaced. That would put the personnel carrier near the State Patrol's billets at the Luxor Inn. Bad luck, but there was nothing to do about it. *If that's the worst news I get all night, this thing'll be a walkover*, he thought. "You get that, Tom, Sam?" McKay asked.

Instantly the other two Guardians radioed that they had, from their positions a block to the west and north of the Methodist Church. Six klicks away, Parkinson and four of

Tanya's junior guerrillas kept watch over the President and monitored the raiders over the large backpack radio from Mobile One, which had been hidden in the Ledouxes' barn.

McKay turned to Rich Smith, a skinny kid with longish black hair spilling out from under a baseball cap. He carried a .270 deer rifle and a walkie-talkie. He was the most reliable seeming of the underage partisans, and a junior electronics wizard into the bargain. "Back around to the front of the house," McKay said. "Tell Strike Team to go."

Smith nodded, moved quietly out of sight. Tanya caught McKay's eye and smiled. He nodded back.

The other five kids stood watching him with eyes big in the starlight. Like his own, their faces had been blackened with camp paint. It was past midnight, and a scythe-blade moon hung low in the west. Crickets sang unconcernedly. He looked his team over: a girl and four boys, armed with a Ruger 1022, two pump shotguns, and a lever-action .375. Tanya carried a Mini-14, a .223 semiauto rifle with a thirty-round clip. Not much to challenge even a rogue detachment of the National Guard. Even with the cumbersome assortment of artillery weighing McKay down.

Grass rustled and Smith was back. His grin was brief and white. "No problem. We should hear 'em in a minute." McKay nodded. "I still think you should let us have some grenades too," the boy said.

"No," McKay responded. The boy grinned and shrugged. The Strike Team, which had been given its portentous name to fool eavesdroppers, had been allotted several hand grenades to help them in their diversion. It was a calculated risk. McKay feared they'd do more damage to themselves than the State Patrol, but they'd still call attention to themselves, and that was what mattered.

They waited. Waiting was never easy, no matter how seasoned you got, but this delay sawed at McKay's nerves. There was so damned much to go *wrong*.

Two minutes passed by on his watch. "Are you sure they got the message?" he asked Smith.

"Yeah," said Smith.

There was a hollow *thump*! from the north. Two of the kids jumped, and McKay prayed the safeties on their weapons were still on. There was the distance-diminished boom of a high-powered rifle, a quick clatter of a .22. Then more weapons joined the far chorus.

"I'm going," McKay said to the other Guardians, and to his squad, "Wait for my word."

He left his M-60 and the bulky tube of an Armbrust anti-tank rocket under Tanya's watchful eye. Cradling his silenced MP-5 across his chest, he glided forward across the yard, over the wall, and across the alley to the back of the supermarket. For a moment he hugged the back wall and listened.

Voices came from across the street. The firefight in the north was a muted crackle, rising and falling at random. It was getting the Guardsmen's attention anyway. He waited, heard motors firing up. Good. Westerfield was sending reinforcements to the besieged State Patrol.

"M-113's are moving toward the motel," Casey Wilson reported from the Knob.

For McKay, gaining the roof was a breeze. An old-fashioned wooden telephone pole stood near one rear corner of the building. McKay slung his submachine gun and shinnied up until he reached the L-shaped iron handholds hammered into the pole. Then he unslung the gun and climbed cautiously higher.

He was unhappy about having the Strike Team start its party before his group and Rogers' made their moves. It would have been safer for them to go first, before the Guard was alerted. But while he had the magic of assured communications with his own men and with Parkinson back at the farm, he'd had to rely on the youngsters' walkie-talkies—and the youngsters themselves—to initate the diversion. The only way to insure everything got underway on cue was to have the six kids in the Strike Team start firing up the Luxor Inn with rifles, pistols, shotguns, grenades, and illegal firecrackers to get the ball rolling. He heard another grenade boom, then a string of the firecrackers. The last were close enough to the sound of a machine gun to panic the State Patrol. Briefly he wondered if kids would ever celebrate the Fourth with firecrackers again.

Or if they'd have reason to.

He went up another rung and peered carefully over the lip of the roof. The diversion was having an unexpected bonus. The sentry was standing up at the north end of the building with his M-16 slung, peering north, trying to see where the firing was going on. McKay eased himself onto the roof, crept forward to the air-conditoner housing. He thumbed his weapon's selector switch to semiauto. He took careful aim.

The sentry scratched the back of his neck. McKay shot him through the heart. Aside from the click of the bolt reciprocating, the weapon made no noise. That was an advantage of the new model MP-5's in .45 rather than the traditional 9 mm. The bullet wasn't moving fast enough to make a supersonic crack, but since it was a full-sized load, there was no deterioration of trajectory—or killing power.

The man collapsed with the bonelessness of the instantly dead. McKay moved back toward the rear of the market to signal Tanya to bring up the others. A word in his ear froze him.

"McKay."

"Here." He moistened lips gone suddenly dust dry.

"Parkinson. We have a truck coming up the road. Deuce-and-a-half—I think it's trouble."

McKay knew it was trouble. "Guardians—you listening?" His three comrades acknowledged.

Parkinson turned up the gain on the radio's mike. Over their earplugs they heard a rapping at the farmhouse door, then a harsh, demanding blur of voices. Sally Ledoux said something in outrage, a man barked back, and then the ripping roar of a Mini-Uzi blazed out over the air.

More shots, a dull explosion. Then Parkinson again. "Got their truck. There're more of them out there." Another burst of his submachine gun. "Don't know how long we can hold."

Billy McKay felt frozen like one of those flies in a lucite ice cube they used to sell at novelty shops. Imperatives pulled in two directions as if trying to tear him in half. He felt a surging impulse to call off the attack and race back to try to relieve Parkinson and rescue the President. But the attack was launched; if they pulled back now they'd never have another chance. And could they reach the farmhouse in time to do any good?

"Billy?" Sloan asked worriedly.

"They know the President's there," Rogers said.

"Right," McKay rapped. "Go for it." The conflict was resolved with the finality of a cable parting. To go back now would simply stave off the inevitable capture of President MacGregor by Westerfield. The Guardians' only hope to fulfill their mission was to get Westerfield *now*—and pray Parkinson, Carl Ledoux, Jr., and the others could hold out.

Silently McKay moved to the edge of the roof.

●   ●   ●

Corporal Joel Hoad of the Iowa National Guard sat in the open cupola of the M-113 parked on the north side of the prison compound, one hand resting on the grip of the big Browning machine gun as if for reassurance. The State Patrol was really catching it north of town. According to what his two buddies down in the box called up to him, the two M-113's patrolling Luxor's streets had been dispatched to help, and a truckload of infantry had just roared away from the school. Everyone else was to sit tight and keep his eyes open.

No problem, he told himself. *They'll never work up the balls to go for us.* Westy was a real man—he had those sodbusters cowed. It was tough on the Patrol that the locals had decided to take their grievances out on them, but the General would make the scumbellies pay tomorrow.

Then a hand clamped over his mouth. Pain flashed bright in his throat as the narrow leaf-shaped blade of a Gerber Mark II knife was punched through the cartilage of his throat. His back arched as Tom Rogers thrust his arm forward, tearing out the front of Hoad's throat and severing both jugular veins. Hoad was aware of being hauled out of the hatch, and then it seemed he was weightless, floating out of the personnel carrier, and then he wasn't anything at all.

"Joel? What the fuck?" A stubble-cheeked face poked out of the hatch. Rogers let the body fall and kicked the face. It disappeared. He pulled the pin on a gas grenade and tossed it into the M-113.

"Hey! What's going on!" Fifty meters away, across a barbed-wire pen filled with sleeping captives, the gunner of the M-113 parked on Sherman Street swung his .50-cal. around to bear on the strange form crouching atop the other carrier. As the heavy barrel came to bear, an Armbrust rocket smacked into the front of the track and blew the gas tank. The gunner was popped up out of the vehicle like a cork from a bottle of liquid fire.

A block north on Sherman, Sam Sloan, lying on his belly on the sidewalk between a parked car and the front of a Pizza Hut, tossed aside the Armbrust launcher. The weapon was lovely, flashless, and almost noiseless; the watchers on the elementary school roof would have no idea where the shot came from. But its effects were spectacular. The burning personnel carrier lit the street a garish orange as he picked up his Galil.

The rear gate of the intact M-113 opened and the two

crewmen staggered out, choking and gagging from Rogers' gas grenade. One of them waved an ancient M-3A1 grease gun one-handed. It was a futile gesture. Standing on the vehicle's deck, Rogers fired two quick bursts from the hip and then slipped down into the cupola.

The machine gunners on the roof of Ames Elementary goggled as the M-113 blew. Muzzle flashes winked from up Sherman. The two emplacements at the north end of the school returned fire.

The assistant gunner in the nest above the armored entryway tugged his gunner's sleeve. "Frank? Frank? Wake up! We're under attack."

Frank's head lolled to the side and his helmet rolled off. The A-gunner grabbed him by the front of his blouse and hauled him upright.

Dead eyes stared at him from beneath a single dark hole in Frank's forehead.

The A-gunner screamed.

Casey Wilson worked the bolt of his M-40 and turned the rifle a trifle to his left. He heard the excited breathing of his two lookouts. He'd started with four, but two had gotten separated in the hike up the Knob and disappeared. He didn't mind. With luck they wouldn't be needed.

The head and shoulders of a Minimi gunner appeared in his scope. The computerized sight was gathering starlight and other ambient light and providing him a digitized picture, automatically corrected for range. He laid the glowing cross on the helmeted head, let out half a breath, and squeezed.

Gunfire lanced from the sandbagged windows of the school, the quick shrill stutter of M-16's and a slower, deeper-throated booming. *Jesus* McKay thought. *Grease guns. Where'd they get those, in a museum?* He snugged the butt of the Maremont against his shoulder and raked the front of the building. Brick dust and sand flew. A giant flashbulb went off behind the school, and white smoke billowed in the blue-white glare of burning phosphorus. Sam Sloan was dropping grenades among the prefab barracks to discourage the troops from interfering.

Around the corner at the church, a lieutenant and several soldiers raced out the back door of the three-story building.

They started down the steps toward the compound filled with fully awake and excited prisoners. They never made it. Tom Rogers had the door covered with the cupola M-2 of the M-113 he'd captured. The .50 caliber bullets tossed the men against the face of the building like dolls.

A few brave souls fired from the windows. At the wire near the M-113, a boy screamed and fell kicking, dropping a pair of bolt cutters. The girl crouching by his side fired her rifle at the church, then dropped it to recover the cutters and finish freeing the captives as bullets kicked up dirt around her. Rogers turned the big machine gun against the building.

The last strand of wire parted. With a roar of triumph the prisoners rushed for the opening. Braving the torrents of fire, several of the freed men ran bent over toward the building. One tall heavyset man ran straight for the chubby blond girl who'd freed them. She dropped the bolt cutters and flung her arms wide. "Daddy!" she shouted.

A burst from an M-16 took her in the side. She stumbled forward, coughed blood on her father's shirt, and died in his arms.

It seemed a miracle that McKay's whole team had made it onto the roof. Tanya lay on her belly, firing over the parapet into the windows. Another boy lay on McKay's other side, pumping rounds from a shotgun. Rich Smith had recovered the dead guard's M-16 and blasted a clip at the school in a long burst. Then he dove for cover as return fire converged on the place where the muzzle flashes had come from.

McKay was systematically dusting the enemy out from behind their windows. Fire from the school had slackened drastically. He figured the defenders' morale was sinking fast. Sloan had popped four Willy Peter grenades into the barracks behind the school, and they probably weren't getting many reinforcements from that quarter. Sloan probably hadn't killed many, but that didn't matter. He'd scared the shit out of a lot of them, and that was what counted.

"Parkinson," McKay said. *"Parkinson!"* His heart nearly stopped.

Then: "Here." A long ragged breath followed the syllable.

"You sound like you've been hit."

"Yeah. But we're still holding." More transmitted gunfire. "They've tried to rush us twice. Couple of the kids are dead.

But we'll—'' A cough. "We'll do what we can, McKay."

"We're going into the school now," McKay said. *Hang on.*''

To his team he shouted, "Back down off the roof! Time to go!" The boy with the shotgun didn't respond. The girl with the 1022 did. She got carried away and jumped to her feet, firing her pathetic little .22 from the hip. A burst of fire yammered from the opposite roof and blew her away. McKay's bullets clawed the A-gunner from his Minimi, and then Tanya and the surviving four pulled back to descend from the roof for the storming of the school.

Casey methodically picked off the machine gunners from the roof of the school, then began to shoot down the soldiers running from the blazing prefab barracks behind. Deep down inside, the slaughter revolted him and he longed for the clean challenge of combat in the sky. But he kept firing, systematically, mercilessly. He was a Guardian, and he had a mission to perform.

At the corner of the supermarket, Billy McKay raised his Armbrust to his shoulder, took aim on the door, and fired. The door blew in with a gout of fire. He tossed down the launcher, picked up his machine gun. "Let's go!" he shouted.

His little force began its dash across the street. McKay fired from the hip, trying to keep the defenders' heads down. Rich Smith had reloaded his M-16 and was merrily busting caps as he ran. A boy dropped and rolled over and over, rifle flying from his hand. Another boy vaulted his body and raced forward, screaming in hoarse anger.

They reached the doorway. One adversary sat inside, trying to stuff greasy loops of intestine back into his belly. Wounded men mewled and moaned in the darkness. McKay spun around the door, fired a waist-high burst. Then he gestured for the others to follow him and plunged in.

Almost at once something came bouncing down the corridor with the thud of metal on linoleum. "Grenade!" he shouted.

Rich Smith whipped past McKay in a long dive. He landed on the rolling grenade. An instant later it went off with a *whoomf!* Smith's body rose half a meter on a mound of light, then dropped back and lay still. McKay leaped past him to the doorway. A Guardsman stood a few meters down the hallway, prepping another grenade. He screamed as McKay cut him down.

McKay turned back to the man with the laid-open stomach. "Where's Westerfield?"

Inside the church, the released prisoners grappled with Westerfield's men. Though they were armed and the captives weren't, the invaders had been taken by surprise, were stunned and horrified that the firepower of one of their own vehicles had been turned against them. They began to throw down their arms.

Sloan glanced across the street toward the vehicle park on the school grounds. Dark forms were running toward the parked 113's. Before he could fire at them with his Galil, one threw up his arms and fell. His partner put on a burst of speed, swarmed past and up the side of the boxy personnel carrier, trying for the driver's hatch. As he reached the top, his head snapped back and he dropped to the asphalt. "Good work, Casey," Sloan said.

McKay's team was across Sherman. Firing from the school had died down. At least two of Sloan's kids were down, but two others started forward, firing as they ran. Sloan felt a crazy urge to follow them, but his place was here, using the M-203 to support his teammates.

It was well he resisted the urge. The two youths were halfway across the street when there was an eruption of fire from behind them. Fifty-caliber slugs swept them along the street like bits of paper in the wind.

Sloan craned his neck. One of the patrolling M-113's was two hundred meters away, lumbering forward like an avenging dinosaur. Hurriedly, Sloan fed an HEDP round into his 203. The shaped-charge heads were supposedly able to defeat M-113 armor. He hoped it wasn't just a rumor. He came up to a crouch, aimed, fired.

Unlike the Armbrust, the M-203 was not flashless. Nor did it pack the Armbrust's punch. He saw the flash of a strike on the left front of the armored vehicle, and his heart jumped.

The M-113 rolled inexorably on.

Well, I tried, he thought as he threw himself down. The .50 roared again, tearing huge rents in the car and showering him with glass from the window of the Pizza Hut. *That'll teach me to volunteer.*

The M-113 veered suddenly to its left and blew up.

A slow drumroll of gunfire, and husky Mike, who had accompanied Tanya and Carl Ledoux in the farmhouse the day before, flew backward out of the corridor he'd ducked into, down which the dying man had told them Westerfield's office lay. McKay pulled up short, threw out an arm to halt Tanya.

From his belt he plucked a small grenade. He yanked the pin and threw it underhand against the mouth of the corridor, bouncing it back at Westerfield's bodyguards. There was a piercing crack and a flash as the stun bomb went off. McKay wheeled around the corner and cut down the two guards as they stood trying to blink the spots from their eyes.

He lunged down the hall, threw himself against the wall next to the door of the principal's office. Tanya ran and pressed her back against the wall on the other side of the door, winked and blew him a kiss. He grinned with fierce exultation.

"Westerfield!" he shouted. "You in there?"

"I'm here," a voice said.

"It's over. Surrender."

"You don't know what you're doing. We came here to maintain order in this town. Without us there'll be anarchy."

"How could that be worse than what your butchers gave us?" Tanya shouted.

"You damn civilians just can't understand. The soft ways don't work anymore. It's time for the iron fist. You *need* it, believe me."

"Come out with your hands up," McKay snarled. "Or I'll toss in a Willy Peter grenade and let you burn."

After a moment, the General said, "I'm coming."

Tanya and McKay stepped back, holding their guns leveled on the door. It opened. Major General Rodey Westerfield stepped through with his hands up, as instructed. He wore his starred helmet and an impeccable dress uniform under a trench coat. He was smaller than McKay had expected.

"Down the corridor," McKay said.

Westerfield looked him in the eye. His right hand whipped down. A paperweight hit McKay in the right eye. He staggered back, discharging his M-60 into the wall.

Westerfield pulled an M-3A1 up from beneath the coat on a sling. Tanya shot him in the right leg. He gasped and fired a burst into her belly.

"No!" McKay screamed, and cut Westerfield's body in half.

Tanya Jenkins thrashed on the floor like a fish on land, hands clutching at the bloody mess of her belly. She was screaming shrilly, mindlessly. She had soiled herself in her shock and agony. The reek of shit and piss and blood filled the hallway.

Billy McKay stared down at the woman he had loved that afternoon. Her blue eyes were open, but no recognition dwelled within. She was gone.

McKay walked out of the corridor. He didn't look back.

Even as the final drama was enacted in the hall outside the principal's office, Westerfield's men were surrendering. The lightning attack had disorganized and demoralized them. Had they understood the new world better, known the pinch of hunger, they might have fought harder for what they had in Luxor. All they knew was that they weren't willing to die so Rodey Westerfield could have a fief.

Leaving the citizens to deal with the hundred-odd prisoners as best they could, the Guardians commandeered a truck and roared out to the Ledoux farm. The eight surviving soldiers besieging the house welcomed what they thought were reinforcements. The Guardians mowed them down. Two tried to surrender. It didn't work.

Inside, Jeffrey MacGregor, President of the United States of America, met them, holding a Remington 1100 across his chest. His eyes were wild. He had killed for the first time this night. More than once.

Sally Ledoux knelt on her blood-soaked living room rug, cradling her injured son in her arms. Of the four youths who had stayed at the farmhouse to help guard the President, he was the only survivor.

And just inside the doorway lay Clete Parkinson. He had over a dozen bullets in him, but he was still breathing feebly. McKay knelt by his side.

"McKay?" The ex-Marine nodded. "It's up to you. Guard MacGregor . . . no matter what."

"I will."

A black hand clutched his arm, still strong despite the nearness of death. "Swear." Bloody foam bubbled from the Secret Service man's nostrils. "Swear you'll stand by him."

"I swear, Clete."

He took Parkinson's hand in his and held it until the agent's grip finally went slack.

EPILOGUE

"So this is it," Billy McKay said.

The four of them were in the Delta-Level recreation room of Heartland Complex, deep below the Iowa prairie. They were the only occupants of the large, sterile room. It seemed to echo with loneliness.

"Hard to believe it's all over," Sam Sloan said.

Tom Rogers nodded slowly and said "Yeah." Casey Wilson just shook his head. He seemed unable to speak.

Hearing of Westerfield's defeat from stragglers fleeing Luxor, the troops holding the cache had disappeared by the time the Guardians reached it in the dawn's early light. Westerfield's group hadn't cleaned the cache out totally; the parts needed to get Mobile One rolling again were still there. With the help of the just released Carl Ledoux and some of his neighbors, they repaired the V-450 and left at once, leaving the remnants of the cached arms and supplies for the people of Luxor. The Guardians had a mission more vital than any farewells. Within two hours the hidden concrete gates of Heartland, each weighing tons, were sliding open in a grassy hillside in response to a special signal.

They had gotten cleaned up in the individual quarters assigned them by Heartland's handpicked staff, and now the

Guardians had drifted into the huge room, drawn by some common impulse.

As McKay looked from one man to the next, he felt a tightening in his throat. So many good men had died on the run. The crew of Mobile Three; Hayes, Turpin, Goldberg and the rest; Clete Parkinson. And yes, one woman, as good as the best.

They were all that remained, the four of them. The moment toward which their lives had been directed for a year and a half was at hand. The mission for which the Guardians had been formed was accomplished. The camaraderie forged in the fires of a burning America was about to be dissolved. Now they had little to say to one another.

Sam Sloan unfolded his lanky frame from a chair. "Well, I hate these long farewells," he said. "Guess I'll mosey on along, and—"

A chime rang from an intercom on the wall. Four heads snapped round. "Lieutenant McKay?" It was MacGregor.

McKay walked to the intercom. It was strange to be without the personal communicators that had linked the Guardians for what had seemed an eternity. "Yes, sir."

"Are the others there with you?"

"Yes, sir."

"Excellent. If you would please all come to my office, I'd appreciate it. Level Sigma, room twenty-three."

McKay looked at the others. Sloan shrugged. "We're on our way."

The door of the rec room slid open in front of them as they walked toward it. A polite tech in a blue jumpsuit directed them to an elevator. They rode it down, each wrapped in private silence.

The door of MacGregor's office opened as they approached. The President sat behind a modernistic desk with computer-console inset. He wore a crisp black blazer, white shirt, and tie, and aside from the dark circles under his eyes might have just come in from a brisk day on the campaign trail. He rose. "Gentlemen, come in."

"What can we do for you, sir?" Sloan asked as they stepped into the office.

"You can start to carry out your *real* assignment," a familiar voice said from his left, "now that you've completed the preliminary stage."

Standing in the doorway, the Guardians turned. Leaning against the wall next to one of those big nondescript abstract paintings that hang in hundreds of corporate offices across America was Major Crenna, grinning at them with half a face.

They snapped him a crisp salute. He pushed off from the wall and returned it wryly. "Glad to see you boys made it. Hate to think I hadn't trained you right."

"Good to see you, sir," McKay said. "But what did you mean, our real assignment?"

"Is that a trace of eagerness I hear in your voice?" He chuckled. "Come in and sit down before you wear out the door."

The Guardians obeyed, taking places on amber-colored sofas and chairs arranged around the office. "I apologize for the impersonal appearance of the room," MacGregor said, resuming his seat. "I haven't exactly had a chance to impress my personality on the place yet. Would you like something to drink?"

"Beer," McKay said. Rogers asked for Scotch, Casey for fruit juice. Sloan asked for fruit juice too, then caught himself.

"After what we've been through," he said, "I think I could use some Scotch myself."

"Wait till you hear what's in store for you," Crenna said.

A panel opened in the wall, revealing a tray holding their drinks. "Isn't science wonderful," Sloan said, and passed them out. "Now, what's going on here, if I may be so bold?"

MacGregor folded his hands on the desk. "Before the war, a top-secret document was drafted. Known as the 'Blueprint for Renewal,' it was no less than a master plan for the reconstruction of the United States in the event of a catastrophic nuclear war. It contains a vast amount of information: technical, medical, scientific, industrial. The means of rebuilding an America stronger and more vital than ever before—and in a matter of years."

His voice rang with crusader zeal. The Guardians exchanged looks. "Sounds great," Casey says. "But where do we come in?"

"The problem with such a document is, obviously, the choice target it provides for foreign espionage. Therefore, the Blueprint was broken into a number of component parts and these components stored with various participating research scientists across the country. The list of locations of these components is known as the Master Code.

"It was in the possession of President Lowell when he died."

Sloan blinked. "And this means—"

"We don't have it," Crenna said. "All we have are a few clues as to where parts of the Blueprint may be found."

He tossed off the rest of his drink and set the glass down on a small round table. His single eye fixed McKay. "Lieutenant, you suspected from the outset that there was more to your mission than simply guarding the President. You were right. From the very first it was envisioned that this team would be instrumental in forging the dream contained in the Blueprint into a reality. From the start, you were intended to be the Guardians not just of one man, the President, but of the destiny of the nation.

"That was your mission, and it still is." He smiled his death's-head smile. "It's just going to be little more complicated than anticipated."

From across the sea, Maximov's voice was soft as silk. "Trajan, my good, good friend, you have failed me."

He could hear a swallow from the other end of the line. "Yes, Excellency. The President is beyond our reach."

Maximov allowed the silence to impale Trajan like a hook. Finally he spoke. "You are a valuable asset, Trajan. Too valuable to throw away lightly. I believe I may give you a chance to redeem yourself."

"I—Excellency, I'm grateful. You won't regret this. The Company has a new lead, one that may render this setback inoperative. A hint of a new option—"

"Never mind." Maximov's heavy voice damned the flow of words. "I have a job for you. The Americans assembled a document before the war. The Blueprint for Renewal. Are you familiar with it, Trajan?"

"We heard rumors, Excellency. Nothing substantial. It seemed unlikely to be more than a figment. Nonoperational."

"It exists, Trajan," Maximov said. "It is the key to America. And America is the key to the world. You will get me this key.

"Or you will die."

•   •   •

McKay looked at Sloan, then at Rogers and Casey Wilson. They had passed together through the fires of hell. Images of that demon run flickered through McKay's brain like scenes from the late-night news: the faces of the mob, contorted with fury and fear, as they rushed the White House in the very teeth of the doomed Secret Service detail and McKay's machine gun; the street littered with pictures of naked women under a boiling mustard sky; the hate-twisted face of the Runner and the searing flash of the final warhead; Chief Justice Shaneyfelt's armored car on its back like a broken beetle, with pale flames dancing on its belly. The lines of refugees trudging single-mindedly through lashing rain. Then the cold feeling of betrayal as the jaws of the trap sprang shut at the Company airfield in Pennsylvania, and the C-130 going to glory in a giant orange-and-black fireball. The sense of comradeship that had grown between Guardian and Secret Service agent during the furtive intervals of peace under midnight skies. The slashing attack of the helicopter gunship, the ambush on the highway, the nightmare drive through regions turned to lifeless waste by invisible poisons. Luxor, Iowa: the shootout at the cache, the innocent fervor of the warrior children, the sight and taste and feel of Tanya under the hot Iowa sun while the cornstalks rattled all around. The flame-shot confusion of the final battle for the school, the hot-blood taste of victory turned ashen by loss. He saw the faces of the dead, Garcia and Mason and Popejoy and poor Tim Hayes, Ben Turpin gasping his life out with a final jest by the roadside in Indiana. Bill Ott and his trained shark Martinez, the Company men in their Blues Brothers suits, the Guardsmen giving way to helpless headless-chicken panic on the road near the cache, Rodey Westerfield firm-jawed as he made his final play. Clete Parkinson lying in his blood, exacting a final oath from his comrade and rival. Tanya writhing in agony on a scuffed linoleum floor, Tanya, Tanya, Tanya . . .

The future held more of the same, of violence and horror and loss. Their search for the far-flung fragments of the Blueprint for Renewal would carry them from one end of the shattered continent to the other, through a strange and deadly post-holocaust world the nature of which none of them could yet conceive. They might fail, they might die in the attempt. They would certainly strive—and suffer—as they never had before. But the mission that had for so long shaped their lives, given them something to live for, some hope of transcendence and glory, was not at an end, had barely begun. The bond of comradeship that had been forged between them would not be dissolved. The purposelessness that had descended on McKay like a weight when the gates of Heartland closed behind Mobile One lifted. *We've still got a mission!* he exulted. He put back his head and laughed.

One by one, the others joined in.

SPECIAL PREVIEW

Here are some scenes from

TRIAL BY FIRE

the second exciting novel in
THE GUARDIANS
series from Jove

coming in May!

Like a panorama from an after-the-holocaust adventure flick, it all unfurled before their eyes as they boomed over a rise in the rolling land south of Osceola, Iowa. One moment Mobile One was making good time along the usual back-country road, hatches closed against the intermittent spatters of rain spitting down from patchy slate-colored clouds. The next they were there, at an isolated farmhouse surrounded by a score or more of bizarre vehicles.

The huge car slewed on the wet red-clay road as Tom Rogers jammed down on the brakes. In the electronic-systems operator's chair at his side, McKay leaned abruptly forward, clamping down hard on the stub of cigar between his jaws. "Shit," he said under his breath, staring through the forward vision block.

It was a two-story whitewashed frame house, with a line of box elders planted to the west for shade and as a break against the wind off the plains, and a real old-timey, storybook red barn out back. A green John Deere tractor was snuggled up against the side of the house like an elephant scratching its side on a baobab tree. An ancient red Ford Apache pickup, now sun-faded to a dusty pink, sat up on cinder blocks in the yard.

Next to it lay a dead Dalmation, as much red as white from the short-range shotgun blast that had killed it. The lady of the house, or so McKay gathered, was the pile of drab clothing slumped beside the front porch at the foot of a broad scarlet smear. A daughter of the household, clad only in a T-shirt, was out in the yard near the dead dog. She was busy being raped by a half dozen burly dudes in Mohawks and black leather.

"Road gypsies," Sloan said from the turret.

Since the dwindling of the eighties, nomad gangs in their stripped-down cars, vans, and dune buggies had plagued the nation's highways. Like the bikers of the fifties and sixties, they had drawn inspiration from the movies: the Australian *Mad Max* movies, the New Zealand *Battle Truck*, and a raft of me-too after-the-holocaust highway flicks. Now it *was* after the holocaust, and the marauders of the open road were getting the chance to live out their Road Warrior fantasies for real.

Of course, in *Road Warrior*, the gangs' opponents had only been armed with crossbows and scavenged sidearms.

"Fire 'em up," McKay growled. "Don't shoot too near the house or the girl." Miraculously, no one had noticed the presence of Mobile One on the hill four hundred meters away. The road gypsies were making enough noise to cover the growling of the car's big diesel. As McKay watched, a pair of the nomads led a bay horse out of the barn and slapped it on the ass. It bolted into a cultivated field filled with some low plants McKay didn't recognize. One of the gypsies raised an FN assault rifle and began spraying full-auto fire after the fleeing animal. His third burst brought it down kicking in anguish at the furrows.

"Bastards!" Sam Sloan shouted. Mobile One rocked with the recoil of its turret MG. The long .50-caliber burst picked up the two road gypsies and threw them fifteen meters into the field, trailing streams of blood like pennants. They didn't even have time to scream as the seven-hundred-grain slugs had their way with them.

Not even the world's loudest heavy-metal group in full throat could drown out the roar of a Browning M-2HB less than a half klick away. The outlaws looked up in open-mouthed amazement, then broke for their vehicles. Afraid of touching off the frame farmhouse with a stray white phosphorus round, Sloan didn't open up with the M-19 automatic grenade launcher. He didn't need to. With a little luck, the .50 cal. could take out an armored car. The chopped gypsy off-road vehicles were nothing to it.

The hood of a dune buggy erupted in debris as the M-2 blasted chunks out of the engine block. Firing in short bursts the way the instructors in Arizona had taught, Sloan walked his fire along a line of a half dozen cars to a black van painted with red flames. A gypsy dove frantically out the rear as machine-gun fire exploded the windshield. An instant later the van vomited real flames out the windows. Apparently gas siphoned out of the tractor and the other farm vehicles had been stored in the back. A dragon's-belch of orange fire engulfed the fleeing nomad. He ran mindlessly into the fields, wrapped in flame. His screams carried clearly to the V-450 in the gaps between bursts of fire from the turret gun.

"Drive on, Tom," McKay said. "We got the fuckers on the run. Sloan, keep 'em movin'." Tom straightened the big armored car's angular snout on the road and drove down the gradual slope at about forty klicks. Sloan sprayed bullets to either side of the farmhouse.

As they reached their cars the gypsies peeled out. The half-naked farmgirl struggled to sit up. A bearded outlaw racing into the house snapped two shots into her from a big handgun, and she went down writhing. From the second-story windows a half dozen of the nomads opened fire on Mobile One as it approached.

With a jackhammer noise bullets ricocheted off Mobile One's alloy hide. "Motherfuck," McKay said. Somebody was shooting a 7.62 mm weapon at them full-automatic—a G-3, or maybe another FN. It wasn't likely to do them much damage. Even the tires, honeycombs of plastic and steel that were virtually impossible to flatten, weren't vulnerable. But McKay believed in making sure. "Take those shitbirds out."

The MG fell silent. "There may be people in there, McKay."

"Then they gotta take their chances." The car bumped down the road. Muzzle flashes flickered frantically from the house, now a mere sixty meters away. "Might be doin' them a favor if you hit them."

A pause, and then the big fifty roared again, rocking the V-450 back on its massive suspension and raking the second story of the farmhouse. The bullets knocked meter-long splinters off the front of the building, punching through both wooden walls—and any intervening nomads—and barely slowing down.

"Billy." Casey Wilson, minus his shooting glasses but with his inevitable baseball cap jammed down on his head, had come forward from the air mattress aft of the turret root and was hanging onto the back of McKay's seat. He pointed out the passenger-side vision block. "The road gypsies, man—they're coming back!"

McKay looked around. *Those fuckers're harder-core than I thought.* A dozen or more of the gaudy vehicles were circling in on Mobile One and the farmhouse like a pack of sharks stalking a killer whale.

A road gypsy broke from the front door, clearing the stoop in a leap and lining out for the trees. He held a chrome-plated

.44 Magnum in one hand. "That's the same one shot the girl," McKay said through gritted teeth.

Without a flicker of expression on his tan face or in his gray shark's eyes, Tom Rogers hauled the huge car around in a turn, its wheels tearing chunks of sod out of the lawn, and rolled past the dead girl in pursuit of her killer. At the hunting-lion growl of its engine, the outlaw cast a look back over his bare shoulder. McKay saw the purest look of terror he'd ever run across—the man's eyes bulged from a grimy, sweat-streaked face, his tongue protruded from the taut ring of the mouth, and his neck tendons stood out in relief like hoses. Then Mobile One's snout hit him low in the back and he disappeared.

The ten metric tons of the car barely bounced as they rolled over him.

McKay almost went face first into the blinky lights on the ESO console as Rogers slammed on the brakes. The turret motor whined as Sloan traversed it to bring his guns to bear on the wolf pack closing in. The M-19 coughed. A high-explosive, dual-purpose round hit a buggy right on the nose. It was built around a Volkswagen of some sort, with the engine in the back. The grenade exploded against the firewall. The blast of superheated gas from its shaped-charge warhead vaporized the driver's legs and blew the car in two. The front tires slewed off to the right, and the rear half of the vehicles blew up.

Bullets whanged off Mobile One's carapace. The attackers behind the wrecked dune buggy veered abruptly and disappeared behind the farmhouse. Then Casey shouted, "Behind us!" from the rear of the car.

There was a loud *whoosh*! and suddenly it got a lot hotter inside Mobile One.

"Molotov!" Casey hollered. McKay fell back against his seat as Rogers goosed the 450.

"Fire on the rear deck!" Sloan shouted down. Casey snatched a fire extinguisher from the bulkhead, popped the top hatch behind the turret, and climbed half out to try to douse the flames before burning gas seeped down into the engine compartment.

Gunfire popped from outside the V-450. There were gypsy cars all around, worrying Mobile One like wolves bringing down a moose. Casey gave a choked cry and fell back down through the hatch.

With a single leap McKay was out of his seat and scrambling to the ex-fighter jock's side. Casey's face was white, his lips a thin line. He rubbed at his left shoulder. "Take it easy, Case," McKay said, easing his hand away. A bullet had punched through his cammie blouse and been stopped by the Kevlar of Casey's Second Chance vest.

"I-I'm okay," Casey said, struggling to sit up. "Arm's like, numb, though—"

"No shit." McKay dug a deformed blob of lead and copper from the fabric at Casey's shoulder. It looked like a jacketed hollow-point from a .357 Magnum. A potent mother—and while the vest had stopped the round from penetrating, Casey Wilson's shoulder and chest had absorbed most of its considerable energy.

"Got the fire out," Casey said stubbornly. If his words hadn't been coming over the intercom to the bone-conduction speaker behind McKay's ear, he never would have heard him, so loud was the yammer of the turret guns through the open hatch. McKay felt an impact on the hull and glanced up—straight into the wild eyes of a road gypsy with a yellow Mohawk who was crouching on the rear deck.

The Mohawker swung up a sawed-off shotgun. Moving faster than he ever had before, McKay swept his right hand back, snapping open the flap of the Kevlar field holster that held his sidearm. He snatched the .45 free, pivoted his hand while his thumb snicked off the safety, snapped two quick shots from the hip.

It was a desperate move. Under any other circumstances it would have been a damn fool stunt—trying to get the rounds out the small hatch without aiming while the armored car bucked and pitched below his boots like a small boat caught in a squall. But no copper-jacketed ricochets whined past his ears. For a heart-stopping millisecond, McKay stared straight *up* the yawning bores of the sawed-off. Then his two slugs knocked the road gypsy up and away. The shotgun discharged uselessly against the impervious rear of the turret, and the nomad was gone.

McKay stuck his head out. The wind whipped at his face. The V-450 was thundering along the road past the farmhouse now while the gypsy pack pursued along the graded strip and through the fields to either side. McKay saw a snarling outlaw standing in the bed of a pickup cock his arm back to throw a

Molotov. McKay snapped a shot at him, missed, and ducked, slamming shut the hatch. The bomb sailed over the car and filled a ditch with brief fire.

The gypsies were smart. Sloan could only depress the muzzles of his turret guns so far. The gypsies were crowding close so he couldn't get them, or maneuvering to stay out from in front of the turret as he traversed it left and right. Glancing out the rear view slit, McKay saw several black columns of smoke rising into the gray sky behind. He grinned. Not all the attackers had been successful at keeping out of Sam Sloan's way.

On the other hand, if the bad guys stayed close it was only a matter of time before one got a Molotov aboard.

"Hold tight, everybody." Tom Rogers sounded as calm as if he were out for a fishing expedition with his two kids. McKay rammed his Colt back in its holster, grabbed a handhold, and clung.

It was a good thing. A stripped Maverick had gotten a little ahead of Mobile One. A nomad leaped from the back of it onto the front of Mobile One and caught hold of the left-hand headlight. Rogers cranked the wheel hard left.

The impact of the V-450's snout knocked the Maverick onto its side. It skidded along in a shower of sparks and dirt. Rogers put the pedal to the metal, the huge car surged ahead, up, onto, *over* the stricken gypsy wagon. McKay was thrown into the bulkhead, and then Rogers had control of the 450 again, leaving the Maverick a twisted ruin across the road behind. Another nomad swerved a heartbeat too late to avoid the wreck.

McKay shook himself and pushed off. He grabbed his Maremont—a lightweight version of the 7.62 mm M-60 machine gun—out of the clips that held it to the hull. It was his pet long arm, a heavy, hard-hitting piece of ordnance. The fuckers thought they were safe, snuggling up to Mobile One. They were about to find out what the firing ports let into the hull on all four sides were for.

He felt more impacts through the soles of his boots. "Billy," Sloan called, "I can't see!"

"Shit." The outlaws had gotten smart. Some of them had climbed up on top and flung a burlap bag over the turret vision block. The servos that moved the turret whined abruptly. There was a shriek, fading instantly behind. Sloan had swung the turret unexpectedly and knocked an unwary nomad off with the muzzles.

Rogers hit the brakes hard. McKay went flying forward. So did two more road gypsies. Rogers rolled them into red jelly and drove on.

Untangling himself from the ESO seat, McKay wondered if any of his ribs weren't cracked. The forward top hatch cracked right above his head. McKay swung up the Maremont's muzzle and fired a single shot into the face that peered in.

Not even the earsplitting bark of a 7.62 next to his ear was enough to flap Tom Rogers. He was so hard-core he damn near frightened even McKay sometimes. McKay jumped up and threw open the hatch.

A burly gypsy in Foreign Legion pants stood prying at the turret hatch with a crowbar. McKay prodded him in the left butt cheek with the barrel of the Maremont. He turned with a curse.

The machine gun's muzzle was six inches from his crotch. McKay triggered a short burst.

Road gypsies were all over the V-450, like baby opossums on their mother's back. Firing the big chopper one-handed, McKay peeled another outlaw off the right-hand headlight. Then he pulled himself up out of the hatch.

The turret was facing to the side. McKay faced a pair of startled nomads across it. He grabbed a metal rung let into the turret and fired from the hip, sweeping the LMG from left to right. The big slugs tore the two to pieces.

A weight descended on his back. He felt a pang in his right side as the outlaw tried to jam a knife through his Kevlar vest. He let the M-60 drop on its sling, reached back with one hand, grabbed, jackknifed forward. The gypsy went over his head—without letting go his handful of McKay's blouse. His momentum tore the former Marine's grip free of the handhold.

Desperately McKay grabbed. He grimaced as his left hand closed around the red-hot barrel of the M-2. "Whatever you do, Sam," he gritted, "*don't shoot*."

He was dangling from the turret with the gypsy hanging off him. He smelled the man's foul breath, put an elbow in his eye. He slipped down McKay, clawing madly for a grip. His boots hit the ground racing by underneath. His face a mask of agony and determination as the hard earth ground at his legs, he hung onto McKay's right leg with fingers like steel talons.

McKay kicked him hard in the face. He let go. For a moment McKay hung off the side of the car, the ground rushing along centimeters below his feet. Then he swung his legs up onto the rear deck and hauled himself back aboard.

Ignoring the pain in his seared palm, McKay grabbed another rung and blasted at a gypsy lunging for him. The man spun sideways, a greasy gray-purple coil of intestine spilling from his bare belly, and rolled off the rear deck. Still shooting the ponderous weapon one-handed, McKay sprayed the V-450 with fire. The three outlaws still aboard went away quickly. He pulled himself upright.

The pickup truck was alongside, the rail-thin outlaw in back gearing up for yet another try with a Molotov. "You never give up, do you, asshole?" McKay said, but the wind whipped his words away.

It didn't affect the flight of bullets he sent hosing toward the beige truck, however. Three red flowers blossomed from the gypsy's bare chest. He dropped the bottle and went over the side.

McKay flung up a hand to shield his face from the sudden savage wash of heat as the other bombs in crates in the rear of the truck went off.

The explosion of the pickup was the signal for the surviving road gypsies to break off the engagement and flee up the dirt track. The bare-bones vehicles were a lot faster than the ponderous V-450. The Guardians were content to let them go, though Sloan picked off another pair of dune buggies after McKay cleared his view slit for him.

Back at the farmhouse three outlaws staggered out, weeping and choking after McKay fired a few 40 mm tear-gas rounds through the ground-floor windows from an M-79, a single-shot grenade launcher that broke open like a shotgun to reload. Reluctantly, Sam Sloan cut them down with bursts from the .50 caliber. He hated to kill them in cold blood, but the Guardians weren't equipped to take prisoners. And not much inclined to.

As McKay and Rogers went inside the farmhouse—cautiously, gas masks in place, and shotguns in hand—they were even less inclined to search for survivors. In the kitchen they found the man of the house pinned to the wall with a pitchfork beneath a knitted sampler that said, "There's No Place Like

Home." He was coughing feebly, drooling blood down the front of his overalls. McKay glanced at Rogers, the team medic. Rogers raised his Smith & Wesson 3000 riot gun and blew the man's head apart. It was the kindest thing they could have done.

They found a boy lying in the hallway leading to the stairs. He must have been about twelve years old. He'd been killed with an ax.

The house had been torn to pieces—furniture chopped up, pictures knocked from the walls, useless TV set blown in with a shotgun. Upstairs was no better. Worse, in fact: to the mindless vandalism had been added the effect of Sloan's .50-caliber bullets.

They'd caught a half dozen of the road gypsies. Two were still alive. But not for long.

They parked in the shade of the box elders while Tom Rogers looked to their hurts. Each responded in his own way to the letdown that followed the hot blood of battle. McKay grumbled and stomped around, Casey sat babbling to a thoughtful-looking Sam Sloan about some science fiction book he'd read, while Rogers, impassive as always, wrapped an Ace bandage around his bruised shoulder.

They were very different types, these four Guardians, from very different backgrounds. Yet each had proven himself on the field of battle.

Sam Sloan, the farmboy from Missouri, had been a gunnery officer on the U.S.S. *Winston-Salem* on station in the Gulf of Sidra almost three years before when an attack by Libyan missile boats had blasted the cruiser's bridge into oblivion—and him into command. From an auxiliary bridge he had fought the stricken ship clear of savage surface and air attacks. His bravery and skill had won him nationwide fame and a Silver Star. A nuclear engineer by training, he was a whiz with computers and anything electronic. He was communications officer for the Guardians. On patrol he carried an Israeli-made Galil assault rifle modified to carry an American M-203 40 mm grenade launcher beneath its barrel.

On a hot summer morning, Lt. Kenneth C. Wilson had lifted his F-16D into a blazing sky from an airfield in the south of the Rub Al-Khali, the Empty Quarter, most evil desert in the world. He was flying MiGCAP on a strike against Aden, capital and deepwater port of the troublesome People's Democratic Republic of Yemen. With two kills to his credit, he was considered quite an up-and-comer—a natural born stick-and-rudder man with a marksman's eye. When a Sea Stallion rescue chopper fished him from the Gulf of Aden where he'd ditched the riddled ruin of his Fighting Falcon, he was a hero, too, with the United States' first five-kill mission since the Second World War. Mellow-speaking California Kid from affluent Silicon Valley and a graduate of USC, Casey was an expert mechanic and aficionado of Eastern philosophy. He was the group's driver and sniper.

Tom Rogers was a war hero too, but not the kind you read about in the papers. He had a decade's experience on active duty with the Green Berets, fighting unheralded battles from the jungles of Central America and Southeast Asia to the deserts of the Mideast and the rocky plateaus of Iran. Some said he had even operated behind the Iron Curtain, raising Muslim guerrillas against the Soviet empire. Others said he had been instrumental in the assassination of one of the Ayatollah Khomeini's favorites by means of a bomb concealed in a tape recorder on the dais from which he was speaking. His comrades knew he had a wife somewhere who'd divorced him and taken their two kids with her, because he could never devote to them a fraction of the attention he poured into his work. Beyond that, and the fact that he was an Army brat who'd grown up all over the world, they knew nothing of his background. A demo expert and team medic, the taciturn, balding Rogers was a jack-of-all-trades. In the field he carried an unadorned Galil—and his two pet knives.

Machine gunner, past master of urban and desert combat, and leader of the Guardians, Billy McKay was the brawling, beer-swilling, cigar-chewing, skirt-chasing son of a Pittsburgh steelworker. Beginning his career with the Marine peacekeeping force in Beirut, he had gone on to see combat with the Corps's elite Force Recon. Subsequently he'd fought his own war in the shadows with the dirty-tricks teams of the innocuously-named Studies and Observations Group, Southwest Asia Command. Major Crenna had found him in a hospital in Haifa and tapped him to head the new ultra-elite team he was putting together: the Guardians.

Now these four men were on the trail of the Blueprint for Renewal, a compendium of high-tech and high-powered experts vital to the reconstruction of a war-ravaged America.